THE STARVING

JON DOBBIN

THE STARVING

JON DOBBIN

Published in Canada by Engen Books, St. John's, NL.

Library and Archives Canada Cataloguing in Publication

Title: The starving / Jon Dobbin.
Names: Dobbin, Jon, 1982- author.
Identifiers: Canadiana 20190058536 | ISBN 9781926903972 (softcover)
Classification: LCC PS8607.O215 S73 2019 | DDC C813/.6—dc23

Distributed by:
Engen Books
www.engenbooks.com
submissions@engenbooks.com

First mass market paperback printing: May 2019

Cover Image: Jud Haynes

To Ashlee
whose support and affection
has made this book possible.

PART ONE
CHAPTER ONE

I

After weeks of hunting, Bill Weston found the Indian named Faraway Sue. Weston and his crew rode into the reservation just outside of Yosemite along the Sierra Nevada and found him amongst the teepees of bleached branches and wood, looking into the fire, and chewing a twig. The local Indians were silent as Weston and his men circled the town on their great horses, rifles at the ready. An East Coast Delaware Indian meant little to them and none spoke for him or to him. When Sue was removed, shackled and bound on the back of an old grey horse, the reservation Indians turned from him, a tepid silence filled the air.

The silence followed them on their way back to Colorado, as did the sun, which seemed to always be at their backs. Occasionally Sue would hum a tune of his people, but that too would fade away with the day. The first night outside of the reservation, as they sat around the fire, Dutch Mueller broke the silence: "So, Indian, why do they call you Faraway Sue?" His faint Danish accent chewed at the words; he spat a cheek full of tobacco juice toward the fire.

A coyote yipped in the distance, and they turned their attention to the chained man for an answer that he seemed to be rolling around in his mouth. Sue looked into the fire, his elbows resting on his drawn up knees so that the chain of his shackles jangled when he brushed some of his long black hair away from his hazel eyes. "I don't know," he mumbled, eyes drawn to the sky. "Why do they call *nipali kishux* the moon, or *alankok* the stars?" He waved his hand at the sky, pulling his chains taut. "Maybe you can tell me, I do not know. I have lost my name, this one I picked up along the way much like that hat." He pointed at Jim Phillips, who stopped shuffling his deck of cards, picked up his hat and brushed it off.

"It's not that bad," Phillips said behind perfectly round spectacles; Dutch and Weston laughed, a clean and bubbling thing that passed to Phillips who tried to hide his smile behind his torn up bowler. Sue studied the three men, and a smile came over him that cracked his face into a million pieces.

II

A week outside of Colorado, the companions and their prisoner rode into the small town of Still Creek. The townspeople kept their distance from the group, dust from the road spilling off them with each trot of their horses. There were few buildings in the town, the church and hotel standing out in prominence a storey above the rest, but a general store and the local sheriff had homes there as well.

Weston guided them all to the far end of the town, Dutch and Phillips looking longingly at the hotel as they passed, a solitary whore waving to them behind a cloud of cigar smoke. They dismounted in front of the sheriff's office, stretched their aching backs and limbs, and hitched their horses. Dutch, burly and thick, helped Faraway Sue from his thin and old borrowed horse lifting him like a man aiding a child.

"C'mon then, Sue," Weston said grabbing the Indian around his bicep and leading him into the office.

The office was small and dark. What little light that did come in was from the windows at the back of the building, but that was interrupted by the iron bars of the jail cells, their shadows making a zebra pattern on the walls and floor. A small, wooden table stood before them, a large pair of brown boots crossed on its surface. Behind the boots a white-bearded man pushed his hat over his forehead and raised his black eyebrows at them, widening his calm grey eyes.

"Sheriff," Weston said tipping his hat to the man behind the counter.

"Mr. Weston," returned the sheriff, putting his feet down with a grunt and some effort, "how can I help you?"

Weston pushed Sue to the side and shuffled around in his coat. He pulled a crumpled piece of paper out and flattened it on the counter before the sheriff. "Hoping to pick up my bounty," Weston said pointing to a poorly drawn caricature of an Indian man that may have resembled Sue.

"Five hundred dollars," the sheriff whistled. "This boy here must've done something nasty."

"Killed two men," Weston pointed to the words on the paper. "Families want justice."

The sheriff nodded and gave Sue a strange look around Weston. "Problem here, Bill, is that this bounty is out of Colorado. Says here that only a sheriff of that state can pay out the bounty."

Faraway Sue watched the two white men speak back

and forth and took a peek over Weston's shoulder at the misused wanted poster. He raised his eyebrows and shrugged before he found a chair next to the door and sat waiting. Sue didn't think it looked much like him. The sheriff continued to give him strange looks from the corner of his watery eyes, Sue responded by making a sharp clicking noise as he picked at the cracked surface of his wooden chair.

"Listen, Bill, the best I can do is put him up for the night. How does that sound?"

"Let me think on it, Joe," Weston said adjusting his hat. "I'm goin' go check out the town first."

"Up to yourself," the sheriff shrugged. "Try to have him back here before six, that's when Lorraine expects me for supper."

Weston nodded, gathered Sue up and left the office, the shadow of the bars slanting more severely than when they walked in.

The dust hit them as they exited, and the waning glow of the sun stung their eyes. Sue brought his hand to his eyes to shield them and stood on the steps taking in the town before him. It was small. The buildings were arranged in a straight line on either side of the town's only road. Few people roamed the streets, the children were fewer still. This was a dying town.

Weston descended the stairs with a gallop and slapped his leather gloves against the hitching post; the horses started a little. "Problem, Bill?" Phillips forced his eyes away from the hotel they had passed coming into town, studying the two men. Dutch walked over to the steps and stood next to Sue.

"We're goin' to have to go to Colorado," Weston sighed, giving the hitching post another slap with his gloves.

"Joe won't do us a favour?" Dutch said, puzzled.

"That'll take us a week or two," said Phillips, stroking his shaggy beard. "And it's in the wrong direction." He shook his head and returned to his horse, rubbing its snout.

"C'mon, let's get to the hotel. I need a bath." Weston began to lead his horse into the centre of town, his companions following suit, even Faraway Sue, who walked at the back of their line, scratching his head and observing the buildings.

III

The red morning sun crept into the small room through a window that faced the main street and woke Faraway Sue up from his makeshift bed on the floor of Weston's hotel room. Shackled around a large oak bedpost, his body was tender and his sleep had been troubled. He sat up, his knees cracking as he ran them over the hard, wooden floor. Above him, Weston sat up in the bed, stripped to the waist, his bare chest a map of scars and battle wounds. He rolled his head to look at the Indian, a bottle of whiskey hanging from his right hand.

"Mornin' Sue," he slurred around his neatly trimmed moustache. "Breakfast?" Weston offered him the bottle.

"No." Sue growled, trying to make himself comfortable in his place on the floor.

Weston nodded and took a swig from the bottle himself, hissing out a breath as he swallowed. He placed the bottle on the floor, stood and stretched his long frame. "We'll get moving again today, Sue. Sorry accommodations weren't more comfortable for you." Weston, favouring his left shoulder, strung about him a faded blue shirt but left it unbuttoned as he strapped on his gun belt and put on his boots.

"Don't you want to know what happened?" Sue was sitting still having given up on trying to find a comfortable spot on the floor.

Weston looked him over, buttoning his shirt over old scars and bumps. "No. Sue, it's not for me to know or care."

"I didn't kill them."

Weston rubbed his hand through his light brown hair and put his hat on. "Don't matter Sue." He adjusted his hat and walked out the door, leaving Sue alone in the quiet hotel room.

Dutch and Phillips came in a few moments later and adjusted his bonds so he could walk freely with them once more. Both men looked worse for wear and their eyes were enveloped by black circles and broken blood vessels. Dutch in particular seemed to have been taken by barrel fever. His face stood pale and unshaven, his blond hair slicked back under his hat. Phillips eyed his friend with a knowing grin and nodded this knowledge to Sue as they both grasped him about the arms. The hotel seemed empty as they escorted Sue through it standing on either side of him; the residents had to have evacuated overnight. Weston was waiting for them out front next to the horses, his keen cobalt eyes focused on the street.

"Something's up," he said as he shrugged into his jacket. "Just saw folks rushing towards the centre of town. See 'em?" He pointed his leather-clad hand back the way they had entered the town. Just over the ridge of a small hill Sue could see the crowd of people gathering around another that seemed to be standing above the rest.

"Let's check it out." Weston started to move in the direction of the townsfolk followed by his companions,

Sue still secured in the middle of them. The crowd was dispersing as they arrived, each person returning to their daily lives as if uninterrupted at all; they all kept their distance from Weston and his crew.

Weston scanned the crowd and raised his hand. "Sam, over here." A small boy of about ten trundled over to the small group of men, his dark hair and pale skin pocked with dust and dirt. He looked up at Weston, a blank and expectant look behind his green eyes. "Hey Sam, what's all this about," Weston said, gesturing towards the dwindling crowd.

"They're wrangling up a posse," the boy squeaked, some excitement in his voice. "A buncha folks are dead."

Weston traded glances with Phillips and Dutch, and sent the boy on his way with a handshake and a pat on the head. Sue saw him slip the boy a dollar as they parted ways.

They waded into the group of stragglers and pushed toward the centre where they found the sheriff dismounting his horse and talking to a few people in passing. The sheriff looked tired and was greeting those who spoke to him with a forced patience. He handed the reins of his horse to someone and moved towards Weston.

"You know, Mr. Weston, I waited at my office an extra half hour last night. I was expecting you to drop off your prisoner for the night." The sheriff took out a pipe and began loading it with some tobacco.

Mighty fine of you, Sheriff," Weston said adjusting his gloves. "Word around town is your starting up a posse. Some folks dead?"

"Is that the word around town?" The sheriff lit his pipe with a long match, shook it out, and took some short drags. "As a matter of fact, I was hoping to speak to you about just such an endeavour."

"Thought so. Must be quite a situation to cause such a commotion in this town, hasn't been anything like that since..."

"Since you were here two years ago," the sheriff interrupted, his steel eyes cold behind a small cloud of smoke. Weston nodded. The sheriff let the silence grow for a moment before continuing, "There's a call for a posse, that much is true; came over the telegraph this morning. Men are dead, yes, but they can't figure what did it." The sheriff began to walk towards his office, a trail of smoke in his wake. They followed.

"Well, it can't be that hard to figure out," Dutch slurred next to Sue.

"You'd think so," the sheriff looked over his shoulder, dark eyebrows raised creasing his forehead, "but they can't. Least, that's what the telegraph said. In either case they're looking for able-bodied men who can hunt and track. Sounds like a few fellas I know."

"Is there pay?" Phillips said, his fingers tapping on his leg.

"No, but the town is just past the Colorado border." They had reached the front of the sheriff's office, and he turned to face them once more. "Sounds like a good opportunity for you to collect your bounty."

Weston looked around at Dutch and Phillips. "I suppose it does."

"Yessir, solves a couple of problems as I see it. You will get your bounty, and I get to sit my ass in that office back there and not worry about travelling to god damned Colorado."

"You're not going to ride with us, Sheriff?"

"Nope, and since I just told all my people that you'd

be heading that way, none of them will be going either. Like I said, solves a couple of problems."

Dutch and Phillips moved anxiously at Sue's sides, a grunt coming from the big man. Weston smiled a dry smile and tipped his hat to the sheriff before he began to move towards the hotel. After a moment he paused in his tracks and turned back. "Where's this town in such desperate need of help?"

The sheriff stood by the door to his office and tapped his pipe against the heel of his hand. "Barclay," is all he said before entering his office and closing the door.

CHAPTER TWO

I

The town of Barclay existed only because of the Gold Rush of 1849. Men from all over the United States, from all over the world even, sought out the Western state and its rivers and lakes rumoured to sparkle with gold and silver. Barclay grew up overnight. It started with Aldon Barclay, a crude business man who had a distaste for manual labour and a love of money. Aldon set up shop in a more or less flat meadow land, building a large wooden store full of mining supplies, food stuffs, and a large copper scale that he would use for measuring gold and silver profits from those that staked a claim on his end of the Rockies. The copper scale took up prominence in the large window of his store to entice customers, but it was never used.

Soon after Aldon Barclay built his store, others followed. Some built small houses around his shop, many others set up tents and camped on their claimed land. Business boomed in and around Barclay. Each customer would comment on the large copper scale, claim that they'd be the first to use it. Aldon just nodded and smiled and said that he had no doubt they were right. More men came, families followed as well, and the town grew up in just a few months.

Only one person found gold during those few months:

Simon Barclay, Aldon's eldest son. By some miracle he found it while casually panning in a lake hundreds of men had panned before him. Strong suspicions grew that Aldon himself may have planted the gold to keep his business running. It worked for a time: more men came, more men panned, and more men left empty handed. Aldon soon found himself on the wrong end of accusations from angry prospectors. Not only did his business suffer, but he also lost his life to a burly Tennessean named Casey Abernathy who shot him through the heart at the door of his own shop, just within reach of the unused scale.

The Gold Rush ended in Colorado with Aldon Barclay's death. Many discovered that it was California that ran rife with gold and silver and pulled up stakes following their dreams. Others returned home, defeated by the backbreaking labour without any return.

Simon took up his father's business. A clever man himself, Simon took advantage of the local tree population and close by lakes to stock logging supplies in the store. Once again, people flowed into the town. Where it had once been a group of multinational men none of which had any skill in particular, now it was large, rowdy but experienced loggers that arrived from the Eastern States and French Canada.

As the town grew, men died, but that was natural for any town. Some residents speculated that the means of death was always more gruesome than other towns, but Simon Barclay (who became the mayor) allayed their fears by reminding them that logging was a dangerous business. The townsfolk would nod and were placated by this, looking around at the loggers of the town who were half-mad even when they were sober.

Barclay lived. The town became large, the buildings

more elaborate, and it became self-sustaining through the miners who stayed behind to make a life with their families as farmers. Barclay lived, its people died.

II

Six men were dead, and four strangers rode into town under a hesitant snowfall. Deputy Tom Baker watched them, three able men and a damn chug all tied up. He spat; the only good chug was a dead chug. There was no mystery as to why they rode into town: the sheriff's message must've gotten out. Still, three men weren't about to be of much help. Baker stood up from his rocking chair in front of the saloon, stretched, and bizarrely thought, 'Arms to the sky,' as he chuckled to himself. He moved towards the sheriff's office, his boot heels clicking on the boardwalk that spread out along the main strip of the town.

Once again, Baker could see the strangers as they set themselves up outside Stella's Hotel. The big'gun they had with them gently brought the chug down from his half-dead horse. He spat again as he got closer.

Tom Baker had been a deputy in the town for five years. He'd come down from Ontario, Canada even before that to try his hand at logging. In his young mind it couldn't be that hard if the frenchies from Quebec were doing it. But it was hard, and he wasn't a damn lunatic like the others that scaled trees and hung from them as they were being chopped down. Baker didn't make much of a living after that and spent most of his time in the saloon drinking and playing cards for money. One night he got into a fight with Jake Gagnon over a bottle of whiskey and he ended up in a cell for a couple of days to dry out. Sheriff Forster gave him a choice then: keep clean or get out of town. Baker chose to keep clean, and the sheriff deputised him right there so he could keep a close look on him. He never turned back, though he still loved his whiskey, but the sheriff didn't mean for him to give it up cold turkey. He wasn't a sadist.

Baker knocked on the door and walked into the office. It was a fairly large space, its wooden floors spotless in the lantern light. Three cells stood at the back of the room with only the middle one occupied, a snoring drunk that was taking advantage of the free cot. To the side Sheriff Forster was hunched over a table reading a newspaper, his spectacles mounted precariously on the edge of his nose. Upon noticing Baker walk in, the sheriff shuffled the paper back together, folded it, and looked at him, blue eyes focusing on him over his half-moon glasses.

"Sheriff," Baker said and grabbed a chair to sit on the opposite side of the desk.

"Tommy, how can I help you?" the sheriff's deep voice boomed. He removed his glasses and placed them on the now neatly folded newspapers.

"Some strangers just rode in, Sheriff, thought you'd like to know. They have a chug tied up with them, seems kinda strange."

"Thank you, Tommy." Forster stood and walked around the table toward the door pausing to put on his jacket and hat. "Where are our guests now?"

"Over at the hotel. Probably getting their pet chug all settled away," Baker said, chewing a fingernail absently.

"Tommy, please don't use that word anymore. You know I don't like it," the sheriff said over his shoulder as he exited the office.

Baker watched the sheriff leave. "Chug?" he said to himself. "That's what they're called, ain't they?" He stood, spit out his fingernail, and followed the sheriff to meet the strangers and their chug.

III

Weston caught a small snowflake in his open hand. As it melted, it was replaced by another that floated from the sky; he wiped it in his pants and returned to his horse. If the snow was going to keep up, he'd have to get Phillips to lodge the horses for the night, he thought, idly rubbing the horse's strong neck. The ride from Still Creek was uneventful. He had feared that they would be caught in some early snow squalls, but even that had been avoided. Faraway Sue began to live up to his name, however, and became more and more distant the closer they got to Colorado. Phillips and Dutch tried to get him into conversation over the days they spent together, but he wouldn't have it and would just grunt or nod.

Weston was born and raised in Colorado. He was the son to a Methodist minister who would travel the state delivering sermons out of large tents and ask for donations from those who attended. He had a fairly loyal group of followers that travelled the state with him, and little Bill Weston was no different. In his early adulthood, Weston took on the role of a scout for the Central Pacific Railroad company, helping the set tracks for the Transcontinental Railroad. In short, Weston had been all over the grand state of Colorado, but he had never stepped foot in Barclay in his life.

Barclay was an entirely singular town to Weston. It was built upon a meadow that was surrounded by lakes, rivers, mountains, and forests. Though it had started as many towns did, with settlers building randomly wherever they could lay down foundations, Barclay's buildings were built in a circle meant to surround the large water well that sat in the centre of the town. This aesthetic reminded Weston of some Mexican cities he had seen in his travels, but he rarely saw it transfer over to American towns. Despite falling into a circle, the buildings themselves seemed to lean into one another for support. The main drag of buildings specifically seemed to be built with no boundaries in mind and no direct access to the back from outside. The residents themselves were an equally singular bunch. Composed of logging families, leftover miners, and their descendants, they were a grizzled and stout bunch that seemed easy to smile, but just as quick to suspicion and anger.

"Good day, friend," a powerful voice came from behind him, interrupting his thoughts.

Turning from his horse, he took in the tall, broad shouldered man who approached him. "Good day," Weston tipped his hat and leaned into the haunch of his horse.

"Just arrive in our fair town?" the man continued, his voice cordial as he pushed back his jacket, put his hands on his hips, and revealed the tin star pinned to his vest.

"Just in," Weston nodded. "I think you're the man I wanted to talk to."

IV

They gathered in the saloon, Weston, Phillips, the sheriff, and his deputy, a squat, pockmarked man with a bald head and red-rimmed eyes. The saloon was quiet, only a few of what the sheriff called regulars sitting at the bar or corner tables drinking from large mugs. The building itself was quite large with a second storey of bedrooms for the whores that worked there. They sat in the middle of the room at a round table amongst at least a dozen more like it. The sheriff didn't think they'd be disturbed.

"So," the sheriff started, "you're here to help?" He

turned around and waved four fingers at the bartender who nodded and ducked behind the bar.

"Maybe," Weston said catching Phillips' eye. "Your call for help seemed pretty vague."

"There's a reason for that: we don't know what the fuck is happening 'round here." The deputy was looking at the table, picking at his fingernails, and a smirk crossed his face as the sheriff said this.

"Maybe you'd care to elaborate then," Phillips said, pushing his glasses up from his nose.

The sheriff leaned forward, his elbows resting on the dark oak table. "Near the end of summer, this year, a young man named Daniel Glacer disappeared. He had been drinking in this very saloon the night before. Most of us thought he would turn up in a haystack or something equally as foolish." The sheriff paused to remove his hat, slicking back his silvery hair; his deputy nodded along to the story. "Well, he didn't turn up for another two days, and what turned up wasn't much to go on."

"How do you mean?" Weston said as the bartender brought over four glasses of straight whiskey and distributed them evenly amongst the four.

The sheriff drained his whiskey and slammed the glass on the table, signalling the bartender for four more before he left the table. "Well, there wasn't much left to see. Tommy here," he cast his thumb toward his deputy, "was the one who found it. A mass of blood and guts and bone."

"I thought it was Paul Tourville dumping his cast-offs from a Mule Deer he'd killed. He's been known to do that, even though we've talked to him about it a time or two," Tommy the deputy broke in.

"Thank you, Tommy. Yes, it looked very much like

cast-offs from an animal picked clean. The only thing that gave it away as human was the skull, still partially corded in muscle and buried under the other remains." The sheriff sat back in his chair and hooked his thumbs into his belt loops, his face ashen.

"Did you arrest anyone?" Phillips said, stroking his chin, sky blue eyes focused on the sheriff.

"Arrest anyone? Boy, why would I do that?" The sheriff sat up in his chair and locked eyes with his inquisitor.

"Seems pretty obvious that it was murder, Sheriff. Did you question this Paul Tourville fella?"

"Well, son, we ain't too sure t'were a human who done it." The bartender had returned, and the sheriff grabbed a glass from his tray and drained it as he did his first. Phillips and Weston looked at him puzzled.

"Teeth marks," Deputy Tommy spoke up, his small grin still touching the corners of his mouth. "It looked like the bones were gnawed on."

"And not just by scavengers neither," the sheriff spoke up again. "Teeth that drew the meat from the bone. Now, how can a man arrest someone for that?"

"Well, there have been known cases..." Phillips started, taking out his deck of cards and shuffling them distractedly.

The sheriff put up his hand. "No, son, no one around here would do anything like that. Them French loggers may be out of their minds in the trees, but they ain't savages. Even if they did do this, I couldn't be seen arresting them for it."

Phillips began to talk, but Weston stifled him with a hand and spoke himself: "And there have been others?"

The sheriff went through the rest of the deaths. There were six in total over as many months. Each amounted to the same thing: a man went missing and a pile of human cast-offs were found a day or two later with most of their meat gnawed off. There had been two separate search parties sent out into the surrounding areas, one went into the tall-treed forests and the other went into the snow-capped Rockies. Neither came back with anything conclusive, and because the remains were left in or around the town, the tracks were compromised by the heavy foot traffic. The sheriff stood at an impasse.

"This town has suffered its fair share of hardships… Death has visited at every corner, but this is something quite different." The sheriff finished with his third glass of whiskey.

"Well, Sheriff, how can we help?"

"Fresh eyes, boy. I'm afraid we're all too close to this 'round here, that we might not be seeing things for what they are. Maybe we're making it more sensational than it actually is."

Weston and Phillips eyed one another for a moment. "Well sir, before we put our eyes to work, there's a matter of an Indian in my hotel room to attend to."

V

Faraway Sue was losing at cards. He suspected that the big man, Dutch, was cheating. That he was hiding cards in his sleeves or pockets. There wasn't much that Sue could do about that though. His hands were chained, and he felt he was going to die soon. He looked down at his cards, they were not good.

"I don't think you have much chance here, Mr. Sue," the big man spoke in his strange English, but then, Sue thought, all English was strange. Perhaps this man's was more so though. When he was a boy, the first white man he met was a missionary trying to teach him about God and Jesus Christ. He was a nice white man, his English was very plain and kind, but Sue could not understand it. The second white man he met, when Sue himself was not yet a man, pointed a gun at his head and made him watch as another man placed a knife to his father's throat. This man's English was loud and angry, but Sue understood it. There had been many other white men since then, but Sue would always remember those first two.

Sue played his cards and lost. Dutch celebrated as he always did by hooting and laughing and snatching up the cards to play another game, and perhaps to shuffle in the extra cards he had in his sleeves. The room they were in was much nicer than the last hotel. There were rugs on the floor, and a painting of a horse on the wall. There was even a small table and two chairs, which they were able to sit at to play cards. Still, Sue would have rather been under the sky and not a wooden roof.

The door opened behind them, Weston and the smart one, Phillips, walked in. They looked serious and stared at Sue.

"How'd that go, gentlemen?" Dutch asked, shuffling the cards, not paying much attention to them.

"Pretty interesting," Phillips chimed in, approaching the table.

"Anything we can help with?" Dutch said, handing out the cards, adding two extra piles for his compatriots.

"I think so." Weston stepped forward now and as he did two other white men walked into the room. "C'mon Sue, time to go."

Sue turned back to the table, glided his chains over the scratched wooden surface and picked up his cards. Dutch turned his eyes up to him, his fingers white on the deck of cards still in his hand. "Damn," said the Indian. "Pair of aces."

PART TWO
CHAPTER THREE

I

Sue's cell was larger than he had expected. He stood next to the barred window, rubbed at the red divots where the shackles had been, and looked out on the dying sun. He smelled the crisp certainty of snow on the air, a cold and fresh scent that his senses welcomed. He extended his hand through the bars, arching his back and twisting his shoulder to accommodate the height of the window. He could feel the small pellets of snow as they fell into his palm, could feel their cold seeping into his pores, but was only met with small water droplets when he pulled his hand back into the cell. He rubbed the melted remains onto the back of his neck under his raven coloured hair. The feeling sustained him, reawakened his muddled mind, and allowed him to sit on the hard, wooden cot in relative peace. He began to hum a song; it was a good song about death and life and second chances. He hummed the song and looked to the sky outside, the snow falling to blanket the land.

II

The deputy couldn't stand the chug's stupid humming. The sound burrowed into his bones and made him shake and shiver. There was no way that Tom Baker was going to let an ignorant savage get one over on him like that. He stood from the desk and placed the ring of keys on its well-worn surface, rolled his sleeves over his thick forearms, tightened his belt and adjusted his holster so he could hold the revolver's handle in plain view of anyone looking at him; he approached the cell.

"Hey, chug," he said, tapping on the cold iron bars with his bare hand. The Indian remained sitting, his neck stretched so he could look out the window, and he still hummed. Tom jiggled the door against its lock, and a loud clanging exploded against the walls of the office. "Hey, Injun." Tom placed his hand on his revolver. "Stop your god damned humming."

The humming continued.

Tom slammed his fist against the bars. A clang rang out, and he pulled his hand back with a sharp inhale of breath. His knuckles were bloody and bruised, but the Indian just sat there humming his savage tunes. Tom growled. He grabbed his gun and pointed it at the chug, threatened his life over and over again, but still the prisoner persisted. Spittle ran down the corners of Baker's mouth, and his hand pained him. His breathing was laboured, and he shuddered after every exhale. He cursed on Faraway Sue, moved away from the cell, and slammed his hands on the table. He grabbed his jacket from the back of the chair and exited the office. He left the Indian alone with his humming, for now.

The snow fell in small flakes as the deputy shrugged into his jacket. That meant there was plenty more on the way, Tom thought, poking a cigarette into the corner of his mouth and lighting it with a match inside his cupped hand. Smoke rolled from his mouth and nose as he turned the corner to the small alley between the sheriff's office and the general store.

The damn Injun had gotten under his last nerve. Sheriff Forster had told him to watch the chug while he settled a few things with those other newcomers. He never had to watch a chug before. What did the sheriff mean, Tom wondered. He figured they were more like dogs; if they bite their owner, then they got shot. Couldn't he just shoot the chug and have it done with? He inhaled another stream of smoke, feeling a surge of satisfaction. Maybe, if the situation was right. The sheriff had a bit of a soft spot for the chugs, the nips; even the fucking bean eaters. Only God knew why. But if he pulled it right, there would be nothing the Sheriff could say or do. The Indian just ran at him, surprised him, grabbed him by the throat. He had no choice but to shoot the poor chug. A smile crossed his face as he took a final draw from his hand-rolled cigarette and threw it into the amassing snow.

As the deputy turned to leave the small alley, he heard a crunch somewhere behind him that caused him pause. He looked above him: the sun was beginning to set and the marble clouds tainted the light that remained; it changed the alley into a monochromatic collection of black shadows between glimpses of white snow and grey buildings.

"Who's back there?" Tom said, pulling his gun from its holster with the smooth creak of old leather. Tom knew the alley well, he often stood there listening to the prisoners whine and bawl. Heard the drunks getting sick, while other times he just sat and watched the town pass by from the shadows. He knew what those shadows held: empty ground and a view of the rear-end of his office and the buildings surrounding it. He'd heard strange and terrible things coming through those bars, heard the chittering of rats and mice, but never had he heard this sound.

The sharp crunch, like a foot through hardened snow, was followed by a short, high pitched trumpeting sound that began to echo through the narrow alleyway making it hard for the deputy to pinpoint the source. He waded deeper into the shadows, gun at the ready.

If hard pressed, Tom would have said it were a deer making the noises he heard, but he didn't have time to think it over. He paused at the threshold of the shadows, cocking his head to the side. The sound stopped.

The deputy squinted, could feel the creases at his temples harden, and set his muddy, brown eyes to see in the dark. At first it was what he expected: the empty alleyway, the buildings just wider than his shoulders and the gathering snow, but something flitted past his vision. He turned to see it pass the exit of the alley, and he heard the high-pitched noise again, now echoed by a low grunt. Tom moved into the shadows, his eyes easing into the darkness with him, and then he felt it. Something was behind him. It was a presence that felt wrong somehow, that made what little hair Tom had on his neck stand on end. Before the deputy could move, he felt a sharp, jagged pain in his neck and a warm sensation spreading below it. He fell to the ground into a blackness darker than the shadows before him.

III

"That's him alright," Forster said, adjusting the legs of his jeans as he made his way into his office.

"What a mess," Jim Phillips said, adjusting his glasses and turning away from the body that was piled in the middle of the alleyway.

Bill Weston stood over the body rubbing his chin and nodded in agreement to Phillips - it was a mess. The body was barely recognizable as human: in some places chunks of flesh and muscle had been torn off by some sort of clawed mandible, while sharpened teeth was the culprit in others. Weston had seen deer torn to pieces by wolves before, ripped apart and left with only bone and stomach. Wolves didn't take their time with their kill, they ate and then hoarded the leftovers. No waste. This though, there was a special pleasure had in this death. The wounds were given singular attention, each in its own order and time. He shook his head and followed the others into the office.

"I didn't see it. Couldn't even see this shit until I woke up with an eye full of it," Tom Baker said, coughing and rubbing the back of his head as Weston and Phillips stomped snow into the makeshift jail. Baker shivered. "All I remember is that… that… sound." He pulled a blanket around his shoulders.

"Like an elk," came Sue's deep voice from further into the sheriff's office.

"Fuck you, chug," Tom said, attempting to rise but fell back into his chair, a green look coming over him that sapped his conviction.

"Easy there, Tommy," the sheriff said from his own seat, bent forward with his elbows on his knees.

The sheriff had rounded up Weston and company, relieved them of their drinks and cards, and called them forth. He had found his deputy face down in the alley, blood dribbling from the back of his head, laying beside the remains that were still in the shadows of the alley now. The sheriff was concerned and afraid, damn near frightened to death. He looked old, weathered. Weston thought it was more than the stress of the murders that was drawing him out so.

"You see anything, Sue?" Phillips had moved closer to the Indian's cell.

Sue sat on his cot in the dark, the orange light of the lanterns lit at the front of the office struggled to reach the bars of Sue's cell. His wet, brown eyes glistened in the darkness.

"Nohm. Heard it though. Heard grunting like that of a deer, an elk. Heard the heavy breathing of the deputy, and heard him fall to the ground. Then I heard nothing."

"Thanks, Sue," Phillips said, running his hands over the cell bars as he turned back to the others. "This brings up a lot of questions." He tapped his temple with two fingers and paced.

"The first of which," said Weston, moving his hand from his mouth, "is 'who's the deadman'?" He looked at the sheriff, who sat back in his chair and rubbed at his eyes with the heels of his hands.

"Well now, let's see." He cleared his throat and spat into a nearby bucket. "We ain't had no people reported missing. Not since Daniel anyway, but we did have a few men go out to do some huntin' in yonder forest a few days ago. Not likely to see them back until next week though."

"It's as good a start as any," Weston said and nodded to himself. "Think you can lead us to them, Sheriff?"

"Myself and Tommy can do that. Shouldn't be a problem."

The door to the office thudded open, snow and wind blew in around Dutch's big boots as he stomped his way in, slamming the door closed in his wake.

"You know," Dutch said removing his hat and brushing some snow from it, "in my country, weather like this could be considered a nice summer day." He barked out a laugh that no one joined in on.

"See anything out there?" Weston said, eyeing the big man.

"Summer is a great time for tracking in my homeland."

IV

The tracks were indistinct as they were partially covered by the waning snow, but they led Weston, Dutch, and the sheriff into the forest to the north of Barclay. Weston had decided it best to leave the injured deputy behind and thought Phillips would be keen enough to put his mind to work on the matter. He would continue to work with the deputy to identify the recently deceased, and they could plan their next move from there.

Phillips was a singular man, thought Weston. An able man, to be sure, but quiet and introspective; the man couldn't turn his brain off. He had met Phillips on the road when they were both in the company of the same caravan leaving Mexico for California. He opened up to Weston on the trails, let him know about his experiences some, many of which they had in common. A mutual friendship grew over that time, but Weston couldn't shake the feeling that behind the thoughtful silences there was something Phillips wouldn't, or couldn't, disclose.

"Fuck," said Dutch over the whine of his horse and he jerked it back toward the footpath they followed in the wake of the killer's trail. The snow made the ground slick and wet which had turned the soft ground into slippery mud that plagued the horses. Sheriff Forster turned in his saddle and held out the lantern he carried in a thick fist behind him.

"Everyone okay?" The familiar boom of the sheriff came from beyond the blazing radiance of the oil lamp.

Dutch grunted, and the sheriff returned the lantern to face forward with a shrug. They had little time to prepare for the trail, and none thought to grab the light other than the weathered lawman. The small group crawled forward on horseback, single file, huddled behind the sheriff's guiding light: a group of spectres roaming out of the snow.

"How's it looking up there, Sheriff?" Weston called from his place at the rear. "Any end in sight?"

"Well, sir, if your man is right, and I ain't about to doubt him, the tracks keep going over yonder," Forster said, halting his horse and leaning to the side with the lantern extended into the trees.

"Anything out here, Sheriff, so far from town?" Weston's voice strained to rise above the wind.

"Not much," Forster said, pushing on, the orange light of his lamp creeping just ahead of him. "There are some farms out this far though, late comers to the town, or just loners." The sheriff snorted.

Weston nodded. There were always some who felt more comfortable on their own. Some who felt less threatened the further they were from others. Perhaps some people got too close for another's liking, he pondered.

They descended back into silence then, save for Dutch's cursing and the heavy breathing of their horses.

V

When they came upon the farmhouse, a small, but sturdy structure, the first dawn's light had begun to turn the sky a smoky grey.

"That's the last of the tracks," said Dutch who had had caught up to Forster once the path had widened out.

"That's Elbert Darrio's house right there," the sheriff

nodded his head toward the house. "He grows the finest tomatoes this side of Mexico."

"Where's the animals?" Dutch said as all three slid out of their saddles and hitched the horses to a fence that seemed meant for holding livestock.

"Oh, Elbert didn't have much in that way. A couple of sheep, a cow, two or three horses."

Dutch gave Weston a hesitant look before turning his eyes to the ground. The three men took a slow walk around the house, Dutch and Weston keeping an eye to the ground in search of more tracks, Forster with his lantern held before him.

"No tracks," said Dutch. "None since those at the fence." He crouched down and moved some snow and frowned.

They wound their way back to the front of the farm house. It looked abandoned in the grey light of the dawn; skeletal. There were no lights coming from the empty windows, and there was no smoke coming from the small stone chimney. It looked as though it had been this way for some time. The three walked up the dirt path to the door and the sheriff knocked.

'When was the last time you saw Mr. Darrio, Sheriff?"

The sheriff bent his head and furrowed his brow. "I can't quite recall. A couple of weeks. Maybe more." He pinched the bridge of his nose between forefinger and thumb. "Ole Elbert didn't like leaving Jacinta and Bethany out here by themselves for too long." He raised a hand and knocked again.

"I suppose it is a little far out. Must be some animal attacks?"

"Oh, there are some to be sure, but that's not what

brought Elbert back here so quickly. That honour went to big Earl Hathaway. Them boys never did get along."

Weston gave Dutch a quick look. "What brought that on?"

"Earl and Elbert? Oh, I can't say for sure, but Earl was never too keen on Mexicans or Indians. Elbert was a little of both, you see."

"Earl live around here?" Dutch said, having another look around.

"Not too far, not too close either. Just over yonder." The sheriff pointed north.

He knocked one more time, the reverberations could be heard even from the wrong side of the door. "I suppose I'll let myself in," he said, opening the door and casting his light in front of him, a bastion in the dark.

The house seemed nice enough: a large cast iron stove stood to the right of the door and monopolized the majority of the space, the rest of which was taken up by a handcrafted table and chairs. To Weston's left was a small sitting room, with a cozy looking armchair and a foot stool. Weston was quite certain he had never seen a farmer with such luxuries in his lifetime. The sheriff swung his lantern forwards to a small hallway and moved a step or two forward. The light cascaded over the bare walls, and the scuffed oaken floorboards.

"There's table settings out," Dutch said, pointing toward the table. Neither man responded. A shiver went through Weston as he passed his eyes over the table once more. Three plates, two mugs, one small glass. The house felt cold.

A thump echoed from the hallway and drew their attention. Weston slipped his gun from its holster and took the lantern from the sheriff, who handed it over without fuss. He moved forward into the hall, and he could feel Dutch at his back, his own revolver loosed.

Their boot heels did not echo on the wooden floor, each one singular and final. Weston panned the light around and focused it on the hallway, his eyes scanning the dark corners for the cause of the thump. The hallway contained two bedrooms, their ill-fitting wooden doors shut just to. Nothing. He turned to look back on the sheriff, his boots now muffled, and sticky as he moved. He looked down to see a pool of blood.

"Dammit." Weston swung the lamp in a low arc in front of him. It looked as though the blood had pooled from the bedroom doors on either side of the hall.

"What is it?" the sheriff whispered and moved toward the hall. Weston held up his hand to stop him and then crouched toward the floor letting the sheriff see the freezing blood. The sheriff's face went hard, and he unslung his repeater rifle from his shoulder.

Weston turned to Dutch and pointed at the bedroom on the left with his gun. Dutch nodded, and they moved toward it, their boots making a horrendous squelch as the moved.

Weston nudged the door open with the barrel of his gun, and an unwelcome screech of hinges cried out in the quiet cabin that made him catch his breath. Weston froze in place, Dutch followed suit, but silence followed. He cast an uncertain look over his shoulder at Dutch and then followed him into the room, pushing the door all the way open. Weston swung the lantern before him, casting the beam of light upon the trail of blood.

It wasn't the sight of the dismembered bodies that caused Dutch to retch, nor that the bodies were surrounded by their own blood and innards. It was the smell. A thick pungency that filled his mouth and nose so suddenly that he had no time to combat the rise of his stomach contents.

Weston moved aside to let Dutch pass into the hallway; he could hear the sheriff coughing at the front of the house as he did. Weston had been in war, had seen atrocities committed on brother by brother, but the scene before him was a new kind of brutality. If he were a religious man like his father, he might even say it was evil that set down in this house and worked the devil's influence on the occupants. Weston backed out of the room and closed the door.

He leaned on the door to collect his thoughts, holstered his gun and focused on the second bedroom.

"How many?" the sheriff called from the entryway, looking a little paler than when they had arrived.

Weston heard the words the sheriff was saying, knew their individual meaning, but could not conjure any significance out of their stringing together.

"How many bodies?" the sheriff clarified.

"Two'd be my guess", Weston said without raising his head.

"What about the girl?"

THUMP

Weston moved towards the second bedroom, his gun ready. Dutch had entered the house again, but Weston waved him off when he saw the big man make to rejoin him.

He pushed the door open slowly and peered into the room. It was a child's bedroom: toys were scattered about the floor, and a small writing table and a child-sized chair were tucked in the corner. The bed split the room in two, with a pink babydoll sitting upon it. In the far corner of the room, beyond the mess of toys and the bed, a blonde headed little girl stood facing the wall. Weston's heart sank. From her fair, almost white, blonde hair to her buckle shoes, she was splattered with blood. He entered the room crouched low to the ground, trying to make himself smaller. His gun had vanished, and he held his hands out before him. The girl swayed in place in front of the wall, her hands clenched at her sides. Weston had manoeuvred close enough to reach for her, had put out his hand to grab her shoulder when she walked directly into the wall before her.

THUMP

It was small impact, but she bounced off the wall, her fists clenched tighter. Weston, closer now, could see a small, red bump beginning to form in the middle of her forehead surrounded by ugly looking bruises. She'd been doing this for some time now.

Weston grabbed her by the shoulder, drew her into his chest and cradled her, his chin brushing the top of her fine hair. He could feel her tiny body relax, melt into his own, and he walked with her in his arms towards the front of the house.

Once they passed the threshold of the hallway, the girl's body tensed, and she made to escape from his arms. He held her tight and tried to soothe her, "Hush now, you'll be alright. You're safe now."

The girl arched her back and clawed at Weston's face and eyes. She beat him about the head and tried to kick him with her flailing legs. The sheriff and Dutch came to his aide and attempted to subdue her lithe arms, but they proved too wiry for their grasp. She squirmed, and scratched, and beat her way out of Weston's arms and ran back into the hallway, and into her parents' bedroom. Weston ran after her but heard her high-pitched wail before he made it to the open door. The girl had fainted in the middle of the room between her parents' unrecognizable bodies.

CHAPTER FOUR

I

Jim Phillips paced the floor of the sheriff's office, ignoring the bewildered stare of Deputy Tom Baker that followed him as he stalked back and forth in front of the entrance. It had been too long; Weston should've come back for supplies or back up if the tracks led them further than a half-day's travel. He stopped in front of the door and peered out the small window that was inlaid within it. The snow had almost stopped, but its cast-offs still swirled on the hard-packed and likely frozen street. Despite the obvious cold, there were signs of activity from the people of Barclay rousing themselves for another day in their city, and unaware that one of their own had been stolen from them during the night, under the nose of their own sheriff's deputy no less.

"I don't know what you're so bent out of shape over," Baker said. "The sheriff will take care of your boys." He removed the towel from the back of his neck and examined the drying blood stain, frowned and replaced it, swearing to himself.

Phillips stared back at the man for a moment, pausing his movement and crossing his wrists behind him. "I have no such worry for my compatriots' well-being, it's just..."

"Just that you don't want to be left out? Get used to that 'round here, son." Baker grunted and shifted himself out of the chair he had been slouching in behind the sheriff's desk. "Sheriff never lets me do anything. I'm surprised I'm even allowed to carry this," he said, producing his tarnished and scrubby revolver, turning it over in his hands with a little sigh.

Phillips turned to the chubby deputy. "Put that away before you hurt yourself." Baker just shrugged and put it away with a grin. "Where did you get that old thing anyway? Did you find it in the woods?"

"Nah, Forster gave it to me when he took me on as deputy. T'ain't much to look at, is it?"

Phillips returned to his pacing. Phillips had been a patient man once; it had served him well in his work as a hangman when he lived down south. Phillips took on work as a hangman after years as a turnkey in a federal jail. He was offered the job by Judge Marlow, who presided over the courts in those parts. Some said it was a punishment, that being given a position to take the lives of men was against God. Phillips thought different. The judge gave him the job because he was the only one with the guts to do it.

It didn't take Phillips long to figure out patience was as good as guts to a hangman. He couldn't count the times he'd been forced to wait for a prisoner, with lawmen as apt as Deputy Baker often putting a brake on proceedings. He wasn't sure if Weston knew this about him, not even sure if Dutch did. It didn't matter, of course. He wasn't that person anymore. He'd left that life behind; he supposed they all left something behind.

"They'll be back soon," a rasping, deep voice said from the back of the office.

Phillips approached Faraway Sue's cell, placed his hands on the cold iron bars, and peered inside. It wasn't much of a cell, but then again, cells weren't supposed to be much of anything. A least there was a small cot and a bucket to relieve himself in; Phillips doubted this was the worst place Sue had been lodged. Perhaps the worst part of it was the barred window that was open to the elements. Snow had accumulated in small piles around the bars, window ledge, and even the floor under the window. As Phillips peered in, the Indian was sitting cross legged on his bunk, long black hair pushed back away from his face, and deep Chestnut eyes staring back into Phillips' own.

"And how do you know that, Sue?"

"Don't you listen to that fuckin' chug," Baker growled from behind, rising from his seat again. "He's like the rest of them Injuns, savages. Trick ya' in an instant and stab ya' in the back while you're looking the other way."

Baker's face was red with boiled over rage. Phillips gripped the pistol he had holstered at his back and took a glance at Sue still sitting in his cell. The Indian offered him a slow shrug and let his hands fall into his lap.

"Shut up, damn you," Phillips said finally, interrupting Baker's litany of racial slurs and curse words. "This man knows more about the world than you know about your own asshole." He took a deep breath. Baker looked like he was going to protest, but sat back in his chair, grumbling to himself, his eyes on Phillips' pistol.

"Now, Sue," Phillips turned to face the Indian once more. "How do you know they'll be back soon?"

"I can smell them on the wind." Sue had untwined his legs and came to the bars speaking in whispers. "They smell of blood and fear." He took a loud sniff, bending himself back to inhale the air around him. "They have company. Someone they are bringing back with them. Someone young."

With that, the office door banged open and Dutch stomped in with a small child in his arms. Weston and the sheriff followed him in, the latter slamming the door.

"Phillips, get over here and take a look," Weston said as he removed his jacket and hat.

Phillips looked back at Faraway Sue, disbelief clouding his eyes, his mouth hanging open in wonder. "How?"

"Nature," Sue said, waving his arms and walking backwards towards his cot. "The Mother Earth has told me, the spirits of the forest and of the wind delivered the message." He paused and sat on his cot once more, raising his knees to his chest he lounged against the cell wall. "Or, I saw them coming through the window." He gestured with his thumb to the snow-covered bars behind him.

Phillips could feel his cheeks turn red, he tried to speak but no words came. With nothing else he could do, he turned on his heel and moved towards Weston and Dutch. As he did, he thought he heard Baker mutter to himself, "Told ya'."

II

The girl was bundled up and laid down on the cot of an empty cell; she hadn't woken up since the episode at her home. Weston pushed his hands through his sweaty brown hair, moving it away from his face. It had been a long day and it was only just past noon.

"What the hell is going on around here?" Dutch had pooled his girth onto the worn wooden floor, his broad shoulders leaning into the corner opposite the door.

"Thought that's what *you* were supposed to figure

out," Baker mumbled from behind the desk.

"It's... I never imagined... it was never like this," the sheriff managed, ignoring his deputy.

Weston walked to the centre of the room. "All right. Let's figure this out. What do we know?"

"We know something is eating people around here," said Dutch, eyes to the ceiling.

Weston gave him an impatient look. "Something constructive."

"We know people are being eaten," Phillips said, stepping up beside Weston. "We know that whatever is doing it leaves a lot behind, so not like a wolf or any other wild animal I've come across. We also know that it is good at hiding its tracks and being stealthy overall."

"It can open doors," the sheriff croaked.

"What?" Baker said at last.

"It got into the Darrio house without any damage. The door was fine, no broken windows..."

"Doesn't sound much like an animal at all," Weston said, nodding.

"So, we're looking for some crazy, fuckin' cannibal?" Baker was near giggling as he said it.

"Sure," Phillips cut across his laugh. "Why not? There's bound to be an old prospector or mountain man living 'round here. Loneliness will drive a man to do some crazy things, maybe even drive a man mad." His words got quicker and quicker as he talked, his feet tapping. Weston thought of Earl.

"It does make sense." Dutch was now focused on the conversation, his sharp, green eyes focused on Phillips.

Weston agreed, it was all very logical, but it didn't feel right. Even after considering Earl, his gut told him that the answer wasn't theirs yet, that they were missing some pieces. His mind raced, but he couldn't figure it out. He knew it was there, but he couldn't place it.

He turned to Baker and Phillips. "What could you figure out about the body, do we know who's missing?"

Baker and Phillips shared a brief glance. Phillips stepped forward once more. "We couldn't come up with much. There was more body missing than we had thought, and it was impossible to survey the town without causing a panic."

Weston nodded and began to pace the room. "All right," he said, breaking his own train of thought. "We still need to check on those hunters you mentioned earlier, Sheriff. Phillips, you come with me. Deputy, you feel up for a ride?"

Baker's mouth dropped open. He looked to the sheriff, but got no comfort there. He managed to mumble an affirmative as he stood and checked on the towel he'd been holding to his neck.

"Good. Dutch, you stay and keep an eye to the young lady. Sheriff, maybe you could fetch up someone who could take care of the poor girl and start asking around to see if someone is missing."

Weston gathered his things and joined Baker and Phillips at the door. He took a look back at the girl now asleep in the cot. How peaceful she looked, he thought, and left not sure if he would see any of them again.

III

"Trevor and his boys usually set up camp 'round this area," Baker said, pushing aside some low hanging branches as he passed the solid oak tree.

They had started to follow the same route to the Dario farmhouse, practically backtracking over the hoof prints they had left earlier that morning, but after a while they turned off into a thicker forest. Weston was relieved. He didn't want to see that old farmhouse again this soon if he could manage it. They were riding for less than an hour before they had to dismount and tie their horses to some thin saplings along a small path that Weston could barely make out, even with his trained eyes. It was a steep embankment that Baker led them along: Weston's ankles bent at an uncomfortable angle, and he had no trouble imagining a horse refusing to take the trail or injuring itself as it stumbled along the overgrown path.

The towering trees, and thickness of the brush, was something Weston hadn't experienced in the Colorado he had explored as a child. Crawling along behind his father's pastoral procession, Weston was accustomed to running between thin trees with flaking bark, hunting caterpillars and frogs in the stagnant ponds and marshes deep in the forests, venturing past anything that most men had cared to explore on those backwoods' carriage trails. And yet, he had never seen a forest quite like the one on the outskirts of Barclay.

The first thing that struck Weston was the pungent, acrid smell that burned his nostrils and made his eyes water. The marshes of his childhood had similar smells, but none so strong or repellent as this. It was like the smell of a long-forgotten death, its rot still lingering in the air. Once Weston became accustomed to the smell, it was the complete barricade the canopy of trees provided that seemed unusual. Within the forest, the sun at midday was reduced to small strips of light fighting their way through branches and leaves. Even the snow didn't take as much of a foothold under the trees as it did back in town. Weston was thankful for that at least and thought with the presence of even a slight amount of snow, the steep embankment would be impassable.

They came out onto more flat land a short time later, and the path seemed to open a bit. Baker halted the small group to take a break leaning against a sturdy tree.

"Won't be too far now," the deputy panted, drawing a cigarette from his front pocket. "Trevor and his crew usually hol' up o'er yonder. There's a little clearing o'er there where they camp." He pointed one chubby finger along the path and took a hit off his smoke, his watery eyes expectant.

"If it's just the same to you, Deputy, we'll keep moving. You catch up when you're able," Weston said, moving onto the path and motioning for Phillips to follow.

"Fine idea, Mr. Weston. I'll be along before you know it," Baker said, barely able to contain his delight.

It wasn't long before Weston and Phillips came to the break in the woods Baker had mentioned, though it wasn't much of one. The treeless patch of forest only spanned the same space as Faraway Sue's cell in Barclay. Even with the lack of trees, the canopy seemed to hold stronger in the small area, and Weston found he had to squint to help his eyes adjust to the lowlight.

"Not much in the way of a camp," Phillips said, walking over the dead and discarded branches, hands clasped behind his back.

"I don't think the good deputy knows as much about his neighbours as he'd like to believe," Weston said, crouching down and poking at the ground with a stick.

Phillips chuckled and examined the path that led further into the forest. He adjusted his glasses and frowned. "There's been foot traffic here, but not recently. I'd say, maybe, two days old?"

Weston nodded, "There's the remains of a fire over here, but it's been cold for some time." He stood and stretched, relishing the creaks and cracks of his bones as he did. "Well, should we get moving, or wait here for the deputy?"

"I think you'd better come look at this," Phillips said, his voice further away and muffled. Weston turned towards the voice, but Phillips was absent. He moved toward the opening Phillips had been inspecting and pushed into the tangle of branches and brush.

Phillips was crouched low to the ground, his hands dangling between his bent legs, yet his head was positioned at a weird angle, looking above him into the trees. He turned to look at Weston as he approached, his face blank. "Look here," he said, pointing at the ground.

Weston moved up behind Phillips and peered over his shoulder. The ground was covered in pine needles, cones, and other tree cast-offs, but, in the centre of the trail, mud and dirt was beginning to peer through from the wear of the path. Weston leaned forward to get a better look at the ground Phillips was motioning towards. It took him a moment, but he saw it: a deep brown stain, something he wouldn't have noticed if it hadn't been pointed out to him. He studied it for a moment more. "Blood?" He stood straight and rubbed his chin. "Could be, but we can't really be sure."

Phillips caught his eye again, waving a finger and then pointing it skyward. Weston followed the direction, his head arching back on his neck to take in the sight.

There were at least three of them: bodies. They were hanging upside down from the thick branches overhead, and were in various forms of dismemberment, missing body parts and flesh in equal measure. Even a head appeared to be missing. Weston shot Phillips a quick glance and slowly scanned the area around them. He was hesitant to make sudden movements, to draw attention to himself. He couldn't help but fear that they had been drawn into a trap that was just about to spring.

Weston made slow movements but placed his hand on his gun without hesitation. Phillips followed his lead and together they surveyed the area.

"Not much to go on." Phillips was casting his eyes back and forth constantly, his hand also on his gun.

"No tracks." Weston confirmed Phillips' suspicion. The field, the path, nothing held tracks nor even a sign that tracks had been scrubbed out. It was just blank. Weston struggled to understand it. How could one man kill three other men and then hang them from a tree without leaving some trace? It wasn't easy work lifting a dead man, Weston knew from experience, let alone three dead men.

"Weston?" Baker broke through the brush and onto the path with a stumble. "There you are. Thought I might'a lost ya' back there some...." Baker trailed off, his eyes catching a glimpse of the hanging bodies swinging carelessly in the breeze. Weston watched the colour drain from the deputy's face and a grimace form around his mouth. "Shit," he said, slumping his shoulders and desperately trying to keep his eyes on the ground.

"These the people we've been looking for?" Weston said, approaching the deputy.

Baker took a quick look up. "I believe so, sir, from what I can see." He forced his eyes back down again before he'd finished answering the question.

Weston nodded and began to walk back towards the horses. "Let's get back to town."

"Bill, we're not going to cut them down?" Phillips

adjusted his glasses, looking up at the discarded bodies. Phillips was a hard man to read. He was a thinker, most of his decisions followed logic and reason. But every now and then, something seemed to pull on one of his heart strings.

Weston turned back, halted in his tracks. "No time." He saw a deepening frown spread across his companion's face. Weston sighed. "C'mon, we'll come back when there's more light left in the day or send someone that can." He looked at Phillips, his eyes focused on the glinting glass surrounding his eyes. "We need to go, Jim. Now." He passed into the small clearing and disappeared from their sight.

Phillips and Baker gave each other uneasy looks, between which Baker avoided putting his eyes skyward while Phillips seemed as though he could hardly take his eyes off the grisly sight. With a final look at the dead, they followed Weston through the break of the campground and into the ever-darkening day.

CHAPTER FIVE

I

Faraway Sue was alone. The daylight slanted through the window and cast a skewed shadow of the bars on the floor. He ran his rough hand over the iron bars, heard the scratch, clunk, scratch, clunk as his hand bounced between them. Sue didn't mind being alone, but he didn't like confinement. Perhaps if they had to ask him to stay put, he would have. Perhaps he would just sit in the open office and wait for them to come around and put a rope around his neck. He couldn't say, and neither could they.

A small sound, a squeak, came from the cell next to his. Faraway Sue was not alone after all, the girl was there. Had she always been there? Sue didn't think so: her cage was open, she could leave, but she didn't. She just slept. The girl had blonde hair with tight ringlets that didn't remind Sue of anyone he knew. Her skin was pale and her lips pink and there was a spot of blood stuck to her earlobe. A speck really. The big man had missed it.

The girl turned in her sleep, wrestled with her dreams and moaned quiet moans that scared Faraway Sue more than it should have. He crossed the cell and stood away from the girl, her breathing slow and quiet as she turned once more, her back facing him. Sue exhaled.

He didn't want to be there anymore, he wanted to be

on his own again, or home again with his tribe and family. But that was the East and he was in the West, and he was afraid he wouldn't make the trip East again. The girl could let him out, Sue thought.

"Hey, girl," Sue whispered and tried to shake the bars. They were sturdy. "Girl. Blonde girl. Wake up!"

She didn't wake.

He crouched down and ran his hand across the rough surface of the wooden floor. It took some time, but he found a small pebble lodged in a floorboard. He rolled the pebble around in his palm, tossed it up and down, and sized up the space. He turned his head sideways, his eyes squinted, and stuck out his tongue.

It was a quick toss that he hoped too late wouldn't hurt the pale girl. The tiny pebble disappeared in the air and then plopped off her shoulder. It hit the floor of her cell, a whisper of rock on wood.

Her back still to him, the girl stirred and groaned and began to sit up. She was slow in her movements and shivered like she was cold. Her blonde hair bobbed as she looked around, her small fists clenched, as her arms stretched above her in a yawn.

Faraway Sue hoped the girl would help him. He smiled, waiting for her to turn around and see him. The girl jumped from the cot, Sue heard her breathing quicken, and she began to scream. Sue's smile faltered.

"Girl," Sue said, moving closer to his cell door. "Girl, it's okay. No one will hurt you."

He watched her pace around her cell and run out of its open door. Sue stretched his arm between the bars, his hand reaching for the girl as she paced in front of his door.

Her sky blue eyes were wide and panicked, and purplish veins stood out against the white of her eye like lightning on a clear night over the desert. The girl's screaming continued. It took some time, but Sue began to recognize the scream's evolution into words and phrases that he struggled to understand.

"Eyes," the girl said. "Eyes in the d-d-d-dark." She stumbled away from Sue's fingers, just out of reach. "Cold. Cold. C-c-cold eyes. Cold eyes in the dark."

Sue's russet coloured hand grasped the girl's blood-splattered yellow dress and pulled her to the cell door. He kneeled in front of her, his rough hands pressing lightly on her cotton sleeves, his hooded chestnut eyes meeting her wide, wet blue eyes. "What have you seen, girl?"

The girl's tears rolled down her cheeks in rivulets, her breath jagged and halting. When she spoke it was in a whisper: "A...a...monster." The girl's eyes were unfocused and she looked away from Sue's face.

"Speak more, girl. It is okay," Sue said, softening his deep voice and smoothing down the girl's hair.

The blue eyes twisted and shot up to Sue's face. "Cold eyes. Cold eyes in the dark," the girl said, her voice venomous as she shook out of Sue's grip to run around the room.

The girl's screaming was like the whistle of a train, a high-pitch that reverberated through the bars and floors. Sue rocked back on his ass and fought the urge the cover his ears. When he tried to speak to her, tried to quiet her, she ignored him and stayed out of his reach as she paced around the sheriff's office.

The girl screamed herself hoarse and yet she continued even through her cracking voice and words. The door opened, and the sheriff stormed in with two women, an older woman and her younger counterpart. They both looked alarmed as they set eyes on the wild eyed child pacing frantically in front of them.

"What in the hell...," the sheriff said, slamming the door as the girl made to escape. His pale eyes widened over his white moustache. "Dammit, Greta, grab the little mite." The older of the women flushed in her cheeks and then went to work organizing a complex plan to cut off and capture the squirrelly blond girl.

"Did she say anything since she got up and around?" the sheriff asked as his hands gripped the bars of Sue's cell. Sue shrugged and swept his hand in the direction of the girl, still screaming and running. The sheriff frowned but nodded before turning back to help Greta wrangle the girl. Sue watched his back, returned to his cot and hummed a song trying to drown out the noise.

II

"I can tell you who's been murderin' and eatin' folks." The deputy spit and stomped on the floor of the sheriff's office. "It's them god damn Injun chugs!" He said these words red-faced and stabbing a finger at Faraway Sue.

There was a silence that overcame the room, complete and resonating. Weston knew that it was what most were thinking now. Indians. It wasn't so long ago that the Lakota and Cheyenne claimed victory up north in Montana, disposing of a small cavalry contingent with ease. Though hostilities were quiet since then, it wasn't so far off that people didn't remember or that it curtailed their fears. It certainly didn't help that there were stories about what Indians did to people during war. Scalping, raping, mutilations, if those things were true. Weston guessed that if they were, it wasn't so farfetched to believe they could eat people. He looked at Sue, the Indian's face blank, eyes closed as he rested his head on the wall of his cell. He couldn't picture Sue eating a man.

"I don't believe that there are any Indian tribes that currently take part in cannibalism," Phillips spoke up after some time, stroking his chin. Baker gave him a hate-filled look and sucked in breath, but Phillips cut him off with his raised hand and a sigh. "But: it certainly can't be just one person after what we saw in the woods, and the tactics could be right for a small raiding party. Sneak in, do damage, and sneak out. Not really sure what motivation any tribe would have to focus an attack on Barclay though, or what reason they would have to kill the men who've died."

"They don't need a reason," Baker broke in with a yell. "They're fuckin' injuns!" He was wide-eyed, shaking until the sheriff put his large hand on Baker's shoulder and whispered something in his ear.

"The girl would know," Dutch said from his place sitting in the sheriff's chair, feet crossed on the desk in front of him, fingers interlaced behind his head. He made the chair and table look small, and Weston feared that if he leaned back on it any further the chair may break. "She saw something."

"Oh ayuh, but it just doesn't make a damn bit of sense." The sheriff turned back to the room, patting Baker on the back as he did. "Greta and Mary are tending to her now, but she keeps saying the same things over and over. Something about cold eyes. About a monster." He looked to the floor and he shook his head.

"She's a little girl who had to watch her parents get torn apart," Weston said, stepping into the centre of the room. He focused his eyes on Sue. "She'd probably say anyone was a monster at this point, and who are we to argue with her?" Baker made to comment, but the sheriff grabbed his shoulder again and shook his head. "Besides, I've never heard of no Indian eating a man." Weston cast a gaze at Baker for a moment and then began to walk toward Sue.

"So, what're you thinking, Bill?" Phillips said, nodding.

"I'm not sure what I'm thinking, Jimmy, and I'm not saying Indians aren't responsible, but there's still a lot that doesn't add up. I think we can all agree now that it ain't some crazed mountain man, or any solitary person. I don't think any one person could kill that many people in one sitting and go away unscathed. Indians. Like you said, Jim, where's the motivation?" Weston stood in front of Sue's cell, the Indian's hazel eyes opened slowly. "I think we need to try the girl again. If she doesn't pan out," he shrugged and turned back to the others, "we have an Indian expert right here." He poked a thumb over his shoulder at Faraway Sue.

III

Greta's house was on the far side of town, near where the trio had escorted Faraway Sue into the town just two days before. It was a small but sturdy house, built of dark pine and oak. The roof's faded grey shingles made it look like a ghost breaking through the fog that had begun to rise with the waning day.

Young Susan greeted them at the door, her ivory finger pushed against her pale pink lips, and her green eyes hooded under furrowed brows in a warning to keep quiet. Weston nodded and took off his hat; he looked back upon Dutch and Phillips who were doing the same.

She led them past the kitchen and sitting room, their

boot heels clicking on the surface. Weston winced with every echo of his foot fall, but Susan didn't seem to notice or care. She slowed as they approached a room near the back and motioned for them to wait. She bent towards the door, her supple wrist turning the doorknob to open it slowly. Once the door was open enough, she poked her head inside. Susan nodded to something in the room, straightened, and looked at the men before her. She nibbled the corner of her pale lips and a lot of the venom left her eyes. Now she just seemed sad and tired. She motioned for the men to enter the room but brought her forefinger to her lips again before she let them past. Weston nodded again and gave her a slow smile as he walked past her and into the room.

It was a large bedroom considering the size of the house. It had a big window at the back centre that looked out over the forest and mountains. The room was lit by an oil lamp next to the door. It was a warm orange light that cast long and strange shadows about it. In the centre of the room, sitting in front of the window was Greta with the girl bundled up and in her arms, rocking her back and forth.

Greta's cheeks were flushed, her hair mussed. Weston could see the strain on her face and behind her friendly, horse-like eyes. The girl had given Greta and Mary a hard go, and now that she was asleep and quiet Weston was here to talk. Despite all of that, Greta smiled at their presence and even attempted to pat down her loose hairs.

"How's she doing?" Weston said in a low whisper; Greta winced. She waved her hand up and down. The girl was okay. Weston doubted that really covered how the girl was doing.

"Greta, darling, I'm sorry to say it, but we need to talk

to the young lady." Weston could see Greta's good nature take a hit with that statement, her tired eyes dropped just a little more and she sighed.

Weston motioned to Dutch and the big man came forward nodding his greeting. "Dutch here will relieve you of the girl. You take a rest, get yourself a tea or a shot of rum." Weston winked over a small grin.

Dutch still held the girl when Greta left the room. It took some reassurance on Weston's part to get her to leave, and even then, she promised to just be in the kitchen if they had need of her.

Dutch rocked the girl back and forth, his girth somehow supported by the rocking chair beneath him. "Now what?" He stared down at the sleeping girl.

"Well, I'm afraid we'll have to wake her up," Phillips said, making to grip the girl's shoulder.

Weston grabbed his wrist. "Let's give her a few more minutes, Jimmy."

They waited. Weston took up space in front of the window. He watched what little light the day had provided disappear into the fog only to be replaced by the dull cold light of the moon. He could hear the slight creak of the chair as Dutch rocked the girl in his massive arms. He fought back a chuckle, the thought of the big Dutchman holding a tiny babe had never crossed his mind before. The gentle movement of the giant man, as though he were afraid he would break the girl, was such an alien image. So strange to Weston that he couldn't suppress the laughter. It was a frightening thing at first, the silence broken, but soon the laughter carried through the room and the others joined him. The stress and worry melted for a moment, forgotten, and as the tears flowed down Weston's stubbled cheeks, the girl woke.

"Hush, child." Dutch looked down on the girl and gave her a wide smile. "Don't you remember us?" He sat the girl on his knee and swept his hand towards Weston and Phillips.

"What's your name, girl?" Weston said, squatting to her eye level.

The girl bit her lip and lowered her eyes to the ground, her blonde hair falling into her face. "Bethany." Her voice was quiet and shaky.

"Pleasure to meet you, Bethany. My name's Bill. This here is Jim, and the big fella there's name is Dutch." Weston smiled as Bethany cast a side eye look at each of them.

"Greta and Mary been taking good care of you? Gave you a good meal?" Phillips said from the other side of the room. The girl nodded her head, sitting up straighter and sticking her chin out.

"I'm sorry to do this to you, Bethany." Weston took the girl's small hand into his own and patted it with his other hand. "But we need to ask you a few questions about what happened to you."

The girl tensed up and arched against Dutch's broad chest, but he held her there as gentle as could be. Her eyes widened, and she withdrew her hand to her side. She remained silent but appeared to be responsive.

"I know this is hard, Bethany, and I'm truly sorry." Weston adjusted himself and went down to one knee. "Did you see who hurt your mom and dad?"

Still tense, the girl arched again with a grunt of exertion, but she nodded her head.

"Good. Thank you, Bethany." Weston kept his eyes on hers hoping to draw her out some more. "Do you know who it was?"

Bethany shook her head. No.

"Thank you, Bethany. How many were there?"

She raised one tiny, shaking finger. Weston looked back at Phillips who raised his eyebrows.

"Thanks again. Only a couple of more questions, darling. Was it an Indian that did it?"

She shook her head, blonde hair wagging.

"Okay, last question. You've been a real big help here, Bethany, but this may be a hard one. The person that hurt your family, what did they look like?"

The room slid into a dark silence only broken by the heavy breathing of the little girl in Dutch's strong arms. Weston caught her eye with his own and tried to draw her out; he didn't want her to go into herself again. Phillips sighed from the back of the room.

"It was tall," her shaky voice began. Dutch rubbed her back and offered a broad smile. "And it was white. Too white. And it didn't wear any clothes, but it was furry. Like, the fur of a deer or a moose. Its horns were so big. I didn't think it could fit in the doors, but it did."

She stared back at Weston, her eyes were rimmed in black and purple, holding his glance and not letting go. "Wait, what did you say? Horns?" Dutch's smile disappeared.

Bethany's hands gripped the arms of the rocking chair and she leaned forward. "Horns. Just like the horns my daddy brought home from hunting once."

"Antlers. Do you mean antlers?" Philips stepped forward and bent over Weston, put his open hands on either side of his head. "Like this?"

The girl nodded her head, a small giggle slipped between her lips and her eyes brightened for the briefest moment before turning cold and sad once more.

Weston stood and took Phillips aside. "Time to go. Bring Greta back in here."

Phillips nodded and exited in a hurry.

"Thank you, Bethany, for everything. You were a great help." He nodded to Dutch. "It's time for us to leave, but we can come back to see you if you'd like." The big man stood and placed the girl in the chair by herself, wrapping the blanket around her. She smiled up at him.

Greta entered, her sleeves rolled up to her elbows and her hair in a better state than when she left. Weston and his companions made their way past the woman, her fists placed on her hips, a smile still glowing on her face.

"He's coming, you know," they heard the girl say as they exited the house, their bodies cutting a path through the fog.

IV

"Antlers? Fucking antlers!" Weston spit into the fog. They wandered through the town heading in the general direction of the sheriff's office but were in no hurry. Around them lamps were being ignited, their orange glow seemed blurred and ghostlike in the haze. Dark clouds crept past the moon above obstructing the chilling blue light it gave off.

"You said it yourself, the girl has seen a horror. She's just seeing a monster where there's not." Dutch placed one big mitt of a hand on Weston's shoulder.

"But it doesn't get us anywhere," Weston said and shrugged off the big man's hand.

"Actually, Bill, some Indians, chiefs and medicine men I believe, wear antlers in their headdresses. Shows their power I suppose. Maybe that's what the sprout was talking about?"

"So, it falls back to Sue."

They walked in silence for some time, following the roads as best they could in the fog and the dark. Weston reflected on where all of this came from. Faraway Sue. His bounty to bring the elusive Indian to justice, and subsequent trek back into Colorado began this mess. Now he was stuck in a town with a series of murders and a possible all out Indian attack on the horizon. Again, it fell to Sue. A man they captured and imprisoned was going to be their guide.

Weston turned to Dutch, a last spark of hope glowing at the back of his mind. "How did it go today, you asking around town?"

"Well," the big man turned his gaze from his companions, "the sheriff did most of the talking, said most people wouldn't answer the questions of a stranger."

"That makes sense," Phillips said, patting the larger man's shoulder.

"Didn't turn up much," Dutch continued. "Everyone was accounted for 'cept the hunters you found earlier." Dutch stopped, thought for a moment and said, "Someone said something about not seeing Earl in a few days though."

"Earl?" Weston stopped walking and faced his friend. "Darrio's neighbour?"

Dutch nodded, "Seems so. Sheriff didn't think much of it. Earl didn't come to town often."

"Shit," Weston said turning back to his path. He didn't think it could get any worse.

"What do you think the girl meant when she said, 'he's coming'?" Dutch said.

CHAPTER SIX

I

The fog wisped around the heavy legs of the Dutchman as he scoured the streets on the far side of Barclay, rifle slung across his arms. It was decided they'd all take up positions to patrol the town. This side of town, just past the main roadway, was left to him and Tom Baker. Baker took up a more central position, closer to the saloon, Dutch noted, while Dutch himself stayed on the outskirts.

He stifled a yawn as he made his way past Greta's house. There was only one light coming from the home, and he was thankful to see that it wasn't the bedroom. Bethany was a beautiful child that reminded him of his own daughter, Adira. He wondered where Adira and her mother, his wife, Lotte were living now. He hadn't thought about them in so long and found that he was blessing himself and was saying a short prayer. Not that Dutch believed much in God, but it was better to be safe than sorry.

He had written them a letter once. A short letter trying to explain himself, but he received no reply. Dutch wasn't truly expecting one. The Americans had had their war, but so had the Dutch. It wasn't brother against brother, but nation against nation. Tooth and nail, each side clawing for victory at every turn. Dutch was a good soldier: he obeyed orders and he killed the enemy. Then the orders started to make no sense. The last order he received was to burn a small village to the ground; they may have been harbouring enemy soldiers. He didn't question the orders and the village burned. Dutch and his men were forced to watch, to ensure no one escaped. They could see little arms flail in the fire, could hear the screams of pain and the cries for help. The smell though, the smell he would never forget. At first, he had the absurd belief that someone was preparing dinner, but the smell took a turn. There was a smell of fat and dirt and he knew it was human. It was acrid and moist and would not leave him for days. He left then, left the army, left the country, left his world; anything to be away from what had happened, from what he had done. The gold rush in America was as good a reason as any. Even that he had run from; had failed.

The foggy night brought a chill to the air and he curled up his collar to shield his neck from the wind's bite. Weston and the sheriff had gathered the few men able enough to keep a watch over the town. There were few, but they would have to do. The deaths made Weston fear another attack, and Dutch thought that was sound reasoning. It seemed likely the Indians would attack the town sooner rather than later. He just hoped he was able to help where he could, maybe keep little Bethany from suffering any more horrors this night.

Baker hated being told what to do. He hated being told where to go, who to see, what to bring with him. Who did Weston think he was anyway? Fucking bounty hunter. The deputy stepped up besides Hattie Walton's house and pissed on the little flowerbed she had set up by her doorstep. Baker chuckled as he zipped up and moved back to the roadway.

The deputy never thought he'd see the day when the sheriff would give way to some out of town mercenaries. He just let them start taking over the town with some foolish preventive plan against Indians no one even knew were there. He rubbed the back of his head but pulled his hand back quickly, wincing. He'd forgotten about the swelling and cut back there.

The darkness was all encompassing with the oil lamps covered in a blanket of fog serving as little more than fireflies against it, but that didn't stop Tom Baker from finding the saloon. The deputy could hear the rumblings of the patrons, the distance clink of ice on glass and the hearty laughter of building inebriation. Fuck Weston, Baker thought; I'll spend my night cozied up to my old pals Whiskey and Rye. I'm not freezing my ass off for some ghost chugs that won't even bother to show up. He hitched up his pants, holstered his gun, and was off and away for the saloon thinking only of spirits kept in a bottle.

The scream came from somewhere ahead of him, beside him, but Phillips couldn't tell in the thick fog. He tucked his repeating rifle to his shoulder and eased himself forward, his bespectacled eyes scanning his field of vision.

He had been assigned the western reaches of town near the church, but in the fog he could only see the ghostly image of the steeple as he moved through the streets. Phillips had been partnered with a young man by the name of Evans, a stout fellow that carried a double-barrelled shotgun and an axe slung across his broad back. He was some sort of lumberjack or logger displaced from Maine. Evans insisted on following at Phillips' heels, but with a glib smile parting his blond beard, he only contributed a heavy breath at Phillips' back.

The scratch of gravel underfoot brought Phillips around the corner of a meek little house that joined in the dozens of other homes that seemed to crowd the church. The house's white paint was chipping, and its windows were dark. He kept the house to his right and let it guide him to its line of neighbours, following the flow of construction laid down twenty years before. He looked up into the shrouded moonlight and saw the steeple coming into his path; he was returning from whence he came.

"That der is my shack," the bulging Evans said in the strained voice of someone who smoked too much tobacco and drank too much hard liquor.

"As fine as I'm sure your shack is, keep an eye out for something unusual," Phillips said, restraining some other, more colourful, words.

"Whut? Like dem noises you've been following? That's just a cat."

"A cat?" Phillips turned on the young logger, rage colouring his face. "Have you ever heard a cat scream like that before?"

"No. But it's possible," Evans shrugged and pushed past Phillips, who took to cursing under his breath before returning to his duties.

"I'm telling you, Mr. Weston, that it is my duty to take care of this town and the people that reside within it. I already have one pile of bodies to keep me up at night, why should I risk adding more?" Sheriff Forster stood behind his desk, hands firmly planted on the oak surface.

Weston worked hard to swallow his growing anger with Forster. The man had been through much in the past few months, especially the last two days, and Weston knew he needed to gain some control back. He just wished it wasn't on this. "Sheriff, the last I checked, he's still under my authority or have you managed to find the five hundred dollars since I deposited him in this shit hole?"

"Now listen here, Weston." The sheriff jabbed a gnarled finger towards him. "I may not have paid your bounty, but I am the sheriff of this damn town, and that fugitive is not leaving my jail until he's going before the judge or going to the gallows."

Weston made to move towards the older man but stopped mid-step; the sheriff had put a hand on his revolver. "God damn it, Forster, listen to me. What the hell do you think is going on here? Do you really think I'm going to drop my pay day for this? Hell no. But I need him. He's a good tracker and he knows more about Indians than you or I ever would." Weston took a deep breath and stood back. "Don't be stupid, Sheriff."

A loud gunshot echoed through the office. Weston flinched and jumped to the side. He kept his eyes on the sheriff who looked just as surprised as him.

"That came from outside," Sue's slow, deep voice said from behind him. Weston looked over his shoulder and saw him crouched down in his cell, a blank look on his face.

"Thanks, Sue," Weston said as he pushed himself back to his feet. The sheriff was already out the door. Weston ran after him.

Dutch's head snapped up and toward the centre of town. Gun shot. He cast a hesitant glance at Greta's house, dark now and silent for hours, and he ran back into town.

It was a harrowing run for the fog only gave him a view of the path just as his feet pounded the ground in front of him. The expectation of running into a wall would not leave him and his eyes watered from bracing himself for the inevitable collision. As he passed into the centre of town, hazy lights greeted him on either side, people taking a hesitant look out of their doors and into the darkness, most with weapons drawn.

Once he got deeper into town, the twisting roads and tight spaces between houses made the foreigner completely confused and lost within the unfamiliar streets. To his right a heavy set, bearded man poked his head out of his door, a lantern and rifle along with it.

"Where'd the shot come from?" Dutch yelled.

The man jumped, his head turning back and forth trying to find the source of the voice, his gun following along. Once his eyes caught glimpse of Dutch his panicked features relaxed into a scowl. "Must be somewhere over yonder." The bearded man pointed in the direction Dutch had been running. "'Round the church, I'd wager."

Dutch tipped his hat and ran on trying to remember who Weston had stationed over there.

The sheriff took a sharp turn around another house, and Weston, slipping on the loose dirt road, followed close behind.

Another shot went off to the south. Weston was close

enough to see the sheriff pull his revolver and so he followed suit. The old man moved with a practiced gait, more stubborn than skill at his age; Weston could hear his breath wheezing even from behind him. It wasn't hard to imagine a man like Forster as glue for a town like Barclay. He held things together and bound those around him to his own sense of justice and law. Even a piece of shit like Tom Baker got in-line when the sheriff asked him too. Forster was old and tired, and he couldn't keep on top of Barclay like he had. At least he recognized that much, Weston thought. And it'd be something he'd have to remember when he revisited the Faraway Sue issue later.

The sheriff had skidded to a stop so suddenly that Weston nearly bowled him over. They stood at a small opening between buildings, the entrance of which seemed clogged with swirling fog and mist. Forster was bent over, hands on his knees, and struggling to draw breath through wheezing lungs. Still, he was attempting to peer around the corner. Weston pushed him aside and took a futile look; the fog seemed to have obscured the entire alleyway.

"What did you see?" Weston pressed close to the sheriff. The old man just shook his head through tattered breaths.

Cursing, Weston swung about and entered the alleyway, stepping over the misty tendrils that seemed to be crawling out of the opening and onto the street. Weston crouched low and prayed that the fog would work to hinder whoever might be in the space with him as much as it did him. He moved slow and tried to block out the wheezing of the sheriff and the echo of his own footsteps. He looked down at his feet, the only thing he could make out in the fog, and saw blood begin to pool around them.

It was a slight movement in the alley that made him look up in time to see a blade swing down upon him. With no space on either side and going backwards just as likely to cause injury, Weston lunged forward with a scream and crashed into the torso of his attacker. They struggled on the ground, Weston's gun dropped somewhere, forgotten as he grappled, trying to disarm his foe. Each man slammed fists into each other about the head and sides, low thumps reverberating in the alley. Weston scrambled to his knees, placing them atop his assailant's biceps to keep them from swinging and began to pummel the man below him.

"Bill?" a voice said from in front of him. "Bill, stop!" Phillips' spectacled face emerged from the fog and his hand gripped Weston's arm.

"Jimmy?" Weston looked down at the bloodied man he had pinned to the ground and recognized him as a local lumberjack who'd offered help earlier. Evans, he'd said his name was.

"Bill, it was here," Phillips said, his face pale and eyes heavy with pain. He crawled forward, and Weston saw blood oozing from his shoulder. "Bill..." he said and fell to his face.

Weston scrambled off of Evans and turned Phillips to his back. He was alive, but his breath was shallow. Phillips' wounded shoulder seemed to be torn to shreds with five long claw marks crossed into his chest. In the distance, Weston thought he could hear a strange growl carry over the fog.

CHAPTER SEVEN

I

Phillips woke with a start, the sense of falling from the gallows still clinging to him from his sleep. He was sitting up in a soft bed, the sheets white and crisp under him. He didn't recognize the small but tidy room he now occupied, but assumed it was in the hotel judging by the view of the street he had from the window.

"Ow," he said, trying to rub his eyes. He was covered in bandages and made a mental note to refrain from moving his right shoulder anymore than he needed. The events of the previous night began to come back to him, but he couldn't quite make sense of the images that fluttered now in his memory. What had he actually seen?

Phillips was up and getting dressed, having found some of his belongings in the corner of the room, when the door creaked open. Weston peeked in, his eyes searching the bed. Phillips smiled and beckoned him in. Weston entered with Dutch at his heels.

Phillips found they both look haggard. Their eyes were bloodshot and pouched in black folds of skin that stood against their pale, almost grey, complexion.

"Glad to see you up, Jimmy," Weston said, twirling his hat in his hands.

"Glad to be up." Phillips eyed Dutch who gave him a

nod.

"How's the arm?" Weston moved further into the room and looked out the window.

"At least he left it behind."

"Who did this, Jim?" Dutch stepped forward, his large hand grasping Phillip's good shoulder. He leaned down and set his blue eyes against Phillips' own.

"I... don't know." Phillips moved away and sat on the end of the bed. "It was dark, and that damned fog, and it all happened so fast."

Weston kneeled in front of him, his eyes hard, a frown on his lips. "Think, Jimmy. Tell us anything you can."

Phillips closed his eyes and tried to remember. "We heard a noise. Evans, that idiot, thought it was a cat. We searched around the church, but in the fog it was just too hard to see. We stumbled into the alleyway and that's when it struck. It moved like an animal, quick and resolute. It took Evan's gun first and tossed him aside. I managed a shot then, but I couldn't have hit it. A moment later, it sliced me open. I heard some scuffling and another shot go off, and then I found you beating the tar out of Evans."

A silence fell over them, neither man sure what to say or do. It was Phillips who broke it: "I can't, for the life of me, picture him. Whoever...whatever it was. He could've been Indian, black, white, even a Chinaman for Christ's sake. I just can't say, Bill. I can't say." Phillips sighed and could feel himself deflating. He felt drained, unwell. There was a growling in his stomach, and an ache that followed it.

"It's alright, Jim. It's more than I expected," Weston said as he patted Phillips on the shoulder. He stood and put on his hat. "Feel up to getting out of here?"

II

The sheriff greeted them with a surly grunt that sent Deputy Baker into a dry round of giggles. The office was dark, the cells in the back only lit by the afternoon light that crawled in through the windows; Sue was there, his face hidden in shadows.

"Some plan last night, Weston," the deputy drawled, chewing on a toothpick. "Did you hope to give an innocent man a beating before or after the real killer got away?" He croaked a humourless laugh, his reddened green eyes boring holes into the three newcomers.

"And where were you, you lazy bag of shit?" Dutch roared and lunged at Baker, knocking him off his chair before being restrained by Weston and Phillips.

"Sheriff, we need to go after it," Weston said, ignoring the hateful glances Baker threw his way.

"Mr. Weston, through all of what happened last night, do you know what I was confronted with this morning?" The sheriff rose from his chair and sat on the edge of the desk facing Weston. "I was told, and just confirmed, that two more bodies were found." He raised his hand to signal Weston to remain quiet. "There were bite marks, flesh and muscle missing, as well as vital organs. Who does that, Mr. Weston? Do you recall I asked you that question when we first met? You still haven't answered it."

"Sheriff, I'm sorry to hear two more of yours have been killed, but we have a good chance of catching the bastard if we leave now."

"Are you saying you think it's just one person now?" Baker stood and walked toward Weston, spitting his toothpick to the floor. "The only kind of sense that came out of your mouth since you arrived was when you said a bunch of damn chugs were behind all this." He was directly in front of Weston now, but cast a look back at Faraway Sue as he spoke.

Weston locked eyes with the deputy. "It was only one thing that attacked Jim last night. Maybe another to do the killings the sheriff just mentioned. One or two at the most. Not that you'd know much about last night, Tommy."

The sheriff laid his hand on his deputy's shoulder and guided him away from his desk and Weston. "What is it you're proposing, Mr. Weston?"

"Me, my boys, and some volunteers head out to find and bring back this thing," he looked at Baker. "Things. We'll head into the forest between the farmhouse and the hunting camp and flush it out. Kill it if we have to."

"No. No one else from this town needs to go, we've lost enough. I'll go, but that'll be it."

Weston couldn't help but picture the winded sheriff, bent over and wheezing. The man was older than he looked, and the age was catching up to him quick. Not only would the trails be hard on him, but he'd slow down the search. And yet he was a proud man that had protected this town for years and wouldn't see it fall to ruin under his watch.

"Sheriff, with everything happening in town right now, I think it's best you stay on here and control the situation. Maybe even wrangle up some volunteers who might help keep an eye to the town."

The sheriff stroked his chin and twisted his moustache. A moment of recognition seemed to light on his face and then a sudden sadness that pushed it away. "I suppose you're right. These old bones aren't much up for riding this time of the year."

"If it makes you feel any better, you can send your

deputy in your stead." Weston's face remained blank in spite of the smirks that overtook his companions' faces. "He could even act as a guard if you wish."

"A guard? Of who?" This came from Phillips who looked confused and pathetic trying to clean his glasses with one hand. Dutch took them from him as gently as he could and cleaned them with his own shirt.

"Him," Weston said, pointing to Faraway Sue. Baker yelped.

III

Deep breaths. Inhale. Exhale. Sweet afternoon air that tasted cool and crisp like snow. In his mind he knew that the air was no different than that he had been breathing under the caged window of his cell, but at the moment that didn't matter to Faraway Sue. Free air was sweet air.

It was brighter too. The lines around his eyes wrinkled and he shaded them with one thick, brown hand staring around the town. It wasn't the same. Not the same as when he'd been locked in the cell. There was a blanket of sadness, fear, which covered the town. Fewer people roamed the streets while women wore black, and clutched their children to their dress skirts. Men shot nervous glances at one another and carried their guns in the open.

"C'mon, Sue, you know the drill." Weston was at his back, shaking chains. Sue frowned as the shackles were clapped over his wrists again, and at the cold feeling of iron gripping tight, too tight to soothe him.

"We'll see how it goes, Sue. If we can, we'll take 'em off," Weston said, inspecting the shackles.

The sound of sucking teeth fell in behind Sue then, followed by a tutting that Sue knew would accompany head shaking. "That ain't how it's going to go at all." Ted Baker strolled in front of Sue's line of vision and feigned a nonchalant look. "If you're dragging me into this shit show, that chug is staying just as he is." Baker refused to put his eyes on Sue, instead he made himself content chewing on the nail of his right thumb.

"You're a real saint, aren't ya', Deputy?" Phillips broke in as he pushed his way past Baker.

"Don't need to be no saint to deal with these savages. Just need short chains and bullwhips." Baker offered a small, curt smile.

Sue took another deep breath. The day was lingering, becoming warmer. He could smell the sweat of Tom Baker as he strolled at the front of their group. He could smell the oil of the chains dropping before him and could smell blood. It was a tacky, unpleasant smell that made him wrinkle his nose. Death. Death was the smell in the air. A smell that would follow him for the rest of his life.

IV

The horses were well rested and eager to stretch their legs as the five men mounted and made to leave the town of Barclay.

Sue was mounted on the old grey mare he was given when he was first found by Weston. She was a crabby horse who liked to bite and hated being given direction. As Sue mounted, he could feel the mare's ribs driving into his calves. She grunted and shook in protest but did not try to buck him. He put one palm on the beast's protruding neck and knew she would die soon. Die and rest.

The others surrounded him on their own mounts, all young and strong. Weston sat at the front of the group, guiding them through the silent town. Under his faded black jacket, Weston's broad shoulders stood straight, his breathing was even. Sue believed Weston would have taken off his bonds at some time but feared what Baker's presence would do to that. One thing was for sure, if his shackles were to come off, he'd have to make some quick decisions. Chief among them were if he should leave the white men behind, lost in the forest.

Sue was still ruminating on his options when a scream went up to his right, and the big man rode toward it. They were all taken off guard by the scream, even Weston, but it only took him a moment to rally the others and guide them after Dutch.

They reined up in front of a small, dark house in time to see Dutch push aside a young woman and tear through the sturdy door.

"Greta's?" Phillips said. Weston barely had time to nod before he jumped from his horse and ran after Dutch.

The girl. Sue made to dismount but felt the deputy's fingers dig into his arm.

"Don't go gettin' no ideas, chug. We'll just wait right here. Let them deal with this shit." Baker had his pistol resting in his lap, the muzzle pointed in Sue's direction. A greasy smile stretched across the man's chubby face.

Sue looked towards the squat house where the young woman Dutch had pushed had fallen to her knees and was crying so hard that she shook. The sound echoed in the empty streets, an eerie presence that went unnoticed and unanswered. She fell back against the wall of the house and hugged herself, her sunflower blonde hair sticking to her wet cheeks. Sue recognized her as he'd just seen her two days before when she came with the older woman to collect the girl.

It was a long time before the three men exited the house, their faces shrouded in masks of anger and concern. Once again, it was the big man who looked to be suffering the worst. Even from where he sat, Sue could see the man's reddened eyes stand out on his pale face. Sue worried about that state of the girl but couldn't imagine it was anything resembling good.

Weston returned after some time examining the outside of the house. He had also spent time speaking with the young woman, but Sue couldn't hear what they were saying. Weston took a hold of Sue's reins, pushed his hat up on his head and scratched his chin.

"Gonna need you to take a look at this, Sue. I want you to tell me what you think." Weston rubbed the grey horse idly.

"No use asking this chug for help. He don't know nothin'," Baker said, his horse coming in closer. "Besides, if he did know somethin', he ain't goin' to tell you. Why would he give away his fellow chugs?" Baker spat.

"Let me put it in terms you may understand, Deputy. When you hunt a wild hog," Weston paused and looked over his shoulder, "or a bear, what do you need?" The deputy gave Weston a blank look. "You need guns, patience, and a good hound or two to sniff it out. Sue here is going to be our bloodhound."

They walked down a slight embankment to the house leaving Baker behind with the horses, looking miserable. Dutch was leaning to one side of the door facing away from them. Phillips patted the large man with his good hand and gave Sue a small nod as they approached. On the opposite side of the door, Susan sat on the ground, hands covering her face, her whole body shook.

"This isn't pretty, Sue, I want you to know that," Weston said, pulling him aside before entering. "And, truthfully, I wouldn't have tangled you up in all this if I didn't have to, but my choices are few and complex." He stood back from Sue and took a deep breath that he released with a sigh. "I know you can track, I know you can hunt and that's what I need. I'm going to wait out here, you go in and see what you can find."

Sue nodded, peered into the house, and thought of many things that didn't include helping Weston and his group of friends. He had no idea the layout of the house before him, but he'd take his chance if it presented itself. Sue cast another look at Weston and stepped into the house.

The scent struck him and Sue's broad hand shot to his nose and mouth, his eyes beginning to water. It wasn't just the smell of death, a fairly recent thing that was just starting to take root in the home, nor was it the rusty smell of spilled blood, which, in and of itself, was overpowering in the small space. There was something else, something old and familiar. It was akin to wet animal fur but stronger, more oppressive. It reminded him of bear's caves, or fox lairs, and yet that wasn't it either. Whatever had happened in this house was wrong. And it wasn't just that a man or beast killed a young girl and her protector. No, that was wrong in a different way. There was something unnatural at work. Whatever it was, it was something that caused the hair on Sue's neck stand on end. He wondered if Weston or his crew had sensed it also.

Aside from the smell, nothing in the front area of the house seemed out of the ordinary. It was larger than Sue had expected, and it appeared very tidy which seemed strange if there had been some sort of attack. There were three closed doors near the back of the room which Sue assumed were bedrooms, one of which was probably the source of the stench. Sue moved further into the house, his shackles rattling as he did. He immediately stood before the middle door, closed like its brothers, and locked. Sue took a moment to check for sure, shaking the door knob. Here he hesitated. There was a sense of being drawn to the door on the right, but he didn't want to face that, not now. He could easily walk to the other door; if it was unlocked, he could enter and look around for anything useful. And yet, he couldn't take his eyes away from the third door, the door on the right.

It was open. At Sue's touch it opened freely with just a whisper of a creak. As he peered in, the strange scent of animal and death overwhelmed him again and he staggered backwards. Despite his efforts otherwise, Sue's body bent him in two and he felt the urge to vomit, but all that came was painful coughs and spit. He forced himself to stand, make his way into the room, and close the door behind him.

The room was in tatters. Furniture was torn apart, broken so thoroughly that he couldn't even begin to picture what it may have been. A cold breeze flowed through the broken window in the back of the room, jagged glass daggers still jutting from the frame. In the middle of this storm of destruction was a bloody mass that had once been a human, though it was hard to be sure.

Despite the churning in his stomach, Sue squat down on the balls of his feet and looked closer at the remains. There was little to make sense of, less of the body remained than that of the other body he'd seen, though it was adult sized. The girl wasn't here, wasn't left behind either judging by the drag marks left in front of the window. Maybe that'd be some solace to Dutch, but Sue doubted it. Nothing good could come from the girl being in the murderer's clutches.

Sue walked carefully around the remains, holding the chain of his shackles in his hands, so he made no noise at all. At the window he stared out at the tall grass between houses, and the edge of a black forest, mist creeping out from around the gnarled roots of the thick trees. He opened the window, surprised at how easily it slid upwards with the shattered glass. And then he was outside, the tall grass brushing his thighs as he ran. Deep breaths. Inhale. Exhale.

PART THREE
CHAPTER EIGHT

I

They rode the horses hard for the winding paths Baker led them on were perilous at best. Trees, thick and slate gray, whirred past and Weston had to work hard to keep his horse on the path, away from the slashing branches that sliced the air next to his head.

It was a waste of time. There was no way that they could pick up Sue's trail: he was in the wind and Weston knew they wouldn't find him unless he messed up. Messed up or wanted to be found, but it was Sheriff Forster's show, and Baker had his ear. Sue's path was clear from Greta's house and Baker thought they could cut him off on a path he knew. All the while, the murderer was getting away.

The deputy pulled them into a small opening in the thick forest, a place where the trees spread themselves in a semicircle of jutting branches and tangled roots. Baker took off his hat and mopped his forehead with a handkerchief, his breathing heavy and face red.

"He can't be too far from here now," the deputy said through his shrill laboured breathing.

"What does it matter?" Weston moved his horse around to the entrance of the small opening, blocking it. "Even if we did catch him up, whoever killed your people will have gotten away."

Baker's eyes bulged from his face; veins stood out on his head and neck, but his voice was quiet and steady. "What matters is we catch the only murderer we had in custody. What matters is that we fix what you done wrong."

"Go to hell, Baker, Sue never did your people harm. And he's owed a trial anyway. Besides, we know there's a killer out here. We've seen what they've done to your people."

Baker gave him a look of such complete confusion that Weston didn't know if it originated at the idea of Sue's innocence or the need for a trial on the matter.

"He's probably out here helping them chugs what did all the killin'," Baker said, shaking his mind back into working order and pulled his horse past Weston and onto the path again.

Their pace was slower as they kicked up again, Baker's head bouncing from side-to-side: alert and ready. Weston stayed at the rear, his eyes scouring the thick wall of trees on both sides for hidey holes or broken footpaths. It reminded Weston of his boyhood, of travelling with his father and his father's congregation, and keeping himself busy in the hidden spots of the forest. His father had told him that he had a knack for both hiding and the reverse, sussing out what was hidden. Looking back on it, those were likely the only kind words his father had for him. The elder Weston was a stern man devout to God and his own flock. His sermons would often focus on the Old Testament, a wrathful God, and punishment for sins. Bill Weston soon learned to keep out of the sight and reach of his father as often as was possible.

When he did see his father, and he wasn't caught doing anything sinful, their conversations were mostly in grunts and nods and silent prayers before bed. Weston often had chores to do, but it was rare that they were exactly the same each day. He would start by aiding the men roll up the tents: knocking over stakes, rolling up canvas, tying it all down, and loading it on the carriages. After that Weston found he would be given chores dependant on where they were. For instance, if they were in town he might be sent to a shop for supplies, or to pass out flyers for any sermons his father may want to advertise. If they were in the country, or on the road, he would more likely get hard labour jobs. Like the time he helped a farmer tend to his animals or shovel shit because he allowed them to spend a night on his land. If he was lucky, he might be asked to go on ahead of the congregation to scout out the roads and pathways, report back any detours they may have to take and the like. That was his favourite job. Weston liked going ahead, being alone, searching for hidey holes, frog ponds, or even just a shiny rock to add to his collection. Whatever it was, it was time away from his old man, from the congregation that constantly crowded him; it was freedom.

"C'mon," Baker's shrill voice rose above the echoes of Weston's memory. "I want to check one more place." Baker kicked his horse onward. Weston and his men followed.

II

Night fell quickly, and Sue was soon stumbling about in the uneven terrain with no light. The chill winds penetrated his jacket and shirt with uncomfortable ease and he shivered despite his best efforts to steady himself. When the manacles around his wrists shook, the tinkling of metal on metal seemed to carry through the trees as easily as if he had shouted his whereabouts. He held them in his hands when he could, but the metal was so cold it bit his skin and threatened to implant itself there, stick in the palm of his hand forever.

They were out there, Weston and his men, out there looking for him. He thought he heard them once, just an hour or so before twilight. The fat deputy was yelling about something in his nasal voice, but they were far enough away and on some sort of path; they couldn't see Sue and he couldn't see them.

Sue avoided the paths he found: instead he kept to the thickest lines of trees, sometimes finding smaller elk trails, and even found one that brought him to some berries and a small stream. For that Sue was thankful. While the pathways Weston and his posse were following seemed to go in zigs and zags which gradually climbed the incline of the forest, Sue took a straighter direction and climbed steadily. His legs burned, and he was thirsty. It'd been too long since the stream.

Now, in the dark, Sue followed breaks in the canopy of tree branches overhead and where moonlight chanced to appear. He was forced to slow his pace, feeling in front of him with an outstretched hand for obstacles he could not see in the dim light.

He'd spent another hour clambering around in the strange forest before he heard it. He stopped short, freezing in his tracks. The noise was up ahead, a snort of a horse perhaps, the hollow crack of a stepped-on branch, the arming of a gun. Sue willed himself still, straining to stop his shivering, one hand loosely gripped upon his chains. I'm invisible, he chanted in his mind, I'm one with nature. The forest surrounds me, swallows me whole, I am part of it, it a part of me. A feeling came over him then, the hair on the back of his neck standing on end, and he felt as if he was back in the house where the girl was taken. The gamey, animal smell wafted past his nostrils and there was something more. A dreadful feeling of bile built in his stomach; he was being watched. Sue could feel the heat of the gaze from beyond the shadows, could feel a need in that gaze.

The noise came again followed by breaking branches and brush underfoot. Sue lowered his stance and waited. He waited five minutes. Ten. Still as a statue.

Nothing came. A sigh rolled from his chest and he could feel himself deflate. He dropped his chains once more and peered into the darkness. It was there that he thought he could make out the shape of antlers moving in front of him. An elk, an old buck by the looks of the antlers. He waited until he was sure it was well out of his path before he moved again, but he could not shake the feeling of those terrible, needful eyes burning on the back of his neck.

CHAPTER NINE

I

They rode into the faded memory of a camp. It greeted them with a vacant smile; its former owners had left many things rotting in the weeds. Baker pulled his horse up to a torn tarp that was the beige-brown of dirt and age and dismounted. His feet sank deep into the unkempt grass and invited the others to do the same.

They had travelled by lamp for some time, but the short reach of their light halted their progress for that night. Now it provided little help as Weston swung it low to see what was buried and tangled, rotting in the forgotten camp. Beside the tarp, a pickaxe lay entwined in grass with its blade pockmarked with rust. Further into the camp was the broken-down frame of what could've been a small hut or storage shed, its timber now an unhealthy grey. A wooden bucket collecting stagnant water that had turned a slimy brown, and not far from the tarp and pickaxe, a cracked wooden handle was cast aside rounded out what Weston could see by lamplight.

"Feels like a graveyard," Dutch said, hefting himself to the ground. Weston thought that was just about right. A graveyard for some foolish want-to-be miner who buried his hopes and dreams in this plot, the broken tools and ruins left as the grave markers.

"Well, this is it," Baker said, turning to the other three. "If the chug was going anywhere, it'd be here." Baker fished a small knife out of his pocket and unfolded it, as he sat alongside his horse on an overturned log. With a singular concentration he began to clean his fingernails with the sharp point of the knife; his downward head and bulbous second chin made Weston think of a frog.

They each followed Baker's lead and set themselves up for a long night. They decided they would spend the night without fire, dealing with the cold because Baker was sure Sue would be along. They did manage to set up their lanterns to provide some light and heat without giving away their location and placed their bedrolls around them as a makeshift screen to the open forest. There would be no watch tonight, Weston doubted they would sleep even if they could; the cold cut to their skin with each gust of wind. They all took to moving in place, rocking themselves back and forth, all except Phillips who relished the light given off by his lantern and took some time to throw cards into his old hat that he had lain in front of it.

Weston turned his gaze to Baker and could see the resolve burning through his red-hooded eyes. Baker would prove himself this time, the need had reared itself within him birthed from his hatred of Faraway Sue. The Indian had escaped; that, to him, proved his need, the hatred, was right. Proved he'd been right all along, and he would finish it with Sue's life - captured or dead. Weston rubbed his hands together. But Baker wasn't right, and he wouldn't prove himself, not on Sue's hide anyway. Sue was more than Baker gave him credit for. He'd not be felled by the likes of Deputy Tom Baker.

"Forest is quiet," Weston grumbled into his coat collar. Indeed it was, for no animals nor birds had made a sound since they settled in and it gave the cadaverous surroundings an eerie silence. It wasn't natural, and it scared Weston more than it should've.

Phillips perked up his head, adjusting his glasses and sending the last of his playing cards into his weathered hat. "That is strange." His eyes darted around the camp.

"It's a cold night, they're in hiding," Baker said flatly.

Perhaps, thought Weston, though he doubted it. Not every animal hibernates.

"You're a damn fool, Baker." Dutch stood with such vehemence that his trail blanket fell from his shoulders in a broad sweep like a bat's wing. Before Weston could intervene, Dutch was halfway to Baker, his teeth gnashed and his massive hands clamped into fists. Baker fell from his log but was up to his feet and backing away from the larger man, his face now pale and eyes hollow.

"Keep that ogre away from me," Baker squealed, one hand grasping for the pistol at his hip, the other wielding his knife. Phillips appeared behind him and grabbed the arm that was seeking out the gun, stopping him in his tracks.

Weston held Dutch back, whispered something to him and sent him back a few paces. He turned on Baker, a sigh escaping his throat. "Here's how it's going to be, Deputy." Weston put his hands on his hips and gave Baker a knowing look. "We're going to follow your lead tonight and tonight only. If Sue shows up, it's your show, we'll give you the credit and you'll get your recognition. If he doesn't, and he won't, then we start searching for the bastard that killed that little girl back in your town. Do you understand?"

Baker's face distorted with a mix of rage, fear, and finally understanding. He tried to make a quick grab at his gun, but Phillips held him in place with a slight wince, and twisted Baker's arm behind him. Baker stopped fighting: his face deflated and his body sagged. Weston nodded to Phillips who let him go. Baker straightened himself and returned to his log without making another sound. Weston gave Phillips and Dutch another look and they all returned to their lanterns, each taking turns watching the deputy, hands on their weapons in the cold air of the November night.

II

The white men made too much noise; that was the first thing. Faraway Sue had heard them long before he found their camp, long before he saw their muffled light in the gloom of the forest. Even now, through the thick trees that surrounded them, Sue could see the lantern light casting its orange glow on their distracted and drawn faces. He wondered why they didn't just start a fire, something they could all sit around. Perhaps they thought he would be fooled, maybe they thought he could be drawn in; it was all very confusing. Then again, at least they had the warmth of their lanterns, and that was more than Sue had.

It didn't surprise Sue when Weston, the big man, and the one with the bad hat turned on the fat deputy. He was a pathetic, hateful man ruled by vanity and liquor. And yet they hadn't disarmed him; that was a mistake. Now, he could see it in their orange-lit faces, they would need to watch him all night and a lack of sleep was almost as bad as lack of heat in this forest. It would be a long night for them all.

A strange compulsion took over Sue after some time watching the white men in their wordless stand-off. He climbed a tree. He had no reason for doing this. In fact, as it was dark and he was shackled, it was a very dangerous action to take. If he were to actually think about it, Sue wasn't even quite aware of the actual act of climbing until he was halfway up the unusually large trunk. He knew his body was moving, knew his hands and feet were finding branches and footfalls to pull himself up, but it was in a distracted way. His main focus had been on the large elk that continued to stalk him in the forest.

Sue hadn't heard the elk since his first encounter with it, but he had seen (or thought he'd seen) the buck's large rack of antlers pushing on ahead of him (or behind him) as he made his own way to the white man's camp. Elk couldn't climb trees, was a steady thought in his head, followed by an almost insatiable urge to laugh.

He settled himself on a sturdy branch that was no more than twenty feet above the ground. The dull light of the camp's lanterns could be seen through the branches and haze, but the men of the camp had almost disappeared from sight. He wrapped his arms around himself as best he could and huddled into the tree. It did little to allay the cold night, but he still managed to doze lightly, his chin against his chest and arms folded across his stomach. As he slept, he dreamt of the massive elk, its black fur matted with blood. It stood across from him in a barren field, its cold, black eyes focused on him; unmoving. Panic surged through his blood, and he knew that if he moved even the slightest the elk would run him down and kill him; beat him to death with its tremendous grey antlers or its massive, blood-spattered hooves. And still he ran, and the elk followed. The ground shook with its murderous intentions, the air grumbled in its wake.

In his dream Sue found a tree, a large and dark tree very much like the real tree he had fallen asleep in; he climbed it. Elk can't climb trees. The world still shook as it came, hunting him, stalking him; getting ever closer. And then it all stopped. Sue huddled close to the trunk of the tree willing himself invisible, but still relieved the elk could not climb his tree. Somewhere in the back of his dreaming mind he heard a scratching sound, harsh, unpleasant sounds like rock crashing against rock. It was a slow but steady sound, and one that seemed to be getting louder; getting closer. Sue peered over the side of the branch he had made his perch and recoiled jumping back in his dream and in reality, waking himself into the cold night that he had somehow escaped if only for a moment. The elk had climbed, and when he looked down upon it, it met his gaze with its black eyes, and it bared its razor teeth at him. It hungered. Sue could feel its hunger emanating like a heat rolling off its body. And the smell. It smelled of death and rotting meat; it smelled of the grave.

Sue cast his eyes over the side of the branch, his heart beating against his chest harder than it had ever done. There was no elk climbing the tree, only the dim lights of the white men's camp below. Elk could not climb trees. Sue closed his eyes and huddled back into the tree as best he could, but there would be no sleep for him the rest of that night.

III

Baker could feel their eyes on him. Oh, they tried to be sly about, that was for certain, but he knew they were watching him. Chug-loving bastards.

He sat bundled up to his covered lantern, the kerosene running low but still giving off enough heat to warm his hands. Baker rubbed his bare hands in front of it now. His plan was still a solid one: wait out the chug, surprise 'im, and kill 'im, after he spilled on his friends, of course. On those that've been doing the killings in town. Simple, but flawless, and everything wrapped up in a pretty little bow for the sheriff. But now, it was all in doubt.

Weston and his cronies agreed to follow his plan, but chug-loving pricks like that, willing to backstab you without hesitation, couldn't be trusted. Baker brought his hands to his face and blew warm air between them, rubbing them against each other, amounting to little comfort. He bowed his head and sighed and did the only thing he could do. He stood up, cast his own trail blanket away from him and said, "I'm gonna take a piss."

The heads of his three captors snapped up so quick he thought that their eyes'd drop out of their heads. Phillips would drop his damn stack of playing cards now, Baker thought; Dutch would sit slack-jawed, and Weston would piss himself in surprise. None of that happened of course, but Baker could just picture it. A smile cracked his face.

"What's that, Deputy?" Weston rumbled from behind him, already standing and dusting off his jeans. He was a tough one, or he thought he was anyway. Baker didn't think much of him. Just another dusty trail bender who was out for an easy buck. Baker suspected Weston even thought he was going to get something out of the sheriff for all this fucking around with the eaten bodies. Well, he was in for a surprise there.

"Gotta take a piss," Baker said, moving away from his lantern and towards the trees on the far side of the camp.

"Hold up there, Deputy." Weston stepped up to meet him his hands on his hips, his blue eyes boring a hole into Baker. "Maybe one of us best go with you, make sure you don't get lost in the dark."

Baker stopped and looked Weston up and down with

a crooked eye, his smile now split his face. "That a fuckin' joke? I know more about these woods than you know about your own cock and balls. I won't get lost taking a piss, Weston."

Baker made to push past the frazzled bounty hunter, but Weston's steely grip closed around his bicep and pulled him back so that their faces were so close they were sharing the same breath. Weston's deep brown eyes flashed, and he snarled, baring his teeth as he spoke. "I don't think that's a good idea, Deputy."

The deputy twisted his arm free of Weston's grip and put a step or two between them, his hat falling askew in the effort. "Where do you think I'm going to scamper off to? Back to town? Back to the bar? Look around, it's dark as pitch and it's not like I can take a horse without you knowing. Use your fuckin' head for once."

Weston continued to stare through him.

"Oh, I see what it is now, Weston. You're a fairy, is it? It's not your cock and balls you're thinkin' about, it's mine. Well, I can tell you right now, I'm not into it. Now, I need to piss. If you want to watch I can't stop you, but I'll shoot you dead if you try to stare at my pecker." Baker pushed past Weston once more, sneering at Dutch as he passed and feeling eyes burn into his back. Baker expected, at any moment, to be grabbed. To be dragged back, pushed to the ground, and stomped on by all three men who stared after him, but he reached the threshold of steel gray trees and not a move was made against him. As his foot breached the tree line, he turned his head to look upon those left in the camp. All their beady eyes rested on him, but it was Dutch who now stood, his breathing ragged and jilted, his eyes aflame. Baker cast another humourless smile upon them and stepped into the trees with a small wave.

The cold was immediate. He quickly lashed his jacket around him and drove his hands into his armpits to stave off the chill. The lamps they had used for heat and light provided precious little of both, but it completely disappeared once Baker broke through the tree line and walked between the cluttered tree trunks and roots that surrounded the small, dishevelled camp. The light was a pervading gray that clung to everything outside of the camp. His eyes attempted to adjust but were met by black spots and a disorientation he was not expecting. He stumbled about, tripping over large roots and rocks that stood in his path, finally planting a hand on the sturdy but rough bark of a massive tree to regain his bearings. He rubbed his eyes with the heel of his free hand and found that it helped the harder he rubbed. After some time, he was able to open his eyes to the gray light and make out shapes of those things that surrounded him, and the disorientation slowly disappeared. He turned back toward the camp and was startled to find no source of light through the pervading gray darkness that now hung in the air. Not surprising though, he assured himself, that's what they had wanted by foregoing a fire. Now, as he stared into what seemed like endless trees in the gray light, he wondered if he should head back. They said they would listen to him for the night anyway. After that he could still take off in the daylight, on horseback, and with some small supplies. Weston and his bounty hunters though. Would they let a prisoner go so easily?

"Too late now." He shrugged and returned his hands to his armpits. Baker shivered and walked into the gloom.

Baker pushed out into the thick bush as far as he dared. His progress was slowed by his need to remain as quiet as possible and was hindered by his constant quivering and inability to recognize a trustworthy, and less dangerous path. Finally, he stopped. He'd been making as straight of a path as he could from the campsite, struggling to keep track of the distance in the haze of the gray forest, and this, Baker wagered, was far enough.

He turned and glanced over his shoulder one more time, still no sight or sign of the camp, or Weston. Baker took stock of his surroundings; he was hoping to head south and toward the town, but unlike his boasts to the contrary, he really did not know this part of the forest well. His short time as a member of the Barclay lumberjacks hadn't even brought him into this area of forest. He couldn't really figure why that was, they'd seemed to have touched every other part of the forest with their axes and saws, but this part they'd overlooked; shunned. Baker had really only been up this far once before, chasing a snake oil salesman out of town with the sheriff.

"This is as close as you come to Barclay again," the sheriff had boomed in his thunderous voice. Baker had sat his horse beside him, and they both stared at the sallow man, in his scuffed black suit and string-like tie, trying to manoeuvre his wagon around to hit back on a trail away from the town. Baker thought the tie might strangle the man had he tightened it anymore, he almost wished the sheriff would do just that. Or that he could. A smile crossed his face as it did back then and he headed as south as he could manage, not caring if it was south or not, as long as he moved further away from the camp.

Weston was wrong, Baker thought as he trundled forward, his legs burning and wobbling as he walked further and further into the gray forest. There were plenty of animals in the brush all around him. He could hear the quaking of brambles, the snapping of twigs. Birds shook loose leaves that fell into his face. Granted there was no growls, no chittering, no squeaks, or grunts, but something was certainly active all about him. They were reacting to his presence was all, he was disturbing their rest, breaking up their shelter from the cold. They were alive and well and all around him.

A thunderous crash exploded from the brush and trees to his left, he leapt back falling to the rocky ground, driving a craggy displaced root into his side and ribs. Baker groaned in pain and shock and rolled to his knees gripping his side with one hand, the other supporting him as he fought the urge to vomit.

Bushes shook and slashed the air around him but stopped as he swung his head around in search of the source. He spit, letting the saliva run from his mouth, catching his breath.

"You're a damn fool..." whispered in his ear, big Dutch Mueller's hapless accent stinging his senses. Baker tore himself to his feet, right hand still grabbing his side, lashing out with his left, a sheet of rage covering his face and a million promises of worldly hurt and torment was hurled in all directions. They'd found him.

"Come out here, you yellow cowards," his scream a high-pitched echo in grey gloom. Branches shook behind him and he swung on them with his revolver in his hand, its coarse handle gripped in his calloused palm.

Nothing.

"Go to hell, Baker," Weston's baritone whisper surged in his ears from all around him. He turned again and fired a shot into the trees. The blast echoed around him and silence followed, final and monumental.

Baker's shoulders slouched, and he breathed through gritted teeth. They knew; of course they did. They were just playing with him now, waiting to sink the knife in. Maybe they'd bring him back to town, or just give him up to their Indian fuck buddies. Baker ground his teeth, eyes scanning the darkness.

"Easy there, Tommy," Sheriff Forster rumbled behind him.

"Sheriff?" Baker turned, dropping his gun to his side. "Sheriff, they drove me to this! They're trying to kill me and let that chug son of a bitch go free," he said, pleading with the shadows.

"It's a cold night, they're just hiding," Baker's own voice croaked in his face, a gust of warm and foul-smelling breath following.

Baker's mouth dropped open, the lower part of his jaw shivering as words tried to rush out but jumbled together and became clogged. The thing that emerged from the brush directly in front of his face stood taller than anything he'd seen before, its massive antlers spreading in an incomprehensible wingspan that cast a pitch black shadow. It was the thing's teeth that made him drop his gun.

Baker didn't so much as feel it when the creature's talons forced themselves into his stomach and tore his skin up to his chest, as much as he understood. The pain was there, the feel of the jagged cutting of old (ancient) talons tearing him in twain, but it was secondary. Above all else was the hunger. He knew its voracity and need that had been dragged through the ages. He knew it was insatiable.

As he was lowered to the ground, his guts spilling before him, steam rising around him like a fine mist, the beast sunk its teeth into his neck. Baker could feel his life draining into the lapping mouth of the creature and he screamed in agony and fear, but most of all in rage. His last breath echoed into the trees and mountains and was lost into the night.

CHAPTER TEN

I

Weston pushed through the thick brush and into the gloom of the forest wall before him. He knew Baker wasn't going to take a piss, and he knew that the deputy would try and put as much distance between him and the camp as he could, but it didn't matter. Weston was content in letting him find his own way back to town. Maybe the chilly air would slap some sense into him. But then the scream bristled the air.

It was one long burst of agony that shook the companions from their places in front of the covered lanterns. A terrible cry that echoed through the forest, and their minds. Without hesitation, Weston broke into the trees beside the camp, both of his revolvers in his hands and his companions following close behind.

It was hard to track anything while they were in the trees with the dark night pervading. They had to stop and seek out any kind of sign, and that took time. Dutch crawled on his hands and knees, his nose close to the ground, barking out a direction that they would run to only to repeat the process again and again. Weston tapped his foot and patted his guns against his thighs.

"This is taking too long," he said, watching Dutch crawl about in front of him.

"It's all we can do," Phillips said from behind him, rotating his sore shoulder and wincing.

Weston looked up to the tree canopy, the night silent save for the small noises of Dutch on the forest floor. There were nights like this in Oklahoma, dank nights with no end to the darkness. Weston and his regiment waited under cover, soaked to the bone and shivering, the Confederates not far away probably doing the same. They'd wage a bloody battle just hours later, but first they sat in a tepid silence their hands and weapons making promises of the pain to come. Weston waited with the rest: dirty, tired, cold, and his stomach empty. His sunken eyes cast to his muddy boots while a man to his left uttered a soft cry. No one could sleep, no one could rest, and there was only anticipation and fear. Weston felt that again now and his stomach turned.

"South," Dutch muttered, dragging his head away from the ground. "He turned here, looked to be going south; trying to at least." He pushed himself upright, dusting off his knees and hands.

They all started to move in the direction Dutch pointed out, the big man leading the way and muttering to himself; his eyes strafing the landscape. "Why are we searching for this man at all?"

"You heard the scream, something happened to him. Maybe it was the killer, maybe it was Sue," Phillips said from the rear.

"Maybe he just fell face first in a hole," Weston interrupted. "It doesn't matter. He's an asshole, but we can't leave him out here to rot and die."

"Why not?" Dutch said, turning to face Weston. "He'd do as much for us. Worse."

Weston nodded. "But that doesn't change anything.

Just because he's a prick doesn't give us licence to be the same. If he's out here, we'll help him," Weston said and began to walk again, his path still blocked by his massive companion.

"Why?" Dutch asked again, his burly arms crossed in front of his sweat and dirt-stained red shirt. Weston looked up into the man's steel blue eyes and square jaw. Dutch wasn't a man who tossed hate around lightly, but, somehow, Baker had earned it. Weston had met Dutch shortly after he got off the boat in Maine. Weston was just finished with his soldiering and found a job as security for the docks. He wasn't quite a lawman, but it felt the same. Really, he just made sure there wasn't too much fighting over incoming goods, or incoming people. Dutch's red face and toothy smile endeared him to Weston, who had to warn him several times not to beat up on the locals. They'd become close and once Weston had his fill of the East coast, he brought Dutch with him back to the west, his home. He was a hard-headed, bull of a man, but beneath his crusty and intimidating exterior there was a loyal friend, and a gentle soul. Which is why it pained Weston so much to say what he said next.

"Because I said so." His clenched teeth made a hissing sound around his words and he pushed passed Dutch with more force than necessary. "Now step in line and let's find this son of a bitch." He didn't care to look back upon his two companions, but he could feel their stares. Could feel their growing concern but ignored it. They had work to do.

II

Faraway Sue was wrong, so very wrong. It was not an elk that had been stalking him through the woods, it was something else entirely.

He bent over the oozing remnants of the deputy's body, a butcher's cast-offs over the bloody forest floor. He had heard the scream and ran to it, pushing through brush and bush until he came upon the source of the noise. The creature's back was to him, a tall but gaunt figure that was squat before its handiwork, sucking and gnawing on what was left of its prey. It attacked the body and fed as if it had been starved, with greedy lip smacking surfaced above the gorging. It appeared ravenous, and Sue could tell why. The beast's ribs strained against its tight, almost luminescent skin. It was truly made of just skin and bones, its muscle seemed to have atrophied or disintegrated some time ago. Quickly Sue moved out of sight to watch the creature, wrapping his chains tightly around his fist.

When it stood, it stretched its too long limbs and back, releasing a horrendous cracking sound that seemed to travel down the thing's spine. Blood soaked claws or talons were spread to the sky, bathing in the little moonlight that broke through the trees. Long, greasy black hair fell around its shoulders and abnormally large antlers stuck out from the human shaped head.

Sue drew in his breath, an image of the thing from his dream leapt about in his head, and he moved deeper into cover behind a thick pine tree. The creature finished its meal with one last slurp followed by a satisfied sigh. Sue turned his face away only for a moment; his stomach churned and rebelled against him. When he had control of himself once more, he turned back, but the beast had disappeared. Panic threatened to overtake him, and he dropped to the ground trying not to think of the old stories that his grandfather had told him.

It took some time for Sue's courage to recover enough to examine what was left of the deputy, though there wasn't much to examine. It was very much like the scene he had reviewed at the woman's house in Barclay: gnawed upon bones still strung with meat and gristle, pieces of innards bitten in half and discarded, and blood. A lot of blood.

Sue picked up a discarded stick and poked through the remains. If he hadn't known it was the deputy that was attacked, they could have been the remains of anything, anyone. And it left no tracks. The scent lingered though, a putrid smell that he now knew wasn't just from the rotting leftovers like he suspected in the woman's home. This meat was fresh. The creature carried the smell of death with it and that wasn't a good sign. Sue sat back and away from the cast-offs, he tried to hum an old song of peace and protection, but his throat was dry and uncooperative. He wished he had his pipe and tobacco.

The other men found him some time later, Sue couldn't be sure how long he had been sitting there, but he was cold and tired and his eyes stung. They stomped into the small area between the trees, Weston and Phillips immediately pausing at the sight of the remains of the dead man, while Dutch backed away and vomited. Sue looked about him in a stiff manner to try and show the newcomers that he understood their surprise, that he hadn't actually done anything, and that, no, the creature was not there, but he was sure it would be by again before too long. They didn't seem to understand any of these things, so he continued to focus on trying to hum his songs. He wasn't surprised when they grabbed him up and were yelling and shouting at him, but he could vaguely hear them over the songs that kept playing in his head. They dragged him back through the woods, the daylight breaking the shadowy gloom around them. He attempted to walk, to help them, but his feet were too slow for their pace, so they dragged him with renewed strength and grunts of exertion. The day blurred with the path they took, and Sue fell in and out of consciousness, songs forever being sung in his mind.

III

Sue didn't come around again until nearly dusk. During his slumber he jumped and let out moans which haunted Weston and the ailing Dutch, though Phillips remained distracted and forlorn. A large fire burned in the centre of the camp, subtlety be damned, and they huddled Sue up next to it to warm him some. Weston had inspected the man, but little was wrong with him aside from some bruises and scratches. His shackles, however, had bitten deeply into his wrists. When Weston noticed that it had caused some sores and cuts on the Indian, he removed them. It wasn't the last stupid thing that Baker had done, but it was close. Weston cleaned and bandaged Sue's wrists and covered him in a trail blanket.

"It wasn't Sue," Phillips said absently after Weston had finished catering to the Indian's wounds, his fist firmly planted under his hairy chin. Phillips said this from a log further away from the fire than the others, his cold eyes staring into the flames without really seeing them. His other hand casually played with his cards, cutting the deck one-handed over and over.

"Agreed," said Weston, cleaning his hands of blood as best he could. "From what I can tell, the only blood on Sue here is his own. What little there is anyway."

Phillips nodded and returned to his meditations. Weston returned to Dutch to see how he was doing. The big man was a shade paler than usual, but he seemed to be improving, despite his need to clutch his stomach with one large, ham-sized hand. Weston patted his friend's thick shoulder and wandered close to Sue again.

The killer had found them. Weston's mind shouted questions at him that couldn't be answered: Did he know they were looking for him? Were they close to his lair? Why did he kill? Did he need a reason?

That last one struck a chord. Weston had met many men during his time in the Union ranks, each with their own reason for joining the cause. Some wanted justice for their fellow Americans, some wanted to honour their family, some were just too poor to do otherwise, but there were some that had other motivations. Motivations to kill and maim without consequence, and to do it in the name of country and justice. Men like Samuel Oswald Tucker. Weston met Tucker just before a short battle in what was now Oklahoma. He was sitting by himself, eyes focused on his hands and he looked tired, cold, and hungry. His blue coat was opened revealing a badly stained shirt underneath. Weston sat on a large rock next to him, examining his weapons before the call to charge. Weston's presence didn't register to Tucker, he was too focused on his hands which Weston noticed were being squeezed closed and then opened time and time again.

"You ready for this shit?" Weston said, checking his six-shooters over before depositing them back into their holsters. The man turned to Weston then and smiled, a deep and broad smile that was as mirthless as it was menacing. Each tooth was displayed in proper order but were yellow and brown in places. His mouth seemed more red than normal.

"I truly cannot wait," Tucker said and walked away

toward the muster points for line formations. Weston's gaze followed the man as he left, a vague recognition that there was something not quite right about him, and then he turned to examine where the man had been sitting. They were two small, furry, and bloody clumps on the ground. At first, Weston couldn't understand what he was looking at and he dropped to his knees for a better look. It was two small field mice, crushed and twitching, but most certainly dead. Their bodies were so distorted that it took Weston time to decipher their particulars. Weston immediately sought out to find the man, but his quick search was in vain; the lines were being formed for battle and he was called away to his regiment. Weston later heard that Tucker had joined a Colorado regiment that took it upon itself to slaughter tribes of Indians, warlike or otherwise, in the name of the United States of America.

Motivations. What was this killer's motivation? That's what Weston had hoped Sue would be able to tell him when he awoke from his tormented dreams.

IV

Sue rose with a start, unremembered dreams dragging him out of some sort of slumber. He examined his aching wrists, turning them over slowly to see neatly applied bandages where his shackles had once been. He wanted to tear open the bandages to see how his wrists were really affected but didn't; not yet anyway. They itched. Sue bundled the blanket he had been covered in around his shoulders and stood, feeling the remainder of the aches and pains from the previous night. It was almost night again now, dusk was on the horizon, and he was still in the forest. A new song began to play in his head and he hummed along as best he could.

Sue became vaguely aware of Weston at his side, his strong arm wrapped around Sue's shoulders and guiding him to sit on the ground once again. Sue gave no resistance to this and, honestly, he thought it was for the best anyway; his legs weren't feeling so steady. Sue was also made aware that Weston was trying to communicate with him, was making crude hand gestures that Sue was sure neither of them really understood. Dutch approached then, his loud and strangely accented voice muddied as if he were shouting at Sue from underwater; all Sue could hear were echoes and a lot of what sounded like groans. The song in his head was sung louder. Finally, he turned to Phillips while Dutch and Weston seemed to be discussing something of what seemed to be great importance. Phillips hadn't bothered to come closer to Sue, hadn't even moved in the last few minutes since Sue was awake, but seeing Phillips, his hand under his bearded chin, his spectacles dangling precariously at the end of his nose, a distracted scowl hanging around his mouth, the song stopped. It was a sudden instant of silence that overcame his mind and then he was able to hear the others, their rambling incoherence as they bullied each other's words with their own and shook Sue violently to help him listen, to have him pay attention.

Finally, he looked at both men and said, "Enough;" and they stopped, their eyes wide with surprise. Even Phillips raised his head from his chin for a moment to study the waking Indian.

"Sue," came Weston's voice as he squatted in front of the Indian. "Can you tell us what happened last night? Can you tell us what happened to Deputy Baker?"

Sue nodded. He could, and he did.

He didn't leave out anything from when he examined

Greta's house, to his strange dream, and then to the night before when he witnessed the attack on Baker. The other men stood around him in disbelief, even Phillips had joined them during Sue's story and his forlorn expression changed to that of worry. Sue sat in silence, actively not touching his bandaged wrists, and still wishing he had a pipe to smoke.

It was Weston who spoke first, the words creeping slowly from his mouth: "Sue, what you're saying isn't possible. There's no such thing."

Sue nodded, it did seem impossible. "And yet it is the truth," he said, continuing to nod.

"What about the clothes?" Phillips said, stepping forward.

"What the hell are you getting on about, Jim?" Weston interrupted before Sue could utter a similar sentiment. From the look on Dutch's face he also had the same question on the tip of his tongue.

"There were never clothes left behind." Phillips started to pace back and forth, he attempted to cross his wrists behind his back, but winced and rotated his wounded shoulder. "If this is a creature that is actually eating people whole, on the spot, where are the clothes? Surely it wouldn't eat those. There's no nutritional value, and they can't taste very good, and, needless to say, clothes would be hard to chew or digest."

"Dogs chew on shoes and bones, I'm sure there's something..."

"Yes, yes," Phillips said, interrupting Dutch's point. "Animals do chew on things for leisure or dental relief, but those things are usually left behind afterwards, chewed and torn, but still there."

"So, what are you suggesting?" Weston said behind

crossed arms.

Phillips ceased his pacing and stroked his beard for a moment. "Perhaps we've discounted a tribe of Indians too soon. Clothes and gear are good salvage, easily turned into something useful for the tribe. Perhaps we've focused a little too much on the more ghoulish side of this. Certainly it is strange that people are being gnawed upon, but not totally unheard of."

"How do you explain what Sue says he saw?" Dutch again, his back now turned to the Delaware Indian.

"Easy enough. The poor fellow admitted to having a rather strange, and rather vivid nightmare the very night Baker died. Perhaps he was still in that place between sleep and awake where dreams still run rampant before wakefulness takes over again. Perhaps he saw something entirely different, but the image of a monster was laid over that from the edge of sleep." Phillips face was flushed red now, but his voice and cadence were still, even, and calm. Phillips' companions nodded in agreement with all of this. It was certainly reasonable enough, thought Sue, if completely incorrect.

Sue stood, his legs wavered once, but he was able to recover. Still, Dutch grabbed him under the arm to help keep him upright. Sue patted the large man on the shoulder in thanks. "When I was a child my grandfather told me many stories. Stories of my people. He told me how we came to be, who we were, and what we were meant to be. Some tales were meant to make us laugh, like those of Crazy Jack or those of Moskim." Sue smiled and looked to the ground for a moment. "Others were meant to warn and scare like those of Mahtantu, a great spirit of destruction. But the worst stories for us young ones were the stories of Mhuwe, the man-eater. What made it the worst was that the Mhuwe could start as a normal man. A man that was foolish, and who fell astray of his path and got lost in the woods, or who didn't stock enough supplies for the winter. It was something that anyone could do. This normal man would make his mistake worse by taking another step in the wrong direction, then another, then another, until he made the worst mistake of all: he tasted the flesh of another man. You see, a man, a normal man, can't come back from that. They become marked. They hunger, they eat, but nothing fills them. They become so hungry that they crave the taste of human flesh. And still they are never satisfied. Their hunger is their curse and their strength. The more flesh they eat, the more their spirit is corrupted, and the more they change. They begin to look as evil as they feel. The Mhuwe cannot die, and it will not be satisfied. It is a terrible existence that bleeds suffering into those around it."

A dreadful silence fell over the four men, broken only by the shriek of wind between the trees. Phillips looked especially disturbed and he would not meet Sue's gaze.

"Is that what you think this is Sue?" Dutch said, his watery blue eyes hesitantly meeting Sue's.

"I know there a killer is out here, I know that he eats his prey, and I know that we are out here with him." Sue shuffled his feet and returned to sitting on the ground, bundling the blanket around his shoulders. "I don't like our chances." Sue looked into the fire and began humming a song.

Weston stared after the Indian, not sure what to make of anything he'd just said. It fit. It was damned impossible, but it fit. He gripped the bridge of his nose with thumb and forefinger, squeezed. One thing was for sure, Baker hadn't been gone long and there was hardly anything left of him by the time they found him. Even a god damned Indian war party would have trouble with that.

Phillips grabbed him by the arm and pulled him around so they were face to face. "Bill, you don't believe any of this do you?" There was a strange, haggard look on Phillips' face. His eyes restless and wild, almost pleading.

Weston didn't want to answer because he did, in fact, believe in it. It made perfect sense in a crazy, fucked up kind of way, Phillips read this on his face. "Jesus Christ, Bill," he stammered. "This is too much. The god damned bogeyman is eating everyone? There's a party of no more than ten Indians out there."

Weston clapped his hand on Phillips shoulder, looked him straight in the eyes and walked away from him.

"Let's make this camp a little less welcoming," Weston said and began to dig through some of the junk that was left around when the miners uprooted. Dutch followed suit and moved towards the dilapidated shed on the far side of the clearing. Even Sue began to sort things by the firelight, keeping some in a pile by his side, while others he just tossed behind him or threw into the fire. After sufficient time passed to show his disapproval of this course of actions, Phillips moved in to help Weston sort through some free roaming piles of refuse, not sure what he was looking for, but hoping he'd know it when he saw it.

CHAPTER ELEVEN

I

They were less prepared than Weston had hoped. Not much of what they were able to scavenge from the camp was of use, so they had to make do with their own gear and what they could find from Baker's saddle bags. Say what they wanted about the deputy, but he rode light. Aside from his raggedy old bedroll and trail blanket, which Sue now claimed as his own, the deputy only carried some extra ammo for his revolvers, a short length of rope, and three packs of matches. Combine that with the two pick-axes, some dust-filled cans, and an old railway flare they stumbled upon and they still had sweet fuck all.

Still, Weston was pleased with the perimeter of noise makers that they were able to string around the camp. It wouldn't stop a lame dog, but it'd give them a little warning if something was looking to pay a visit. They had finished rigging everything up just after dusk and each of them gathered around the waning fire. Sue had fallen into an unsettled snooze soon after, his face a mask of discomfort. Dutch had agreed to take first watch, but Weston couldn't rest with the events of the day playing over and over in his head. From the look of the dancing glare on Phillips' spectacles, he looked to be doing the same.

It boiled down to Baker being dead, killed the same

way as the others, and the someone who did it and did it quick. But that was the problem. Phillips had the sanest idea, a bunch of angry Indians rampaging the countryside. It wasn't unheard of, the Lakota and the Cherokee were famous for attacking and burning small towns, and killing on their way, but they had no presence this side of Colorado. Then again, he wouldn't have thought an east coast Delaware Indian like Sue would ever be this far west. Sue had a theory himself and it made sense if you believed in ghosts and ghouls and things that go bump in the night or if you were insane. Weston had seen some strange things on the dusty trails, but nothing like what Sue described. He shook his head; how do you kill something that's immortal? For that matter, how do four men kill a rampaging Indian War Party? He didn't like their chances in either case.

"In my country, in the Netherlands, we have a saying: 'Hunger eats through stone walls.' It is a good saying." Dutch's words cracked the darkness. The large man sat with his head down, greasy blond hair lit in dim orange firelight. "It fits Sue's story, yeah? The beast, he won't stop, he is driven. Walls can't stop him, weapons won't stop him, people can't stop him. We should leave here, leave and not come back."

The words hung on the air, thick and potent, the fire crackling under their weight. Smoke flowed through a small break in the heavy tree canopy, stars dotted the sky above. Weston looked up into the broken sky where the view of the stars was a sigh of relief in the oppressing forest. Weston had been in every sort of environment on his travels, but he enjoyed the open air and trails of the mountains most. It was freedom in a very real sense. There was nothing to bar you in, no one to bother you or tell you what to do. It was just the open air, the sun on your face or your back, and your thoughts. Before the war, he often thought of building a little cabin in the mountains and making a go of things. He was never a farming man, but he had a notion of how to do it and thought with enough hard work anything could be accomplished. That, of course, was when he had Mary.

"Are you buying into this too?" Phillips' haunted voice came from far away, almost as if he was in the forest, an echo of his voice calling on the wind.

"Not much else to buy into." Dutch didn't lift his head to respond. Instead he spoke to the ground, one of his big hands running its thick fingers through his hair. This was met by an unmistakably flabbergasted grunt from Phillips, and a moment of shuffling as he turned himself away from the fire and the rest of the group.

"Let's just get through the night," Weston said, plucking the hat from his head and placing it over his eyes. "If we get through tonight, we'll make a call in the morning."

"Call about what?" Phillips had turned his attention back to the fire.

"About whether we stick around or get the hell out of here."

II

It was a restless night for everyone, save for Faraway Sue. When Weston was finally awoken for his shift on watch, Sue joined him in a silent vigil over the camp. There hadn't been a sound through the night, none of their traps had been tripped, and there were still no animal noises to be counted upon. Nothing seemed right in these woods.

They packed up as quickly as they could after a small

breakfast of coffee and some jerky that Dutch had stored away in his saddle bags. Baker's old steed took to Sue right away, and the Indian rode him around the camp just so they could get a feel for one another.

The path was easy enough to follow on the way out from the camp, but it wasn't straight nor was it direct. Often, they would get a good gallop out of their mounts when they would have to slow for a sudden turn or dismount to walk the horses over uncertain watery patches or rocky areas. At times they would just stop to try and get their bearings about them. They had only travelled this path once with Baker in the lead, and it took some time to ascertain if they were heading in the right direction. When they were faced with a diverging path, they would often have to just make a judgement call based on if they could remember landmarks or by trying to backtrack their own course coming up this way. Sue was little help during these times, not remembering the trek to the camp in the same way as the others, but he would jump from his horse and try to aide in tracking and guiding.

About an hour into their flight from the camp, they came to a three-pronged fork in the road. They all sat on their horses contemplating the three separate paths that diverged from one another, Sue giving the other three of the group an impatient look.

"I don't remember this place," Weston said, squinting at each path and trying to discern any telling features they might have. None presented themselves.

"Think we got turned around, boss?" Dutch dismounted and looked to the ground, kicking rocks and sticks aside as he tried to eye any sort of tracks.

"Could be," Weston said, but he wasn't so sure. It was a rough trek so far, but they were doing everything right:

they took their time, studied the area around them, and eventually one of them found something that was familiar or showed some sign of their being in the area previously. This place was different, perhaps even new, but he didn't think they made the wrong choices bringing them here.

Sue dismounted as well, his boots crunching and slipping on the loose gravel around the path. He began to skirt around the trees next to the path, sometimes squatting low and smelling at the ground or grass or roots. Weston tried to rack his brain for any path they may had taken two days earlier that would have led them past this place, but nothing came to mind.

"Do you remember this place?" Weston said, turning to Phillips. The man's complexion had grown pale and it crept around his bushy beard that normally hid his angular features, but now seemed to only draw them out more. Phillips had dark purple circles under his glacial blue eyes, which were now staring, unfocused at the ground just past his horse's nose. Jim Phillips was always a man trapped in his own mind, and it wasn't strange for Weston to speak to him at length without disturbing him from his studies, but at that moment Weston thought that he was looking at the spectre of his friend. Weston grabbed the man's shoulder. "Jim, you okay?" was all that he could manage to say as he jostled Phillips to and fro.

"Bill? Bill? Yeah, yeah. I'm okay. What are you doing?" Phillips said, turning toward Weston, his eyes focusing. He was still pale and had a general look of unwell about him.

"Are you sure you're feeling okay?" The pale man nodded and stifled a cough, covering his mouth with his fist. "Do you recall this place on our trek up here?" Weston said after he was sure that Phillips wasn't about pass out or fall from his horse.

"Here? No. No, I don't remember anything like this, Bill," Phillips said, his voice and eyes distant again, but now slowly surveying the area around him. Weston squeezed his friend's shoulder one more time and then left him to surrender to his own mind.

"This way," Dutch said pointing to the path to the far left. "I found a pack of Baker's matches, and, judging by the path itself, it looks like there's been more traffic here, especially lately."

Weston nodded to the big man and he turned his horse around. Sue was still bent over by another path, sniffing at the different vegetation and poking through the overgrowth with a stick.

"C'mon Sue, let's go!" Weston shouted to the dawdling Indian. Sue turned to Weston with a questioning look on his face. "Dutch found us a path. Get on your horse, we're getting out of here," Weston said, pointing to the left most path.

Sue's face collapsed on itself for a moment. He looked over his shoulder at the path he'd been inspecting and shook his head, but returned to his horse and mounted it without any further question. All mounted, Weston led the way down the left most path, their horses following one after the other.

The path closed in around them as they pushed their steeds forward, low hanging branches swatting at their faces and arms. Weston slapped away those that he could with his free hand, but spent more time urging his horse to dodge protruding roots or rocks that spotted the treacherous path. Finally, after each of them had almost been dislodged from their saddles, they were forced to concede to the danger of the path and slowed to a walking trot. Weston directed Dutch and Sue to scout ahead, leaving him behind with the still sickly Phillips. It was a quiet walk on a dark path. Phillips' skin was so pale it seemed to glow in the shade cast by the thick foliage that now surrounded them. His gaze was blank, his eyes unfocused, and he seemed to be breathing in heavy rasps. He rode his horse with a drastic slouch, his wounded arm clutched desperately to his chest, reins held loosely in his other hand.

"How you doing, Jim?" Weston said, hoping to break Phillips from his doldrums as before. Phillips just sat in his saddle being jostled gently forward by the steady motions of his horse, a stream of saliva running from the corner of his mouth. Weston reached over and grabbed his shoulder once more, shaking him lightly, but to no effect. Weston gave up with a heaving sigh and made plans to pull Phillips and his horse to the side once Sue and Dutch returned. They couldn't keep moving with him in this state.

"Do you believe Sue?" Phillips' croaking voice rose up from his chest. It took a few moments for Weston to register that anything was said, his keen brown eyes falling on the man riding next to him and not seeing any change in his demeanour or posture, an unfocused stare at the ground in front of his horse's nose. There was no way he spoke, Weston thought, chalking the voice up to a hopeful day dream as he turned away from the afflicted man.

"Well, do you?" Phillips' spoke again, a belch of air that rose from his chest, watery and unpleasant. Weston turned to face his ailing friend once more and was startled to see the unfocused stare now upon him. Phillips looked extremely ill, his sunken face clear under his ragged and unkempt beard. Looking at him face-to-face seemed to give his black-pouched eyes a crazed, heretical look. Liquid with a yellow tinge trickled from his nose and mouth which now hung agape and uttered a wet and wheezing noise.

"What do you mean, Jim?" Weston said, hoping he concealed his surprise and fright.

"Aaabout the monsterrr?" Phillips said in that same dragged out croaking noise, his mouth barely moving as the noise erupted from his jaws. "Aaabout the monster thaaattt eats people?"

"Well, I don't really know. Doesn't make much sense in the real world does it? Maybe only in our dreams…"

"Nnnnightmaresss…," Phillips broke in, his head nodding some, a flicker in his eyes. Life seemed to be returning to him.

"Yeah, nightmares too. Why do you ask, Jimmy?" Weston sat back in his saddle; with his reins in his hands and his hands gripping on the pommel, he looked around. It would be getting dark soon; he could smell it in the air. Night came earlier and earlier this time of year, and it wouldn't do to have Phillips on the road much longer. Each passing comment seemed to cheer him some, bring him back from whatever was ailing him, but they'd better not chance it. He was hoping to find Sue and Dutch just up ahead to help him wrangle the man and the horse.

"Iiit cannn't be real. Jjjjust a fffew Indians. Just a few little Indians." Phillips returned his gaze to the narrow path, his breathing unsettling but constant. It was an uncomfortable silence that followed, Weston felt the need to keep Phillips going, to keep his mind off things, but Phillips had escaped back into his own thoughts once again.

Dutch and Sue came sauntering back within the next half hour, Dutch wore a sour look over his broad mouth.

"You're not gonna like it," he said, unable to hide his surprise at the degradation of Phillips, who seemed to be only sitting in his saddle by a pure act of will. Sue also gave Phillips a strange look and urged his horse to keep its distance from Phillips' own.

Weston followed the two men, Phillips and his horse ambling along behind the rest, but still moving forward. The path opened suddenly, the trees that had entangled it falling away on either side leaving only open grass and swampland to appear unexpectedly. Out in the open air with the waning orange light of the sun as it began to hide beyond the horizon, Weston could just make out what Dutch had been referring to: a flowing stream that seemed to obliterate the path just a few yards from where the trees ended.

"What the fuck is this?" Weston took off his hat, giving his scalp a rough scratch. This was not the trail they had taken earlier. He dropped from his horse and handed the reins over to Dutch before stomping over to the edge of the stream. It had completely washed out the path. He hunkered down and looked at the water for a few moments. It was a steady rush of strong current that would likely end up flowing down the side of a hill or mountain. The stream wasn't something new, it had been around for quite a while and wasn't the result of some sudden rainstorm or untimely thaw.

"We tried to take the horses through it, but it's too rocky. The water is too rough," Dutch said from behind Weston who now took to kicking loose pebbles into the running water.

"Did you look around for another route?" Weston stood and looked out over the stream. It was just as good to him now as having the Atlantic Ocean before him was.

The other side of it was clear to see from where he was standing, but it was impassable. How could a river sneak up on you, he thought to himself and stifled a chuckle.

"Not yet, boss, we were waiting to get your impression on this."

Weston could've told Dutch his impression of it. Could've told him that he thought it was their death sentence, that if Sue's creature or a pack of Indians were truly roaming this area, they didn't stand a chance. Weston also could've told him that he didn't think that Phillips would last the night in his state, or that they seemed to be lost. Weston could've said all of those things, but he kept them to himself. Swallowed them down and tried to take no heed to their nagging worries; their deadly consequences.

"Good enough. Well, I think that'll be a top priority for us, Dutch. Sue and yourself will need to take care of that for us once you help me get Phillips down from his perch over yonder."

Dutch nodded and went to work helping Phillips down from his horse. He removed the man as if he was a child, gentle and slow, placing him on the ground on unsteady feet.

Sue crept closer to Weston, eyes scouring the stream that stood before them. "This is the work of Mhuwe. He has led us from our path, fooled us into believing that we could escape, all the while his hunger swells in his belly, gnawing at him, goading him. He will come tonight, and we may all die."

Weston turned to Sue, ready to scream at him, to tell him to shut his mouth. He wanted to tell him that he didn't know what he was talking about, or that he was no better than Baker and all his loud-mouthed bravado. But

Sue was gone, returning to his horse to pet its nose and hum something to it.

A sigh escaped Weston's broad chest and he moved to help Dutch with Phillips. They eventually sat him in some soft grass where he managed to keep himself upright with bracing from his unwounded arm. His puzzled look held firm to his face.

The dusk had begun to set in again, darkness encroaching on the final moments of daylight. Weston directed the others to set up camp around Phillips, and he went to work starting a small fire. It wasn't hard to get one going, there was plenty of grass and twigs around, and some nice branches to keep it lingering.

"Bill," came Phillips' dry voice once more, now even more muffled as his head lolled onto his chest.

"Jim?"

"I'm hungry, Bill. I'm hungry."

III

The night came on quick once they had set up camp. The four of them sat around the fire, its crackling heard above the eerie silence of the wilderness. Still, Weston felt much better in the open air and away from the stifling forest. The moon was concealed behind thin black clouds, the stars breaking through the cloud cover like flares at sea, dipping up and away with the changing wind. Weston filled his lungs with the unoppressed air, his chest heaving and falling with the exhalations. It felt good, he felt good. Phillips even seemed to benefit from being out of the woods; his eyes had cleared, and his pallor had improved. He still seemed to be favouring his wounded arm, but he was interacting with them more and hadn't mentioned his hunger again. In fact, he didn't eat much of anything offered to him, though Weston couldn't entirely fault him there; Dutch's jerky was losing its appeal quickly.

Dutch and Sue had made an effort to suss out any paths or trails that may lead them away from the stream, but there didn't seem to be many other options available of them. In the morning they'd have to backtrack the way they'd come. They had to make it through the night first.

It was still too silent. In the two days since they left town, Weston hadn't heard a single animal, nor did he see any signs of their presence. No droppings, no burrows, not even bones. It was as if all the animals had deserted the forest without warning or need. It left Weston with a very anxious feeling, as if the entire forest had just taken a deep breath and it was waiting to be let out. Or burst.

Weston, Dutch, and Sue had divvied up the watch duties, hoping to give Phillips some extra rest to recover. Weston sat up on the first watch, his knees drawn in front of him, arms hanging limply over his knees, and he took in the cold light of the hazy moon as it glinted off the rampaging stream that blocked their path. It all troubled him: the path, the stream, and the signs that brought them there. Dutch was a fair enough tracker, had even proven so just recently, and Faraway Sue bet his livelihood on his ability to read trails and guide people to safely. "And yet," he grumbled into his chest. And yet they had led them wrong. Baker hadn't brought them this way, and it seemed to be the least used and most untraveled paths that they were now following. Weston didn't like it, nor did he like the implications that it brought to his mind.

Weston couldn't quite say when the rustling of trees at the edge of the path had begun, but he became all at once aware of it. His body reacted faster than his mind, and he jumped to his feet with his six shooter in his hand. The area around the path was dark, a gaping maw of shadow that seemed to beckon to him. The noise raised once more, and Weston could just see some movement at the tree line; branches dancing, brush shaking. He turned to his companions, but found them still asleep, undisturbed by the now steady noise. He took stock of them and decided to leave them be. "Probably just a god damn squirrel anyway," he said under his breath and he moved toward the dark path.

Weston kept his movements slow, hoping not to startle whatever it was in the bush. His stomach hoped for a rabbit, but his mind had already decided it was probably just a rat or mouse, nothing that would even come close to a full meal. Still, if it happened to be something that, with the right preparation, might make Phillips feel all the better after a helping or two, then it was worth the extra effort.

It got harder and harder to see as Weston moved into the darkness of the shaded path. Still though, bushes and branches on either side of the jagged opening would continue to shake and move even with his approach. He started to wish that he had brought his lantern with him, and contemplated turning back to grab it, but as he did the noises erupted again and he forced himself to move on ahead. Weston was in pitch black when he was within arm's reach of the source of the noise. A faint orange glow from the fire behind him made the darkness and its shadows stark and unsettling, like tentacles of some unheard of sea monster waging war with the light. Weston stretched out one leather clad hand, his other hand holding his gun on the source of the noise as steadily as possible and began to separate the bushes and brambles in front of him. He restrained himself as he felt the bushes move against his hand, and managed the slow movements still hoping to surprise whatever creature was making the noise.

There was nothing there. He pushed back the bushes, his gun thrust forward ready to fire, but there was nothing to shoot. Weston strained his eyes, squinting into the now open space in the dim light, but it still stood empty. The noises and movement had stopped.

A strange feeling crept over him, and his neck crawled with a nervous tickle. Hundreds of thoughts ran through his mind; warnings and assurances. Something's behind you, screamed louder than the rest, carrying above the torrent like a cannon shot over a battlefield. A strange cold feeling made his spine between his shoulder blades numb, and his body fought to agree with his mind and turn around to face the unknown. He couldn't -- wouldn't. Another thought wailed in his mind, struggling to be heard; 'Turn around and you're dead,' it said. It was a thought that had grown from a childlike logic that made no sense in the real, adult world. Still, it was there, and it had an appeal that he could not deny.

Weston fought to regain his composure. He appealed to his senses, allowed the bushes to slowly return to their natural position, and listened. There was the scratching noise of leaf on leaf, twig on twig as the bush fell back into place, but he could hear nothing else aside from the smouldering of the fire. The shadows hadn't changed, still they struggled, winning, against what little light extended toward the path. But something else prodded at him, nothing that he quite understood, just a sense of warning.

With a quick twist he was facing the opposite direction, his long jacket billowing behind him. He brought his free hand to bear on the hammer of his revolver and squeezed off two shots before he could focus on whatever was behind him. Nothing. He was confronted with a clear path back to the stream, to the side he saw the heads of his companions shoot up from the ground, groggy but ready to act. Dutch was up first, cursing and struggling to strap his belt around his waist.

"Bill, what in the hell?" Dutch shouted as Faraway Sue moved to calm the horses that were thrashing against their bonds. Weston smiled and waved off the alarm he saw on his friend's face.

"Sorry, boys," he yelled back. "Just a case of the heeby jeebys, I suppose." He laughed then, holstering his gun and pressing thumb and forefinger to the bridge of his nose. When was the last time he laughed? Weeks ago perhaps. He used to laugh more, would laugh openly and loudly. Slap his knee, bang on the table kind of laughter that left him breathless and teary eyed. That was a lifetime ago, in a different place; a life with other people. A life with Mary.

Weston started back towards the others, his smile had faded a bit, his thoughts wandering to another time. It was hard for him to believe that he had once thought he could have a quiet life, a life so remarkably different than the one he was leading. Back then, when he was young and foolish, he thought anything was possible, that life was as easy as picking apples from a tree. Perhaps it was at that time. He was a hardworking boy, and that's all he wanted: to work hard. Of course, he had Mary with him then and that certainly made even the hardest of work seem easy.

"Hey, Billy," Mary said in his memories, he could remember the sad smile on her lips the day he left the house, that last day before she was gone. Before everything had been lost.

"Turn around," her voice was so clear, so close. He

could feel her breath on his neck, her hands on his shoulders. But it was all wrong. Everything was cold: her voice in his ear, her breath on his neck, her hands on his skin. Cold like the chill of a winter wind, sending shivers through him. Cold like the grave.

"Billy," came the voice once more, and it wasn't Mary's. Weston tried to turn, but he could feel a great pressure on his neck, a sensation of floating, and then he descended into darkness.

IV

Sue shrank back in fear releasing the horses as he did. The Mhuwe had arrived. The horses snorted and thrashed with fright until they broke free from the log they had been tied to, and they scattered into the night. Sue wished that he could do the same.

It had come for Weston. It had followed him out of the dark and gnarled path, laying its long, thin fingers around his neck and whispering something that Sue could not quite hear, but it was in a woman's voice. Sue wished he had not heard it at all. The tales his grandfather told didn't say much about the Mhuwe, only that it was a spirit that possessed a man who indulged in the flesh of another person. In those tales, the Mhuwe wouldn't be denied its hunger, wouldn't stop until it was satiated, though it never would be. It was meant to be a punishment, but it was a punishment that spread to everyone around it. His grandfather's tales never said how it could be stopped.

Weston was slow to realize the danger he was in, slow to turn and face the beast that was preying on him, and when he did turn, the Mhuwe was ready to devour him. It was the big man, Dutch who saved Weston's life. He had grabbed Weston by the jacket, dragged him from the creature's grasp and tossed him away from it. Sue watched as Weston landed a few feet away, unconscious. Dutch, with a great roar, grappled with the beast, his large bearlike hands gripped around the stick like wrists of the Mhuwe. Dutch was dwarfed by the height of the Mhuwe, which now looked down upon him with cold black eyes full of rage but was as thick along the shoulders as two of the beasts stood side-by-side. Despite this, the beast was winning. Its pale grey skin strained in effort, but it was forcing the man's arms down and away from it. Dutch's grunts and groans could be heard, and Sue was able to see the man's broad back heave to no avail.

The beast pressed its advantage and swung its immense rack of antlers toward the large man, but the angle wasn't quite right to gore or skewer and all it did was beat Dutch about the arms and shoulders. Tiring of this, and saliva spilling from its gaping, abhorrent mouth, it began to take flailing lunges with its snapping teeth at Dutch, who avoided it as best he could. Sue didn't think he could do so for very long.

Sue looked about him with his heart beating in his chest. He had no weapon, and he wasn't sure that even if he had one that it would work. He thought of running to Weston, grabbing his weapons, but the creature and Dutch were nearly on top of the fallen man. He turned back to the fire and to the still prone Phillips and moved toward him. He could hear the grunting of the man and beast behind him.

As he approached Phillips, he could see that the man was anything but lying prone. The man was shaking, his back arching, and he grasped his arm so furiously to his chest that it looked like he was trying to tear it off. Phillips was uttering a low guttural moan, but his mouth was twisted in pain; his eyes were wide open, and they almost appeared to be utterly white. Sue moved closer and made to grab for Phillips' sidearm, as he did Phillips grabbed his wrist, squeezing hard.

"Hhhhelppp meeee...," the man whispered, the muscles in his neck sticking out with effort, his teeth clenched. Sue jumped back, tearing his hand away from Phillips.

"I'm sorry," he managed and moved back into the fray.

A scream pierced the night, high-pitched and horrible. Sue turned towards it and saw Dutch pushed to the ground, the Mhuwe on top of him, its teeth sunk deep into his throat. Dutch's face had gone slack, but his hands were beating against the monster's arms and shoulders. Sue looked around him once more. Weston was still down, but he was moving now, slight movements of his legs and arms. With no other options left to him Sue grabbed a junk of wood from the pile next to the fire and ran toward the beast. He slammed the makeshift club into the Mhuwe, splintering it into pieces. The beast showed no sign that it had been harmed at all. The squelching noise of its eating continued unabated. Sue stood back, not knowing what else he could do.

A loud bang echoed from behind him and the beast twitched, its feeding halted. Weston was struggling to his feet, one arm outstretched and a gun in hand. He fired again and the creature flinched and unfolded its too long torso, its black eyes scanning about it.

Fully recovered, Weston dug his second gun from its holster and began to fire both his weapons at the monster all the time walking it down. Each shot that landed drilled dark holes into the Mhuwe's chest and arms, and black ichor dribbled out of each of them. The beast flinched and twitched with each shot, a look of confusion crossing its inhuman features.

The beast recoiled, a terrible growl escaped its split and blood reddened lips and it stood to its full height on disjointed, animal like legs. It raised one too long arm to shield it from the bullets that shook it and let out another howl of frustration and pain as Weston landed more on its arm. The Mhuwe grabbed the ankle of Dutch, who continued to thrash weakly in a pool of his own blood. The monster didn't register his objections and began to drag him backwards towards the enclosed path, its shadows now seeming to reach out to greet the creature's own.

One of Weston's revolvers clicked empty and he threw it to the ground, using the now free hand to grasp his remaining weapon more securely, and fired two more rounds before it too was empty. The clicking noise of this second gun echoed through more attempts, before it too was discarded. Still Weston stalked the creature. Sue had a moment of panic fearing that the Mhuwe would recognize that no bullets remained and the man brazenly walking it down was, in effect, defenceless. But the creature seemed to take no heed of this change and continued to drag the large man away, its face hidden behind one pale arm.

Weston reached into his long jacket and pulled out an eight-inch blade, his face twisted by anger and bloody from his landing. Sue grabbed at the man and received a thunderous blow to the chest for his efforts that made him cringe and fall to the ground. The air driven from his lungs, he couldn't help thinking of the terrible scars he had seen on Weston's body that morning in Still Creek, Sue looking up at him from the floor of the small hotel room. Weston paid no attention to Sue, nor to the delirious screams now coming from Phillips, he just continued to move forward.

Sue regained his feet and clasped his strong arms around the torso of the fury driven Weston, his feet sliding in the mud and dirt as Weston continued to struggle forward.

"No, Weston. It's gone, it's gone!" Sue yelled, tightening his grip and hooking his feet around Weston's to bring him to the ground. They hit hard, and Sue's still recovering breath was knocked free of him once again. Weston struggled, cursing and kicking, but Sue would not let him go. Over the flailing form of Weston, Sue watched as the creature slid into the shadows of the trees, its clawed hands wrapped around a now still Dutch. He watched it disappear. Blink out of sight as if it had never been there at all.

Sue released Weston who jumped from the ground and ran towards the shadowy tunnel of overreaching, overgrown trees. He slashed at the shadows and the bushes, clashed against the tree trunks, and stabbed at the barren ground. When his rage subsided, he was left in a crumpled form, his shoulders rising and falling with his exaggerated breaths.

From his position flat on his back, arms stretched to either side, his air returning with his shallow breaths, Faraway Sue felt a tremendous sorrow for Weston. The rage that erupted from him was buried deep within him, an old wound that was reopened in the clash with the monster. The aftermath was still yet to be seen, and he felt a dread at discovering what that would come to be.

A cool breeze fell upon Sue making him shiver. He rolled to his side and wrapped his arms around himself to control his shaking, so he could listen to the growing, expectant silence. Hesitant footsteps approached, a slow march. Weston fell to his knees beside him, his face a mask of confusion and despair. He drew his knife up to his face and studied it, his steady brown eyes dancing over the blade.

"It knew her. How could it know her?" Weston's voice cracked in a whisper, his eyes wet in the study of his knife.

"It's a spirit, a horribly twisted spirit, corrupted by the evil of humanity. It has tasted a dark and dangerous power in the depths of human evil and craves more. Hunts for more. It knows what it needs to know, sees what it has to see, all to satiate its desires," Sue said, hearing his grandfather's words in his own voice.

Weston would not look at him, could not meet his gaze. "And now it has taken Dutch." Weston slid his knife back under his jacket. "Taken Dutch in my place." He stood and helped Sue up with a swift pull. "And what can we do now?"

Sue dusted himself off and shrugged; he did not know. His grandfather's stories never told of how the Mhuwe was defeated, they only spoke as a warning against sin and evil and temptation. Sue rubbed at the back of his neck and took a deep breath. He didn't think the Mhuwe could be killed. It was damned forever, cursed with the eternal. Living its horror until the end of time.

"Where's Phillips?" Weston said, bending to pick up one of his revolvers.

Sue held his finger to his mouth and perked up his ears. Nothing. The terrible screams, and unnatural groans had stopped completely. He ran to the fire site, the nearly dead fire casting hesitant light on the wreckage that had been their camp. Weston came up behind him, his eyes screaming questions that his mouth did not have time to ask.

"He was here… in pain…" Sue said, throwing the discarded bedrolls around looking for any sign of the missing Phillips. Weston followed suit and studied the area around the fire, kicking things out of his way with great swings of his long legs.

"There," Sue said pointing out towards the blockade of water. A shadow in the glimmer of the moon staggered in the flowing stream. Weston ran toward the shadow, casting aside his jacket as he did, and trudged into the stream, his legs quickly disappearing in the rapid undulations of the water. Sue ran after him, taking a moment to grab whatever blankets he could. It was only a few moments before Weston emerged from the water with Phillips in his arms. Wet from top to bottom, Phillips shook in Weston's strong arms, and he continued to do so when he was passed into Sue's arms and covered with a rough trail blanket.

The two men dragged the third back to the fire where Sue worked on stoking it back to life. Phillips lips were a purple color, his blue eyes rimmed in a sickly red, and his skin was a stone gray that told Sue he didn't have much life left in him. He looked at Weston and could see that he had the same thought. His face was drawn into a deep frown, his forehead creased and eyebrows furrowed. He wrapped an arm around Phillips' shoulders and helped him huddle next to the fire.

"What can we do now?" Weston repeated as he stared into the dancing flames.

CHAPTER TWELVE

I

They didn't have a watch the rest of the night. Part of it was they didn't think they'd sleep with adrenaline still coursing rip shod through their veins, their senses screaming at the subtle movements of the grass in the wind. The other part of it was that they didn't think it mattered. The beast would come, or it wouldn't. It would take them one at a time or all at once. It was a certainty, not an option.

There was some sleep to be sure. Sue had eventually nodded off, his head between his knees, and a stiff blanket wrapped around his shoulders. Weston thought he might have caught a nap leaning into Phillips during the night, a few brief moments his body had clambered for, demanded. And Phillips, well, Weston wasn't quite sure, in his state, if he was either awake or asleep. Perhaps he was something in between.

The sun rose with an opulence of oranges and reds, cracking the gloom that had surrounded the woods throughout the night. Weston steadied Phillips and rose with the sun, his arms held to it in a stretch that produced more than a few cracks and creaks. During the night a horse had returned, Sue's horse, that he had recently taken ownership of from the deceased Baker. It was a large brown mustang, a little too chubby, but smart and quick.

It now stood over its new master nudging at him with its nose and snorting in his face.

It wasn't long before Weston had found the other horses; none had much room to roam with the stream before them and the unnatural path behind. And so, they grazed in the tall grass and came back to the camp with no complaint.

Sue made breakfast and coffee as Weston took stock of what they had, but it wasn't much. Weston drank his coffee as he called it out to Sue at the fire.

"Two rifles and ammo, three revolvers and ammo, coffee, jerky, and a pack of matches." He took a loud sip of his coffee. "A small length of rope, an old flare (probably doesn't work), some empty tin cans, the last of the ham (which you're cooking), and this coffee," he said and took another loud slurp.

"Plenty," Sue said, turning the ham over the fire. He was squat down with his knees gathered before him, his chin resting on them, and yet he seemed completely comfortable.

Weston shook his head, "Oh ayuh. We're practically bountiful."

Weston took a good look at Phillips, still sitting the way Weston had left him, seemingly propped up by some unknown and unseen barrier that kept him from keeling over to his left. Phillips' sunken, half-lidded eyes twitched as they watched the fire, but Weston doubted he saw it at all. He bent down and looked closer at his travelling companion's face: washed out and sickly as it was, he hadn't noticed that Phillips' once bountiful, chestnut beard had begun to shimmer with a gray fading to white.

"What the hell is wrong with him, Sue?" Weston turned toward the Indian who had begun to eat a thick slice of ham, and who simply shrugged in response.

And that was it. That was enough, Weston thought, and skewered his own piece of ham with his knife. He looked up to the dour sun squinting, a frown falling across his face.

"Strip him, Sue," Weston said, still gazing into the cloudy sky. The Indian was just staring at him when he brought his gaze down to ground-level, eyebrows cocked in a questioning, 'are you serious?' kind of way.

"Let's see his shoulder," Weston said and took a knee beside the catatonic Phillips. Sue finished his ham in two quick bites and shrugged an affirmative before he removed the blanket from Phillips' shoulders.

"Easy there, Jimmy." Weston reached in to begin unbuttoning Phillips' shirt, but the reaction was immediate. Phillips flinched and drew away from the two other men, his face contorted in confusion and he clutched his wounded left arm tightly to his chest.

Weston felt heat build in his face and his chest tighten. He clenched his teeth and grabbed Phillips by his biceps and forced him to the ground. Phillips, for his part, struggled like an animal, teeth gnashing and legs kicking. Buck as he might, the steel grip of Weston wouldn't waver.

Weston crossed his knee over Phillips' stomach to hold him still and called for Sue to help remove the shirt. It was a terrible struggle and though they undid all the buttons, Phillips held it closed with both arms. Weston roared and grasped the injured left arm and pushed it to the ground with both hands. Phillips cried out in pain.

Sue sat back on his heels watching, afraid to get between the struggling pair, but frozen in place next to them. "His arm," Weston spat, still struggling to hold Phillips in place. Still Sue sat back, not moving.

"Grab his fucking arm," Weston growled and pushed Phillips' left arm back to the ground.

Sue approached Phillips slowly, dodging flailing limbs, and fighting to grapple the loose and unwounded arm. Phillips managed to strike two blows to Sue's chest and ear before he could subdue him, his ear paining fiercely for his troubles.

Weston nodded to Sue, sweat beading on his forehead, and he tore open Phillips' shirt. Phillips stopped struggling. His breath was laboured but rapid, his stomach was moving in and out with each hissing breath he took. Weston and Sue were able to let go of his arms that now stood rigid by his side, his hands in fists and his knuckles white. His wounded left shoulder was a mess. Black blood oozed from each shallow scratch made by the Mhuwe on their last night in Barclay. Little filaments, or hairs, seemed to be growing sharply from the wounds in a greasy black matting that somehow rejected the black blood. Immediately around the wounds a pinkish red color faded into a pale gray that then seemed to spread in thick, jagged fingers around Phillips' heart.

Sue drew back upon taking in the full sight of Phillips' affliction, but Weston hovered near, his face drained of anger and color and replaced by a strange thoughtfulness. He placed his hand on the rigid man's chest and drew it back quickly.

"That hot?" Sue said, noting the look of infection and fever of such a terrible wound.

Weston just shook his head. "Cold," he said in a whisper as he moved around the man he had just been wrestling with, hugged him in close, and placed his head into his lap. "Cover him up, Sue," Weston said and stared off into the forest beyond.

II

Phillips came around a short while later, a bewildered look on his face as he wrapped himself in his shirt and the blanket Sue had strewn over him. He clutched his left arm to his chest with a new ferocity and gave the men now on either side of him a fearful look. He retreated to the opposite side of the low burning fire and adjusted his shirt buttons while shooting anxious glances at his campmates.

"Where's my guns?" he said after a long silence, his gaze shifting between Weston and Sue.

"We took 'em," Weston said, poking the fire with a thin stick. Sue looked on, cleaning one of the rifles that had been recovered from the horses.

"Well, I want them back. Where's Dutch? Does he have them?"

Weston cast a cold look at the man before him, his mouth a grimace of pain and anger. He pointed one thick finger at Phillips. "What's wrong with you?"

Phillips wrapped his blanket around him tighter and coughed into his right hand. "Nothing. I just want my guns..."

"WHAT THE HELL IS WRONG WITH YOU?" Weston jumped up and bounded around the fire, grabbing Phillips around the collar of his already misused shirt. Weston shook the cringing man where they stood and said again, pointing at the wounded shoulder, "What is wrong with you?"

"Just a few scratches really, it's noth--"

Weston gave Phillips another furious shake and then released him. Phillips crumbled into a pile on the ground, sobbing into the grass and dirt. Weston drew his big colt revolver and pointed it to the crying man's shuddering head.

"What the hell is wrong with you?"

Sue made his way around the fire and grasped Weston's wrist. Weston hesitantly pulled his gaze from Phillips and locked eyes with Sue. The Indian nearly fell backwards under the scrutiny of that stare but managed to hold his ground against the rampaging Weston, even gripping the gun arm tighter in their silent struggle.

"I... I don't know," Phillips said through heaving tears and shuddering breaths. Sue and Weston lost interest in one another once more. Weston put his gun back in its holster, and Sue stepped back giving the companions some space.

"Bullshit, Jim, you're too much of a smart ass. You know something," Weston said, backing away a step or two and letting Phillips sit up.

"It's terrible, Bill. Torture. At first it started with a burning pain in my shoulder, but then it -- it changed." Phillips turned to look at both men, his face streaming with tears and dirt and grass. "I don't know what's happening to me," he said, putting up both hands to stop the verbal assault that Weston had ready. "What I do know is that I'm cold. Cold all of the time, but it's not an uncomfortable cold, just something that is there, ya' know? Like I'm used to it, but it feels... strange. I have horrible dreams. Dreams about eating. Eating so much that I feel like my gut's going to explode. And then it does, in my dream. But you know what, Bill? I just keep on eating. The pain disappears and the hunger returns, and I eat and eat and eat and it all happens again." Phillips fell silent and turned his eyes down to the ground, wiping them in the blanket strung across his shoulders.

"I fall into fever dreams, for lack of a better term, because it doesn't really fit. When I'm there, I don't dream. I just twist and hurt. Some part of me is awake though, because I remember bits and pieces, just nothing clear enough to do anything about." He shook his head and smacked it twice with his open palm. "And it's spreading. I can feel it moving across my chest, across my back. Maybe it's like blood poisoning, maybe I've been infected with something. It feels like an infection, it moves like an infection, but it's not hot. It's cold. So cold." He shivered for a moment drawing the blanket around him again.

"Don't worry, Jimmy, we'll get you some help. We just got to get back to town," Weston said, kneeling beside his travelling companion and patting him on the back.

"What if this is it, Bill? What if this is how it happens?" Phillips began to rock back and forth in place, his eyes wild and flashing around the camp. "What if this is what it does, how it passes on its curse?"

"What are you talking about, Jim?" Bill said, quieter now. Softer.

"What if I'm turning into that thing, that monster?" He cast his pleading eyes up to Weston and Sue but found no answer or solace in their confused and scared faces.

III

Weston stared into the dark and shadowed entrance of the path back into the forest. The opening was very much like a circle, the recently bare and jagged tree branches rounded and curled above the traveller's head entwining with the branches of evergreens to shield the path from most natural light. In the same vein, the craggy tree roots exploded from the ground like hands prepared to grab those who rode too quickly or too distractedly to pay them much heed. Weston had a momentary urge to set the whole thing ablaze, see how the beast enjoyed that, but now there was the sick to worry about.

He looked about him. They were all on horseback; Phillips had managed to mount with little help from either Sue or Weston and was more alert than he had seemed for several days. Sue sat close to Phillips and gave him a strange, appraising look from time to time. None of them took pleasure in the thoughts of returning to the forest, least of all by way of that path. But it was but their first step to escape from this forest and its demons.

Weston had no plan to confront the creature, nor did he want one. At this point he just wanted to get everyone that was left out of the forest without suffering the same fate as Baker or Dutch. He couldn't have more deaths on his hands.

The smell of dead leaves and rot hit them as they entered the forest once more. They kept a slow pace and were on guard. Weston kept one of his revolvers in hand and Sue, having claimed a rifle for himself, had it resting across his saddle and lap. Phillips was the only one unarmed, but he rocked uneasily on his steed. Grim concentration was the only thing to keep him in his place.

The path swallowed them as they proceeded down its small trail edged with old, desolate trees. Looping, reaching roots seemed to slither upon the ground as they passed, sometimes pointing like an accusatory finger and other times flailing as if trying to catch the passersby. The trees ensured that the light of the outside world did not penetrate their firm grasp, and there was a seldom ray of sun that might break through, casting a yellow hued beam into the gloom that walked before them. It wasn't long before Weston could no longer see the break in the tree cover and the grassy space where they had spent the previous night had disappeared completely.

Phillips slumped in his saddle, as if something heavy was weighing on his shoulders. A fresh new pain was erupting from his wounds and he was forced to clutch his arm to his chest so tightly that he could feel his muscles pop and strain. Already his eyelids felt heavy and he knew he would start to see all the images he had fought to forget, images that he had refused to mention to Weston. Thick fingers of cold penetrated further and further across his chest and into his skin, the clawing feeling of a bug skittering. He could feel his breath quickening and his vision blur. It was happening again.

From behind Phillips, Sue started to hum. He started quietly enough, just catching the rhythm, and then he rose in tone and speed. The ears of each horse perked as he did, but they focused on their task and moved ahead without sparing him a glance. Soon Sue was singing a throaty song in the language of his people, his voice carrying along the wall of trees on either side of them and echoing back. His voice was dry and rasping, but it was pleasant in its repetitions and enunciations. Weston looked back at the Indian who sauntered along on his horse, rifle hung at an angle before him, and sang with closed eyed passion. Phillips seemed to be sitting straighter and more confidently than when they had started and he cast a sly smile at Weston as they both listened intently to Sue's words, of which neither knew the meaning.

Sue finished his song just as they exited the path. What greeted them was no different from the day previous: three trails divided around a small break in the thick of trees. And now they were still faced with a choice of which direction to take. Sue leapt from his horse without bringing it to a stop and began to scour the ground around the other pathways.

"I thought I'd seen something here before," Sue said, running his hands over the ground and roots around the centre path. Weston dismounted as well and looked around the edge of the path to the right. He could see nothing out of place, nothing at all. If this path had been used, it wasn't recently. The tell-tale signs were not there; the grass was not disturbed, rocks hadn't been moved in ages, and the brush had begun to reclaim the beaten down and muddied track.

"Here it is," Sue said, kneeling at the entrance of the path. Weston joined him, peering over his shoulder and failing to see anything that might give reason to believe this path was the right one. "You see," Sue continued and pointed to the very edge of the path where some flowers and grass were turned down. "You can see the light underside of those leaves, not as light as it used to be, but that just means it is a few days old." Sue stood and moved into the path, pointing at a smudge on a mossy rock. "And here, some scuff marks made by a horse on a slow trot. It isn't much, but it's all I can find."

"You did good, Sue, thanks." Weston climbed onto his horse once more.

They began to travel down the new trail which was much larger than the last and so they were able to travel side by side. Weston wanted to push the horses faster but didn't think that Phillips was in any shape to hit the trails that hard, no matter how much he had improved since the previous night. He had certainly perked up, but he was still pale, and his bright blue eyes still looked glazed and red-rimmed. Sometimes, not often, but sometimes his mouth would twitch, he'd cringe. He was still feeling pain and trying not to show it.

The road opened up before them, and a break in the canopy above let some of the daylight through. The orange and red beams of the setting sun reflected off snowflakes that lazily fell around them. They managed to break into some short gallops but didn't maintain it for long. Phillips tried to keep up with them, but just wasn't able for too long before his strength wavered. The new path opened before them as if it were a crack in the Earth, a never-ending horizon. As night settled in, they used their lanterns to help them find their way along the path, but it did little to guide their way. After some time, Weston reluctantly called a halt to their movement and they set up a small camp.

It was a broken sleep that got them through the night, Phillips' moaning keeping the others awake, but they heard no noise and sensed no movement outside of that. The next morning was an early one, the sun wasn't yet rising when Weston raised them to keep going, eating what was left of Dutch's dried jerky as they rode.

It turned out to be a short reprieve for Phillips, as the night and sleep did him little good. He could barely sit in his saddle as they started down the trail again and he refused to eat or drink anything. He held his arm to his chest savagely and refused any offers to look it over.

The ride was slow with Phillips lagging behind, and Sue rode ahead to try and get a better lay of the land. Weston allowed Phillips to catch up with him, but they rode in silence. Weston knew very little of Phillips' life before he met him, nor did he expect Phillips to know much about him. They didn't talk about such things. Now Weston came to wonder what road Phillips had taken to bring him here. Was there a Mary in his life? Was there a memory he was running from as steadily as Weston was?

That moment, as the dark red sun broke the surface of the black horizon, Weston wanted to know; wanted to ask. It was on the tip of his tongue, but he couldn't force it between his teeth. Then he wondered, what did Dutch leave behind?

"Can I have my gun?" Phillips' weak voice broke through Weston's thoughts. Phillips was leaning precariously toward him, his eyes focused on Weston's own.

"Why don't we hold off on that until we get you back to town, Jim?" Weston kept his eyes on the path, his own gun was still in his hand.

"I'm doing fine, Bill. My arm is a little sore and I'm a little tired is all. I can handle having it hanging on my belt. Really. I'm feeling kind of naked over here without it, ya' know?"

Weston's mouth tightened and he looked over at Phillips, saw the growing desperation on his pale and sickly face. "Sorry, Jim. Can't do that, buddy. You're not yourself."

"Well, what if that thing comes back, Bill? I'm going to need something to protect myself, right? I can help god dammit. I'm not a fucking invalid. I can hold my--"

Weston clicked back the hammer of his gun and Phillips drew back. "Alright, Bill. Alright. I just don't want to end up like Dutch is all."

Weston looked over at Phillips, but he was already slowing his horse and backing off. The truth of the matter was Weston didn't really know why he had taken Phillips' gun from him. Phillips had done nothing that would have made them think he would harm them, and if push came to shove, another gun would only be helpful with the creature roaming the woods. Still, something told him that Phillips shouldn't have it. A gut instinct that he was loathe to ignore.

"Weston, you need to come look at this," Sue said as he rode back into view before turning and riding ahead once again. Weston and Phillips sped up to meet up with him. It wasn't much further up the path where they found Sue, sitting back on his horse and staring into the sky.

"There," Sue said as they approached, pointing to the edge of the trees with the barrel of his rifle. Laying there half in and half out of the trees was the fresh carcass of a large cougar, strips of fur and flesh missing from places all over its body. Weston looked around the large cat, trying to see if there were signs of anything that may have done such a thing to the animal, but nothing seemed out of the ordinary.

"What's the big deal?"

Sue dismounted and approached the dead cougar. It was a large animal, its fangs bared in a death scream that would have pierced the forest for miles. He lifted one of its large paws, the talons still descended, and let it fall to the ground. "This is the first animal I've seen out here. We've not heard any form of life aside from the Mhuwe, but that is easy to do for animals that do not wish to be found. To not be seen, to not leave any signs, that is something else entirely. Here is the first creature we've encountered, and it looks to have been torn into, but not from any other animals, none that I know."

"The Mhuwe?"

"Perhaps." Sue paused and took another look around the beast. "Perhaps, but we know what the Mhuwe leaves behind. This is far too much meat for it to let escape. So, either…"

"So, either it escaped, or it put up too much of a fight for the monster?"

"Yes. Or, maybe, the Mhuwe's lair is close by. We need to be very careful." He returned to his horse looking around the forest as he went.

"That's it, Bill, give me a god damned gun. If that thing is around here, I want my gun." Phillips pale face had managed a watered-down shade of red.

Weston looked over to Sue who was patting down his horse and gave him a shrug when their eyes met.

"No," he said after a short silence. Phillips face dropped and he slapped his knee with his good hand. Tears threatening to crack the corner of his eyes.

"Listen, Jim, I don't know what's wrong with you, but I can't trust it. Even if I gave you the gun, you'd likely be no good to use it if the time came. Or did you miss that you're worse when that thing is around?" Weston leaned over his saddle and looked at Phillips now, his brown eyes drilling into the other's blue eyes.

"Now, myself and Sue are going to take a look around in those yonder woods. This may be the only chance we have to get any semblance of Dutch back. To do right by him. If I can find anything of Dutch, I'll bring it back, if not we'll bury whatever he left behind at the hotel." Weston swung down from his horse and drew his rifle from his saddle holster, checking that it was loaded. "You can stay here with the horses."

"And what will I do if the bloody monster shows up," Phillips said, dejected.

"Yell."

IV

There were no surprises held for Weston and Sue as they broke the tree line and entered the forest. Darkness assailed them under the heavy tree canopy, darkness and gloom and silence. Weston sighed; it felt as if the forest atmosphere clung to him, stuck to him like a layer of dirt that he could not get rid of. Sue echoed his sigh as he bent over the cougar and fell to studying the area for any kind of trail or footpath.

"It's not so easy in this light, but you can see the cougar's path, it almost shines." Then, pointing at a lighter shade of green through the underbrush, "See?"

Weston could see. It was blatant and clear, but it didn't bring him any joy to recognize it. He cocked his rifle and chambered a round. "Better get moving then. I don't want to spend too much time out here." They pushed on further through the underbrush and low hanging branches.

It was a thick bush, much like they expected, but the cougar's trail was easy to follow. Aside from the shine that Sue had seen, there were droplets of blood, signs of urine or excrement, and even some pieces of flesh. It wasn't a pretty sight, but it felt good. Finally, they were searching from something that was tangible, something that they could see and feel and smell. Weston's heart started to pound with a rapidity he knew as excitement. Finally, he could do something other than react, other than sit and wait to be killed and eaten.

They didn't have to go far to find the source of the cougar's undoing. Weston almost walked right past it, but Sue stopped him with a light grip of his arm. Leaving Weston where he was, he climbed over a fallen tree and circled a small area of grass and dirt. "It was here," his voice was hoarse and distracted. "The cougar fell from that tree." He pointed one thick finger above him. "It was already being attacked, landed on its back and scrambled forward. But the beast followed it." He squatted down next to some nearly invisible indentations, circles what looked like faint prints in the grass and moved on. "That must be the creature, but it's strange. They seem too small to fit the beast we've seen…"

"There's another?" Weston said, his voice more panicked than he had hoped.

"Maybe, but I don't believe it to be so. The creatures my grandfather told me of were solitary, loners, which is why eating human flesh was easy for them. Once their bloodlust kicked in, I don't think they could abide having another person with them, even if they were changing into the Mhuwe. Their need requires satisfaction."

Weston nodded, looking about him. "Is this where the path ends then?"

Sue poked his head up from where he squatted, looking at another indentation in the underbrush. He fixed his chestnut brown eyes on the ground and then shot a quick look up to the trees, at the branches that were covered in a thin layer of green moss. "I don't see anything else. I fear this is all there is." Sue stood and leaned the barrel of his rifle on his shoulder before he turned back the way they had come. Weston followed.

V

It didn't take them long to return to the tail end of the cougar. Sue took a few minutes to look over the dead animal again, poking his rifle barrel into the places missing flesh and muscle, but it amounted to about the same as before; he shook his head as he pushed through the trees and out onto the path.

That's when the screaming started.

Weston forced his way through jabbing branches and scratching brush, rifle ready as his feet touched the course dirt road that lay outside the tree line. Sue was off to his right, hands held in the air, but rifle still gripped in one strong hand. His face was serious, but his eyes were filled with fresh panic.

"Hands up, Bill," Phillips' familiar drawl said to him, and Weston turned to face his friend. Phillips was wet, completely soaked from head to toe. His hair and beard took on a greasy look as they dripped a steady stream of viscous amber liquid. His hands were held in front of him holding something small in both, angled in a threatening way that Weston was still trying to understand. At Phillips' feet lay three empty lanterns, their glass broken and whatever kerosene remained dripped onto the ground beneath.

"I mean it, Bill, hands up." Weston was surprised to see how limber the previously ailing man was; his wounded arm now in full use holding the match packet steady for the unsheathed match in the other.

Weston raised his arms. "What the hell are you doing, Jim?"

"You should've just given me my gun," the man standing before him muttered, eyes dancing between Weston and Sue rapidly. "Now I've had to resort to this. This!" He shouted allowing himself a quick and jerky motion with his right hand.

"You know, I think I was right," Phillips said, his voice manic. "I think it is some sort of blood poisoning. Some kind of corruption that was leaked into my system the night it clawed my shoulder to pieces."

"What…"

"I've had dreams, Bill. Dreams that I'm hungry, so hungry. Dreams in which I gorge myself on every type of animal, fruit, or vegetable I can find, but nothing soothes. I can eat until my intestines burst and still feel that gnawing hunger driving me to eat more. But, in my dreams, I don't just want animals anymore, Bill, no, I want to taste human flesh. I dream about that. Dream about eating people. And, in my dreams, I do. I've eaten you, Dutch, Sue, and even Baker and the sheriff. Anyone and everyone in my life. I thought about digging up Sarah. Digging her up and cleaning off her bones. Why the hell would I think about that? Why would I dream that?"

"You're sick, Jim, you're just sick. They're fever dreams. That's all."

"No. No." Phillips stomped in place and spit, sending off some of the thick kerosene in a spray. "It corrupted my blood, Bill. Somehow that fucking thing corrupted my blood, and now I'm going to be just like it. I'm turning into it; can't you see that?"

Weston shook his head, "This is insane, Jim. We just need to get you back to town, get a doctor to…"

"No doctor has seen anything like this. I'm not going to do it, Bill. I can't do it. I won't… I won't do that to Sarah. I can't." The spark was lit before Weston could react and the flames erupted in a violent explosion of intense heat that drove him back and scattered the whining horses. And then there was the wailing. Sue ripped a blanket off one of the retreating horses and rushed towards Phillips, but the screaming and thrashing man was already running into the trees, fire blazing around him in the dry brush.

Weston levelled his rifle and fired two rounds that put Phillips down; they echoed in the thick line of trees. Flames spread and crackled around the fallen man. Sue rushed to the fire and beat it out as best he could, leaving a smouldering heap of dead branches, black and crackling and dead.

Phillips lay among them.

CHAPTER THIRTEEN

I

The horses were long gone. The open path didn't hedge them off as before and they didn't pay much attention to where they ran. Weston walked over to Sue who was squat down in the path studying what supplies they now had.

"Not much came off with the blanket." Sue was running his hands over the small pile of items he had gathered before him. "An old flare, some rifle shells, a knife."

"Plus the rifles, my Colts, and--" Weston sat down hard, his breath a sharp exhale and he drew a gun from the back of his jeans. "His gun." He looked over to the body, looked upon his last dead friend, and coughed away tears. Another soul he couldn't save, another person he couldn't protect. He'd lost count of how many people had died around him. He started scraping away handfuls of dirt and gravel. "Sue, gather up some rocks."

They buried Phillips in a shallow grave on the path they had been travelling and would continue to travel upon. Weston wasn't sure if the man was religious but made a rough cross out of some fallen branches just in case. Sue hummed a song as they stood around the grave. It was a light song, soothing but morose, and it didn't help Weston. He hoped it'd be of some benefit to Phillips, wherever he might be going.

They gathered their meagre belongings and started to walk down the path once more. Sue pointed out the tracks of the horses as they walked, but there was no sign of their stopping or waning in their full gallop away from the sudden fire. The men couldn't hear them either. The galloping hooves, their heavy breathing, snorting and snuffing, all of it was swallowed in the trees that loomed above them.

Their trek was silent save for the cracking branches, swaying of trees, crunching leaves, and dropping of water. The sounds were strange -- the pathway, the forest was breathless, and no wind was able to break the barrier of trees and brush. There was no sign of animals around them other than the fading tracks of the horses that stamped further and further away from them. Each noise brought Weston around, craning his neck and straining his ears to detect the source, but never being able to do so. He fumbled with Phillips' small revolver, spinning it in his hand absently, cocking the hammer and then releasing it. Absent but purposeful. It kept his mind off his hopelessness.

They set up camp just before dark; they had no lanterns to keep them going after the sun had set. They had made little progress on the road and had no doubt that the horses were long gone now, and they'd never catch up with them. They started a fire without matches, Sue taking care of that with some sticks he found on the edge of the forest. It was a small fire, but then, they were a small number. Weston's stomach rumbled, and he groaned with it. The last food they had was on the trail, the remnants of Dutch's jerky. It was a taste he didn't enjoy but would trade just about anything for the salty taste of that dried beef right now.

"How far do you think we are from town?" Weston said, staring into the fire, still playing with Phillips' gun.

"Hard to say." Sue was looking down the path, back the way from which they came. "The wind doesn't blow in here, and the stars…" He waved a lazy hand toward the sky. "Those, I cannot see. This is a fairly well-used path though. I'm sure it leads somewhere. When? Well, hard to say."

Weston blinked at him, shrugged and asked him what he had wanted to ask him all along: "Why don't you think it's come back?"

Sue looked at him over his shoulder, his face lit by the dim orange light cast by the fire. "That is also hard to say. Perhaps it cares not for us, perhaps it has found other things to eat, perhaps it has returned to the town. Perhaps we hurt it." He lowered his eyes to the fire, the shadows playing across his face creasing it with wrinkles and time, making him look much older than he was.

"Is that what you think, Sue? Do you think we hurt it?" He could hear the desperation in his voice, which he tried to stifle too late.

"I don't know. When you hit it, it backed away. It ducked into the shadows and disappeared. And it bled. But does that matter to a creature such as that? I just don't know. The black blood may be the only thing remaining of its humanity, rotten and dried and disappearing. Maybe it was just its evil spilling out of it." He shrugged then and turned his attention back to the road.

"I was in the war, Sue, did you know that?" Weston stopped playing with his gun. "Do you remember the war?"

Sue nodded; it wasn't all that long ago. He remembered well how it ran through his people, how they joined armies to aide one side or another, to show them paths and trails to sneak up and kill their rivals. It was a war, and many people died, including many of his own.

"I was afraid a lot of the time then. Afraid of death, of injury, of losing, but I went where I was told. I followed orders and did what I had to. One time, we were a day's ride out from a charge on our enemy and it got particularly bad. I had the shakes, I had cold sweats, and I was barely able to hold a gun. I was young, I was afraid. Word of this got around to my commanding officer who called me to him. I practically had to be dragged by two of my fellow soldiers, because it made everything worse, being called to him. So much worse. I didn't want anyone to see me like that, to know I was so scared, to think that I couldn't be a soldier any more. What if I was kicked out? Could I live with that?" Weston's eyes were drawn to the fire, the orange light reflecting in the brown pools there. Sue had turned back, his scrutinizing eyes following Weston's lips.

"When I was brought to my commanding officer, he just looked at me, you know? Just stared for a little while over his long beard. Stared. I could feel his cold blue eyes bearing down on me, and I knew -- I knew -- that he was going to put me in irons or send me on my way, strip me of my uniform and my guns and that'd be it. The worse was, of course, that I kind of wanted that. I wanted to be released from the responsibilities, the fear of battle, of death. But do you know what he did?"

Sue shook his head.

"Well, he said in this quiet voice he had, 'Boy, I'm told that you are afraid of battle. Is that true?' I couldn't answer him, I just nodded and fought back tears. 'Well, boy, welcome to the war.' I just sat there, real still like. I didn't really know what that meant. Then he goes, 'Boy, everyone is afraid of war. Only the dead stop worrying about dying. I'll tell you a little secret that might help: the enemy, even Lee himself, they're afraid going into battle. Just afraid as you or I. Death is a great equalizer, son, in more ways than one.' And then he sent me back to my bunk. Christ, I wish I had a smoke." Weston patted his chest and jacket pockets, but came away with a frown.

"I can't really explain it, but I felt better. That night anyway. My shakes stopped, I could breathe easier, and I was able to get some sleep. Now, it all came back the next day, Sue, don't get it twisted up. I was still quite afraid. I was able to ride into battle though. I rode with my fellow soldiers, to hold my rifle and pistol and unsheathe my sabre. And all we found was an empty camp. There was no battle that day. The commander did a general pass of the troops after we all arrived and he gave me a slight little nod, and I knew what he meant. I knew. It was just like he said, they were as afraid of us as we were of them. That got me through the war, that got me through everything else I've done since. Everyone's afraid. It keeps us on level ground. You see what I mean?"

Sue nodded his head.

"If we hurt that thing, if we really hurt it and we really scared it, then that means we can kill it. That means despite everything else it has or can do, we can hurt it and it brings us back to the same level. It's a good thing, Sue." Weston could feel the apprehension lifting from his chest and back, could feel a lightness replace the weight that was dragging him down for what felt like endless days.

Sue returned his gaze to the path behind, his face a stony expression that hadn't changed since Phillips had killed himself. "That's if we did hurt it," he said in a quiet voice, watching the shadows of the road dance in the fire's gleam. "If a thing such as that can be hurt."

PART FOUR
CHAPTER FOURTEEN

I

The next morning, they set out again, dashing the remnants of their fire with their boots and then starting on down the path. Weston was cheered, despite the hunger clawing at his stomach, but was worried about Sue. The Indian seemed to be distracted as he walked down the road, his eyes not alert as they normally were, but wandering over the tree line, the road ahead, and particularly, the road behind. Sue continued to look over his shoulder, straining his neck and eyes to pay attention to whatever was drawing his mind back there.

Weston attempted to goad him into telling him what was distracting him so, but Sue would just shrug and push ahead, leaving Weston to look over his own shoulder to make out whatever it was in the unchanging wild landscape that they faced ahead or, it seemed, behind.

It was a milder day walking and Weston had to remove his jacket after a short while. Sue didn't seem bothered one way or the other. As the morning drew on, a sickly looking mist rose about the tree roots all around them, and soon they were walking ankle deep in a thick fog that Weston could hardly penetrate with his sight. Sue would sometimes stop and wave at the fog, hunched over on the balls of his feet, trying to make out if there were any prints or signs of life other than themselves on the pathway. The horses still roamed the path it seemed, and he could make out their tracks from time to time, but there was still no sign of them around. Otherwise the road remained quiet and devoid of life.

They took a rest about mid-day, or what they judged it to be. The fog had risen around them, and it had started to drain away any of the light that had been filtered through the trees above them. They sat in the fog barely able to see one another and neither of them would talk. They didn't have much to say to one another.

Their walk started again before too long, legs and feet now aching. Weston vaguely wondered about what was happening in town, if the sheriff had sent out a search party for them, if the monster had begun to visit there again, if there was anyone left. Was Barclay a ghost town now, were they truly on their own?

"Where do you think the animals went?" Sue's voice cracked the fog, around them, his eyes facing forward, and his feet stumbling up the road.

"I just thought they were afraid. Afraid of the monster and left. Migrated to another part of the forest. That's probably why the beast moved on to the town. Started eating people."

Sue nodded. "I think it ate them all. I don't think there is anything left out here. No birds, no wolves, no gophers, no elk." He shivered at the last word, but it didn't stop him, or slow him down. "I think everything is dead."

The rest of their walk that day was quiet, the fog building up around them until they couldn't see anything but what was right in front of them. They decided to call it a day and set up a quiet camp.

They woke in the middle of the night. The fog had

dissipated enough that they could see the glowing stars through the small breaks in the tree cover overhead. There was a skittering noise that seemed to come from all around them; it was the noise of claws or talons on rock, and it drew them from their slumber and had them on their feet, weapons drawn. They tried to get a sight on what was harassing them, but the noises stopped, and they were left in the quiet once more.

"What the fuck was that?" Weston said, holstering his guns.

"Sounded like a rat?" Sue ventured, but he didn't seem too convinced.

Weston chuckled, "I guess it doesn't like rat."

Sue chanced a smile, the dying fire casting a million shadows on his cracked face, and he laughed a deep and hollow laugh that echoed into the night.

II

Weston and Sue started out once more at first light, weak and weary, but cheered by their midnight encounter.

More and more they saw the signs and heard the sounds of animals about them. Sue particularly brightened as a small red fox crossed their path at a distance, and already Weston could see designs on trapping such animals run through his mind.

Town must be close, Weston thought to himself, and a fresh load was lifted from his back. Food, drink, reinforcements. A plan could be made to deal with the monster. No man left behind, they'd hunt it in force. If it could be hurt, it could be killed.

No more animals passed before them, but the forest came alive with their noises. It was almost thunderous compared to the silence they'd endured for days. Sue continued to stop and check for markings and tracks and would often report the different animals that had been on the trail recently. He was the most excited about the paw print of a black bear he found near the tree line. Sue seemed to be in his glee surrounded by the skittering, tweeting, and growling of the alive forest.

And then it all stopped. Silence hit the forest like a fist, so sudden and so shocking that it almost pushed Sue and Weston back a pace. They both looked about them, confused, when a horrible roar sounded through the echoes of the forest all around them. The roar was followed by inhuman laughter and a sudden growling that bubbled up around them. They drew their weapons, stood back to back, and turned in a slow circle trying to study the entire forest and its movements all at once.

"We were so god damned close," Weston hissed through clenched teeth, eyes flicking all around him,

"It knew. It knew we were close. It doesn't want us to leave." Sue's breath was even and calm, but he shook. Weston could feel him as they pressed their backs together.

"Maybe we are close enough," Weston said and took a wild sprint down the small roadway, boots slipping on gravel and stone as he ran as fast as he could. Sue followed behind him.

The trees passed quickly beside them, and Weston imagined he could see the glare of many eyes staring at him from the shadows of the bent and twisted trees that stood on the side of the path. Eyes that were intent on one thing, but unable to act on it. Yet.

Not so far away, another roar echoed on the air like the thunderclap of a storm overhead. Weston ducked as if it were a physical thing, and kept moving, a strained hope of the town rising before them at the distance, but it never came.

Sue had seen something move in the shadows out of the corner of his eye, a quick movement that drew his attention and made him stumble mid-step. He managed to keep on his feet but fell behind Weston who ran on in the centre of the trail.

The shadows came alive just in front of Weston and the Mhuwe revealed itself. A roar spewed from its throat as it grasped Weston and threw him through the air and into the trees to the left of the road. It roared in triumph, its slender arms stretched above its head.

It took no heed to Sue -- whether it considered him no threat, or it was too focused on Weston, Sue could not say, but he took his opportunity. He steadied his rifle as the beast started its hunt for the out of sight Weston. He had a clear shot, nothing in his way, and the beast was unaware. He slowly squeezed the trigger, exhaling as he did, and the rifle bucked in his arms. There was a confused and angry whine from the beast as it spun towards Sue, a large chunk of flesh missing from its upper chest, and then it collapsed to the ground.

Sue was hesitant to approach, but he reloaded his rifle and moved forward slowly. The creature wasn't moving, even its stomach seemed still of any breathing. "Weston?" he called, hoping to rouse his companion. "Weston?"

No response.

The closer he got to the creature, the fouler the smell. It was the evil stench he'd discovered in Greta's house: the acrid smell of death and rot. It lay on the ground, very still, black ooze bubbling on its chest. He looked up to the place where Weston had been thrown and tried calling for him once more to no avail. As he looked back to the Mhuwe, he saw its eyes flick open, and it had him.

CHAPTER FIFTEEN

I

Weston woke with a start; the crisp linens wrapped around his naked torso were cool and pleasant, slicked in sweat. Rubbing at his eyes to clear his blurred vision, he threw back the covers and placed his bare feet on the coarse wooden floor. He became vaguely aware of the hazy sunlight drifting in from an open window, a light breeze making the transparent white curtain float lazily in its wake.

He knew the room. Had lived and slept in it for nearly five years, but that was so long ago. He stood on uneasy legs, gripping the large armoire for balance before stumbling towards the door. He made two lazy criss-crosses of the room, bouncing off a small dresser with little flowers painted on it before finally landing on the solid oak door, one hand gripping the brass doorknob. He turned it, feeling and hearing the familiar light jiggle as he did, and opened the door into the hallway he'd helped build, a hallway which he had travelled countless times. He turned to look back on the room, hazy in the morning sun, and he found the painting that hung crooked, just a fraction. He had never tried to straighten that picture because he liked it better the way she hung it. And it was hers, her painting of roses. It was Mary's. He took a steadying deep breath and flung himself into the hallway.

He leaned a shoulder into the wall opposite the door and used it to help him walk down the short hallway. The small kitchen lay ahead of him, the same hazy sun lighting it, glinting off the small crystal vase that was rolling in a slow circle on the round table where he'd eaten countless meals, held innumerable conversations, laughed until his stomach hurt. The little water that was in the vase now lay in a liquid circle that mirrored the vase's slow path. The flower was nowhere to be seen.

"Mary," he called in an echoing voice he wasn't sure was his own. His head hurt and he rubbed at his eyes once more. "Mary?"

She was there when he dropped his hand and opened his eyes. Her long, flowing red hair tied up in a messy bun, little ringlets falling around her big blue eyes and her smiling, pale pink lips. She held a cloth over one hand, a red dot growing out from where it was placed.

"Are you okay; did you hurt yourself?" Weston said, making to move to her, but having to fall back against the wall on his still unsteady legs.

"Oh, Bill, I didn't wake you, did I? I was hoping you'd get some extra sleep, you had such an awful time tossing and turning last night." She moved to him, blue eyes full of concern.

He took her in, her soft Irish features, her floral perfume, her quiet voice. He grabbed her shoulders and drew her into him, kissing her cheeks and forehead and neck. She giggled in his ear, her breath on his skin.

"Oh, you foolish man," she whispered, another giggle escaping her throat.

He pushed her just far enough away from him to grasp her covered hands, a grimace crossing her face. "Have you hurt yourself?"

"No, no. I was just putting a fresh flower in my vase and I pricked myself was all." She allowed him to remove her makeshift wrappings and inspect her finger. "I was distracted." Her voice was a sigh.

"It must've been an ambitious thorn to dig as deep as a needle," he said, a smile in his eyes as he kissed her fingertips.

She laughed again and pulled away from him, covering her finger before fixing the vase and wiping up the spilled water. Weston's head swam, his smile plastered across his dumbfounded face. Here she was, and here he was. There was something strange about that though, something familiar, but something off. He pushed himself forward, his legs steadier than before, and he leaned on the small table that stood before the window. He cast his gaze out at the familiar land, soil rich for farming, though he had yet to start. He bought this land just after they had married, and that just after the war.

She had waited for him of course, his sweetheart, waited four years, hoping and praying that the boy she knew would come back in one piece. He did come back, with some extra scars, a dirtier mouth, but more or less whole. Of course, he had gotten used to killing men, and had grown accustomed to sleeping under the stars, in the mud, and waking to cannon fire and gun shots ringing in his ears, but he came back. There were many who didn't.

"Mary, darling, what was it I was supposed to do today?" he said, eyes studying the untouched field.

"Silly, Billy, would forget his head if it weren't attached to him." She ruffled his hair from behind, his smile growing.

"I... I really do forget, hon," he said, turning now, his

legs stronger still. "Was I supposed to go hunting?"

"Hunting? Oh dear, I don't think so," Mary said, absently tidying around the kitchen.

"You sure, darling?" Something about hunting struck a chord. It made sense.

"I think you said you were going to buy some tools for farming. Mr. McDonald was going to go with you, help you pick out some things, maybe even get you a decent price. Remember?" Mary's pale face was turned down to her scrubbing, her loose curls bouncing with the effort.

He did remember something about meeting up with Mac, about seeing someone about a couple tools, maybe a plow? It felt so distant and strange; he couldn't quite place why, but it did. And fear. He felt fear around it, around leaving the house, about leaving Mary.

"What do you say I just skip all that today, Mary? Skip all that and we spend some time together. We could go to town for the day, spend some time looking in the shops, maybe even head out to the lake, watch the sunset like we used to. What d'ya' say?"

"Why, Billy, you old sweet talker, you sure do know how to make a girl feel special." She let out a gust of laughter, sweet and warm, that bubbled up from all the way down in her toes and just fell out of her in gusts of pleasure. Genuine pleasure.

"Come on, Mary," Weston said, wrapping his arms around her from behind and squeezing her into him. "Let's just forget about all this old stuff. We can play hookey for one little ole day, can't we?" He kissed her neck and nibbled her earlobe.

"You do know how to tease a girl," Mary said in a breathy voice, eyes closed and head back. "If you're not careful, I may take you up on that offer." But she turned around and gave him a gentle push, laughing.

"Go on with you, Mr. Weston." She wagged a finger at him. "Get yourself ready and out the door. We have a farm to build!" Her smile was too much to refuse.

Giving her one last tickle, he walked back down the hall, his legs forgotten about. It felt nice to wash up, to dress in clean clothes. Not just clean but cleaned by Mary. They smelled of her. He dressed in his favourite pair of jeans and an old plaid shirt, put on the boots laid out by his bed. He felt like a new man, renewed after a long day of riding. He felt like himself again.

The picture was different. He had glanced about the room making sure he'd not forgotten anything (where were his guns?) and noticed the picture was no longer just a little crooked, but completely askew. He noticed as well that the room had become much darker, that the picture now fell in a shadow, its bright colours unreadable from where he stood.

It had to be fixed. He grabbed the picture around the frame and drew it out from the shadows in order to hook it back on the nail more centred and in place. But it wasn't the same painting. What had been a simple rose, painted by his lively wife, was now small red dot; a red dot that was growing. It was as if a drop of paint was absorbing through the material meant to clean it but was instead widening. Like Mary's cut finger. It had bled and bled, had spread so easily on the cloth she used to wipe it. He didn't want to hang that painting up again, so he placed it on his dresser, afraid to look at it and see its changing face.

Weston backed away from the painting, afraid to look upon it, but unable to look away. As he reached the door, he saw it change once more. It wasn't just a widening dot on the canvas, but a large red mouth, open onto the world and everything within it. It was hungry and needed to be fed.

He stepped into the hallway, trying to pry his eyes away from the growing maw that wanted to swallow the paint canvas whole, and he called to Mary. No answer. He rushed into the kitchen, as dark as the bedroom.

"Mary," he said, his voice frantic, his heart beating out a rhythm on his chest. "Mary!" he yelled as he stomped around the small home trying to find his wife.

She wasn't there; she was dead. He remembered that now, remembered that she was murdered the day that he picked up the farm implements, remembered how he didn't find her body as much as pieces of it scattered everywhere. Remembered finding her perfect face on her perfect head in the grass nearby. Discarded.

The kitchen with its round table overturned and crystal vase smashed, like a pane of glass smashed and scattered all around him in a jagged rain that left nothing behind but the bluish black background of his empty dream.

He screamed. Screamed as he did that day when he had found her, screamed a long and horrible bellow that was full of anguish and helplessness. He screamed until he didn't think he could scream anymore, but he did. He continued screaming, until his throat was sore with the iron taste of blood, until he sat upright in the cold forest floor moaning and writhing and thrashing. And then he screamed some more.

II

The forest remained dark, but he could still see the trees sliding past him in a blur of motion. His feet pounded the ground as he ran, the returning fog floating around his thighs. The soft clap of wet leaves on the path were like footsteps and he had to look over his shoulder to be sure the beast was not following him. It was not and, for that, Sue was happy.

The inconsistent sleep and lack of real food made it hard for him to keep up his pace. Already he felt winded, a growing pain in his side and a dull ache in his legs. He would need to rest but was sure that once he did, the Mhuwe would attack again. The creature had slashed at him when he'd approached it, foolishly thinking he'd killed it, his rifle taking the brunt of the abuse and now had three jagged gouges to prove it. He hadn't been spared though and his right wrist and forearm now bled slowly through two open slashes in his sleeve. Looking down at his wounds kept him moving despite his exhaustion, though he didn't know how long he would be able to keep it up.

Sue was unsure as to what happened with Weston. He hoped that the man died with the beast's vicious throw, hoped that, being dead, Weston wouldn't have to face the pain and torture of the creature eating him alive. Sue had no such hopes for himself; the Mhuwe was solely focused on him now, he was sure of that. All the time Phillips' death seemed more and more appealing. Sue drew the rifle closer to his chest.

It wasn't long before his prophecy came true and he was bent over in the middle of the path, hands on his knees and lungs aching for breath. His side burned with each breath, but he forced himself into a quick, if somewhat laboured, walk, hoping to see an end to the path and an end to the forest.

Not much further up the path a large fallen tree blocked his way. It was so immense that he could not see over its tremendous side and his vision was limited to cold grey bark. Sue had a thought to go over the tree, to scale its craggy bark and slide down the other side, but he doubted his injured arm would support the climb for long. He scanned the tree line on either side of the path. The wilderness still maintained an eerie silence; the Mhuwe was near.

Faraway Sue scuttled into the tree line, ducking under the oversized roots that came free in the tree's terminal fall. Within the thick forest he made his way around the fallen tree, dodging branches and roots alike to try and make his passage back to the path as quick as possible. Passing through the trees, hands running over the tough bark as he passed the tight spaces around him, Sue thought of his grandfather, Maxkwikee.

His grandfather was very old and very well respected amongst his people. He was a huge man, stout and barrel-chested, and the scars he carried over his thick wrinkles told of many battles fought and survived. Maxkwikee taught a lot of the young children of Sue's tribe the stories of their people. Stories that would make them laugh, like that of Moskim the rabbit or Crazy Jack. Other stories he would tell them were meant to teach them lessons about the dangers of being greedy or ill prepared. Other stories still, like that of the Mhuwe, were meant to frighten. Sue never believed any of those stories. He thought they were silly things only meant for the little children, much to his grandfather's chagrin. Sue was more interested in Maxkwikee's war stories, his travels abroad in the territories, and his time with the white settlers, but his grandfather rarely spoke of that time. Instead he taught Sue how to hunt, which placated the young man as much as it frustrated him.

"They are wise," Maxkwikee had said when he first took Sue to hunt deer. "Wise enough to move with the wind. You must get to know him. Follow his path, learn his ways. If you do not, you will never earn him." On Sue's first solitary hunt, he stalked a mature buck for three days. Three days without notching an arrow or pulling his knife. He followed droppings, and the sparse tracks it left behind, willing himself to believe that he heard grunts and snorts just in the distance, out of reach and beyond the next tree. On the fourth day, he crouched low, notched an arrow, and followed the path out of the trees and into a valley. Surveying quickly, Sue moved back into the edge of the trees and watched, waiting for the buck to emerge, and graze, watching for it to present itself to him. He had earned it.

Hours passed and the buck didn't show itself. Sue's hand cramped from holding the arrow in place and he was forced to relax it. His feet and knees were straining, and he was made to sit on the root of the nearest tree. Sue began to panic; did he miss tracks? Did he time the buck's movement wrong? Was there a stream or watering hole close by that he didn't think about, didn't know about? He struck the ground with his fists and stepped out into the plain, kicking grass and rocks. Finally, turning to face the trees again, he heard the grunt, heard the harsh exhalation of breath and saw the animal, tall and proud. In the shade of the trees it looked grey and black, its eyes gleaming and wet, and its antlers spread in beautiful angles and curls. Sue locked eyes with it for a brief moment, and it stared at him passively, regarding him with mild interest, and a sense of regal disappointment hit Sue. It turned and walked back into the forest and out of sight.

Maxkwikee smiled when Sue told him the story,

clapped him on the back and laughed when he walked away, but there was something in his eyes. His grandfather was disappointed in him, Sue could tell. It wasn't in his words or actions, it was in his eyes. His grandfather's large, brown eyes wet with age and knowledge, knew of Sue's impatience. Knew he had lost the buck. Sue left his tribe soon after. He never saw Maxkwikee again.

He'd learned much since he last saw his grandfather. Some he learned on his own, some from other tribes he found, other Indian people. He even learned some from white men. What would his grandfather say about that?

When Sue finally broke through the tree line, he could see the dots of flame in the distance, could see the lights of town. It cheered him little. Safety from the beast was within reach, but safety from the gallows was uncertain. He was a dead man, but at least he got to choose his own death. Neither appealed to him. He hummed one of his grandfather's songs. A song of life and death, of battle and freedom.

The roar came from all around him. Fell all about him, splashing down like rain in water. Faraway Sue cocked his rifle and ran toward town.

III

Weston stood in the darkness, trying to regain his bearings. He had landed hard, his legs taking the brunt of the fall in the tight confines, and the branches he struck on his way through now lay around him. He examined his wounds, mostly scratches, and one large gouge up his right thigh that would cause him trouble, but he'd survive.

He crashed back through the tree line, limping as he did, cursing under his breath. A roar broke the gloom somewhere ahead of him. He shivered.

Weston called to Sue, looked about him for any sign. After some looking, he found two spent rifle shells, and a small puddle of black blood.

Moving was painful, running was out of the question, and his walking was hindered by a severe limp to his left. But he continued. Sweat stained his brow and thoughts coursed through his mind. Part of him believed that if the beast was ahead of him, he should find another way, he should turn back. But what was the good in that? He'd only be delaying the inevitable. The beast would find him, and it would eat him. The only way out of this god forsaken forest was to kill it, he decided. Kill it and be done with it.

The path was straight, the tree line hedged off by the beaten down trail, the thick fog tendrils that spread tentatively through the cracks in the trees preventing him from checking for any further signs that Sue had come this way. Weston had given up on tracking the monster itself, and instead decided to track what it tracked. Prey upon its prey. He was sure he would find it if he found Sue.

Another roar echoed off the thick fog and Weston pushed himself to move faster. The monster had found its prey.

IV

Faraway Sue waited in the shadow provided by a craggy hill that stood on the outskirts of a small patch of flatland he'd come to along the path. The silence of the forest persisted and, except for the steady thrum of his own breath echoing in his ears, Sue could hear nothing. There was no sound, but Sue was not alone.

He had taken flight upon hearing the beast, readied

his weapon, but had not seen the Mhuwe. Sue knew it was near though, that it was stalking him, but a quick look from his cover in the shadow of the craggy hill told him nothing. Sue's vision was lit by moon and stars, and in it he saw the tall grass of the flatland as it swayed in the cold, gentle breeze of the night. Snow had started to fall in small flakes that floated to the ground and stuck to the tips of the grass, glittering there for their brief life span. In the distance were the lights of Barclay, burning now as they had before and calling to him.

Sue leaned back into the hill, his shoulders being jabbed by jagged rocks that had become lodged there some time ago when Kitanitowit created the world. He'd asked his grandfather once if Kitanitowit placed things around the earth because he knew one of his people would need it sometime, somehow. "For instance," he had said in his small boy's tongue, "did he give us deer and elk and fish so that we could eat? Or did he leave stones and trees so we could have tools and weapons?"

Maxkwikee, just looked at him, a broad smile crossing his scarred face. "We have what we need when we need it, why ask for any more." It was a good answer, Sue reflected, but why did he need jagged rocks poking his back as he leaned against the craggy hill instead of extra bullets, or a knife? Perhaps Kitanitowit had a sense of humour.

A gentle snap of a twig brought his attention around once more. He held his breath and prayed that he didn't give away his position. Forcing himself to swallow his fear, he moved his head ever so slightly so he could peer around the edge of his jagged hill. The tall grass still waved, the snow still fell with no urgency, and nothing was out of sorts. Out of the corner of his eye, as he turned away from the field, he saw a black shape move in the shadow. It was slight, barely even a movement really, but it was there. Sue checked his rifle, slowly bringing it to his eye; it was loaded and ready. He reminded himself to breathe.

Sue's father had been killed by white men when he was a boy as they were forced out of their home. His grandfather held him in his arms as the blood of Sue's father, Maxkwikee's son, ran down his face. Sue was very young, but he remembered it. He remembered the warmth of the blood as it dropped down his face and onto his chubby, balled up child's hands. But that was all he remembered of his father. He'd asked his grandfather how he did it, how he watched his own son die and not react. Not kill the man who did it. Maxkwikee shrugged. "I took a breath. One breath after the other, boy. That's all you need to know."

One breath. He braced his feet, digging them into the soft grass, and slid up the craggy hill, his back taking the abrasions of the sharp rocks on through his thin shirt. Another breath. He peered into the shadow across the small flatland, searching for the gleam of eyes, a glare from fangs. He brought his gun to his shoulder. One breath. The sudden movement of the pure darkness so fast that it was a mere blur. Another breath. The Mhuwe appeared, its horned head bending forward to prepare its charge, its blood blackened teeth agape in a broken smirk. One breath. Sue moved from his cover, rifle poised at his shoulder, and he walked towards the charging monster. Another breath. Fire; the rifle bucked against his shoulder losing a bullet into the Mhuwe. One breath. Fire. Another bullet in the air. Another breath. Fire. One breath. Click.

The monster was struck two times by Sue's barrage; it flinched away and twitched as it took the shots to the chest, black blood leaving it in a fine spray. It hissed and slashed at the air around it, pain crushing over its already distorted features. Standing to its full height on its disjointed, buck like legs, it tossed its large antlers and roared an ear-piercing squeal that struck Sue like a wave cascading over rocks.

Sue looked sidelong at his empty rifle and tossed it into the high grass. No weapon available to him now, he continued walking, stalking the beast that stood watching him with a tilt of its antlers.

Sue broke into a run and jumped onto the Mhuwe, arms wrapping around the creature's too thin waist, and his left shoulder pressing into its concave stomach. He squeezed as hard as he could, feeling the thinly stretched flesh, old and dry, wrapped around the sharp bones of the unnatural beast. Sue could feel a grunt as it reverberated along the Mhuwe's spine and ribs, and then he felt its long-fingered hand wrap around his already ill-used shirt. With a flick of its stick thin wrist, the Mhuwe tossed Sue to the side, flipping him to his back with as little effort as a wolf throwing a rabbit from its jaws.

Sue's lungs constricted, and he arched his back against the pain from the landing. A chittering sound spilled from the creature's throat as it moved toward him once again. Still gasping for air, Sue began to crawl away from it, blood or saliva running from the corner of his mouth. His hand fell on something hard and cold in the grass, the barrel of his empty rifle. He grasped it in his hand just as the Mhuwe dug into his left thigh with its hand full of razors. Pain, cold and piercing, raced around his leg. He bellowed into the ground, the grass and dirt absorbing it. The creature began to drag him backwards; Sue kicked and flailed, but the creature's grip would not fail.

Sue pushed the pain and fear out of his mind, adjusting his grip on the rifle barrel. Sue turned onto his back, a fresh blast of pain bringing another cry from him and drawing the beast's attention. It looked down upon him, its blood-stained face a smattering of both purple and black over the Mhuwe's thin, wrinkled mouth and sharp teeth. Sue brought the rifle up in a clubbing motion, its shoulder stock landing on the side of the creature's face with a resounding thud that echoed over the field. The creature's head snapped to the side, a low gurgle rumbling in its throat, and it released Sue's leg, which he gladly took back. The shoulder stock of the rifle had broken in the crash, splinters of it lay throughout the grass and atop Sue's shirt and chest. The creature stumbled backward.

Sue regained his footing, despite not being able to move his left leg, and began to limp away from the beast that stood wavering in the middle of the field. He reached the ragged tree line before the creature had a chance to recover, and tried to pull himself into the trees, his arms and hands grasping at the flailing branches before him. The thin roar of the beast erupted from behind him and he almost fell back into the field. Instead, he was able to make his way into the trees, collapsing under his own weight.

Faraway Sue was crawling once more, and he could feel the fallen branches and embedded rocks as he crawled through the overgrown forest floor. Sue's leg had locked up on him, a cold feeling still circling within it, and it stuck out completely straight. He tried to stand but the straight leg made it hard without additional help, so he crawled as best he could, his hands falling upon broken branches and sticks that lay discarded before him.

A heavy crunch sounded in front of him. Sue's head shot upwards, eyes running past the snow coloured hoof and fur of an overgrown elk before landing on the snarling mouth and cold, black eyes of the Mhuwe. It reared up before him, its thin fingers spread on both hands to rake down across him. Sue's fingers wrapped around a thick branch and he jabbed it upwards into the monster's stomach. A terrible scream lifted from the Mhuwe's throat. High-pitched and ear shattering. Sue recoiled, both hands rushing to cover his ears.

The scream went on for what seemed like eternity to Sue, but it ended abruptly with another gurgle from the creature's mouth. Sue looked up at the creature, hesitant to remove his hands from his ears in case another screech was let loose from the Mhuwe's birdlike chest. It was hanging there, the stick piercing its stomach, the other end digging into the ground. Its arms were limp, the body lifeless.

"Kitanitowit provides," Sue said, a watery giggle seeping from his chest.

It took him some time, but he was able to crawl into the tall grass of the flatland, tumbling over the small rise that separated it from the treeline. His leg felt frozen, and he rolled to his back trying to rub some life into it, but the pain kept him from kneading it as much as was needed. He tore some cloth from his shirt and wrapped it around the punctures in his thigh. The blood was oozing out of the wound, slowly but steadily, but the makeshift dressing seemed to help.

Sue remained on his back, watching the lazy snowflakes land on his face and the grass cushion his head. The stars above glared in the sky, bright and observant. The moon was hidden behind a thick band of clouds that concealed its yellow light. Still, it was a bright night, and the fog had dispersed. Perhaps he could make it to town.

The cold had penetrated his bones by the time he had forced himself to his feet again, a chill that shook him to the core. He flailed across the flatland, arms wrapped around his chest, but thinking only of the warmth he may find in Barclay.

He'd crossed onto the main path, the light from town now closer than ever. Barclay wouldn't welcome him with open arms, likely he'd be in shackles before he could explain anything, and not long after that he'd be blamed for the loss of Weston, the deputy, and everyone else. Most white men wouldn't believe what had really happened.

"God damned Injun," the deputy rumbled from behind him.

Sue spun on his good leg to see the Mhuwe staring down upon him, black blood spotted around its gaping mouth, its tentacle like tongue running along the edges of its sharp teeth. It grabbed his arms with both clawed hands, squeezed tight, and pulled him towards its own body. Sue struggled, twisting his shoulders back and forth, kicking his legs, arching his back, but the strong grip held.

Smelling the sour scent of the creature as it pulled him closer and closer to its waiting mouth, Sue began to hum a song. It was a good song, a song that his grandfather had taught him. It was the song of Kitanitowit and the creation of the world. With all things good must come all things evil; Kitanitowit was told that in a vision, for that is the nature of the world, and life.

As the Mhuwe sunk its teeth into Sue, the creature's body shaking with anticipation, he smiled. His humming had finally come to an end, his suffering in the cold and under the white man had come to an end; he would see his father again soon. Faraway Sue dwelled on these things as his vision faded into the final darkness at the end of things.

As the clouds cleared the skies, the limp form of Faraway Sue lay cradled in the emaciated arms of the Mhuwe. The terrible sound of it greedily sucking and biting and gnawing on the young Indian's neck and chest resonated off the trees to either side of them. But that too would soon be silent, as completely silent as Sue's humming, lost to the eternity of time.

CHAPTER SIXTEEN

I

Weston studied the immensity of the fallen tree that blocked the roadway and his release from the forest. At every turn, the forest provided as complete a prison as any jailhouse that he had witnessed in his life. If he weren't so exhausted, he'd probably be quite impressed.

He stumbled through the trees and brush to go around the tree, following the path Faraway Sue had taken just hours before. The overgrown passage gave him no repose, and he crashed through it, cursing loudly as the tangled branches and brambles slashed his wounded leg. Returning to the road beyond the trees was even more of a challenge and he chose to fall the short distance rather than try to brace himself on his heavily abused legs. The fall was short, the drop small, but he discovered fresh new pains when hoisting himself back to his feet.

A persistent darkness of the night halted him once more, but overhead he heard the hoarse calling noises of crows in flight, and their presence cheered him; Barclay was close. He peered into the distance and saw what he thought must be the glowing lights of the town before him. An unhindered smile cracked his dirt encrusted face.

Weston limped down the roadway, trying his best to walk quickly despite the throbbing in his legs and feet. He was comforted by the fact that each new step, no matter how painful, brought him closer to town. The roar had gone unanswered after he had heard it last, its horrible screech echoing in the tall trees of the forest. It did not repeat itself. Perhaps it had found Sue, and during their battle Sue had killed it. Perhaps it went the other way and the monster had found a new meal. Weston doubted that either possibility was so cut and dry but prepared himself for the worst. Sue was likely dead by now, the beast was likely feeding or well-fed, and Weston would have no way to hunt it, let alone kill it.

By the time the sun was threatening to break the horizon, the sky lit in pale yellows and oranges, Weston could see the outlines of Barclay's buildings blurred by the morning haze. He'd taken to using his rifle as a walking stick, using the stock as his extra foot, his hand gripping the barrel. It wasn't something he would of have done normally, but his situation facilitated the need. It made his gait quite strange, three rapid thumps that corresponded to his steps. Thump thump thump. It was a strange triumvirate of sounds, echoed by the hollow slap of the gun's shoulder stock on hard ground. It was in this manner that he came to a small patch of flat land overgrown with tall grass. The sudden end to the tree line jarred Weston for a moment, and he peered into the small area, scanning the top of the tall grass. There, in the middle of the high grass, he saw the Mhuwe, its gangling frame facing away from him, its bony arm stretched behind it; dragging something.

Weston fell back to the cover of the tree line, obscuring his view of the beast. He took a deep breath to try and calm himself, and then another to slow his heart which felt like it was going to beat out of his chest. Weston took still another breath, holding it, and looked into the flat land once more. The creature was now crouched down, its large rack of antlers swaying above the high grass, the noises of its eager feeding carrying over the small space. Weston pulled himself back, released his breath in one slow exhalation, and drew his rifle from the ground.

Bringing his gun to his shoulder, Weston turned around the tree he had used for cover and entered the high grass. He did little to conceal his movement, but the monster was too intent on its meal to hear him. Trying to get as close as he could before opening fire, Weston had a moment to think on Phillips and Dutch. If he were Phillips, he would have some sort of plan developed involving traps or some ploy; he would have tried to stay three moves ahead of the beast. If he were Dutch, he would have snuck up on the beast and tried to deliver one single blow that would end the fight before it started. Weston had his own ideas on what would work and began to fire at the beast in a steady walk towards it with his limping gait.

At the first shot the monster twirled, snarling. Weston fired six shots from his rifle -- the beast twitched and flailed, but Weston wasn't paying too close attention to his hits. After emptying his rifle, he dropped it to the ground before his hands swung low and came back up with his Colt revolvers, firing them both with a practiced one-handed cock and fire. Weston knew this would cut down on accuracy, but he was closing in on his target and it would be harder to miss than hit. Again, the creature flinched and reeled with each bullet it took, its foul smelling, black blood trickling from small wound appearing all over its upper torso and face. When the Colts clicked empty, he slung them back in their holsters, waiting.

The Mhuwe fell to the ground during the barrage

of bullets, a harsh, wheezing breath emanating from its punctured chest in its rapid rise and fall of lungs. Weston stood above it, reaching into his jacket and removing the knife he had hidden away in a sheathe under his arm. It was the first real look he gotten of the beast without fear or disgust influencing his evaluation. The creature's revolting worm-like skin seemed to crawl under his gaze, moving and quivering in places that almost caused him to step back. Now, as he took it all in, he realized it was female, its breasts shrivelled against its rib cage, decimated by the creature's inability to eat its fill or its unearthly old age. Weston didn't know and didn't care.

The creature twisted against the ground, writhing in pain, but still very much alive. Weston bent, adjusting his knife to a stabbing grip. The Mhuwe's claw-like hand swiped at him; Weston fell to his ass just barely avoiding the eviscerating blow. He scuttled backwards in time to see the monster jump to all fours, like some evil mockery of a buck Elk snorting and growling, its blackened tongue lashing over its horrible teeth.

It bounded after him, casting its claws at him with every step. Weston dragged himself backwards with his hands, avoiding it as best he could. He rolled in a backwards tumble and followed his momentum to get to his feet and, ignoring the pain, slashed out at the charging beast with his knife. It reared back, fresh black blood sprouting on its cheek. A grunt rumbled in its throat and it cast a large, slender backhand at him, connecting with his shoulder and sending him spinning back to the ground.

Getting up was much harder this time, and the beast was on him before he could fully recover, its face close to his own, its cold breath stinking as its tongue lashed out between its teeth, saliva dripping from it. Weston shoved his forearm into the creature's neck to try and maintain some distance, and stabbed furiously with his knife, piercing the creature's stomach repeatedly. Cool liquid began to drain upon him.

The creature reared back, its face contorted, and its lips pulled back in a vicious snarl. Weston took the opportunity to roll away from the creature and tried to get to his feet once more. He tried to ignore the pain in his legs, but they just would not support him any longer, and he struggled to stay on his knees. The creature had no such issues with its multiple wounds and bullet holes, and it ran at him once more, its growl urgent and its black eyes intent. With his limited mobility Weston could only wait for the beast to come, and when it did, he attempted to launch himself away from it, hoping that his legs may be persuaded to work on the third attempt. The creature was too quick by far and lashed him across his back and side, tearing open his jacket and the clothes underneath, but not his flesh, though he could feel its razor-sharp talons scratching at his side and ribs.

The Mhuwe was atop Weston before he could recover yet again. He slashed at its guts and sides, but the creature swallowed the pain and brought its deceptively strong hand down upon Weston's knife hand. Weston could feel the bones in his fingers crack to the point of breaking and he released his knife to avoid it. Quick as ever, the beast pushed its full weight on Weston's hand and he felt a snap and immense pain. He screamed and the beast smiled, raising its head to roar in victory.

Weston ambled about beneath the creature, his unbroken hand flailing in the grass attempting to wrap its fingers around anything that might be used as a weapon. The beast turned its attention back to Weston, its black eyes wide and watery. It was a look that reminded Weston of a wild animal, wary but unconcerned with human activity, staring at anyone who gazed upon it as if they were just another part of the scenery. Its face dove into Weston's own once more, its teeth snapping as it fell towards him, and Weston shoved his forearm into its throat once again, while his good hand flailed about. When his hand landed on something, he grabbed it, and brought it to his face to see if it would help. The creature pushed its neck against his forearm, black blood dripping onto Weston's face. As it did this, it placed both hands behind Weston's back and began to pull itself forward getting closer and closer to Weston's face and neck. Weston couldn't look away, afraid that once he turned the creature's jaws would be around his neck. But it was getting so close.

He caught a glimpse of something red in his hand and knew what he had. With no time left, he struck the top from the flare from the old mining camp hoping that it would still be active after all those years in the abandoned camp. Its red flame came to life; it sizzled and burned at the air around it. Weston pushed against the creature's neck with all of his waning strength and pushed the flare into the Mhuwe's stomach.

It was an unexpected, but not unwelcome ignition of skin and sparse hair that caught quick and spread quicker. The beast was engulfed in the flames within a breath, the heat that erupted from the roaring flames and sizzling flesh, burned at Weston's face and hands. He scuttled away from the Mhuwe's grip, welcoming the cool air and damp grass he gathered himself in.

It was Phillips all over again. The flailing body, the boiling fire, and the intense screams. Howls, roars, and whines erupted from the beast as it staggered around the open field. It scratched at itself, and batted at its own arms, and still the fire burned. Weston watched in the monster's dying light, waiting for it to die, but hoping it wouldn't be too soon. When it collapsed to the ground, the flames continued to arch and roll over the blackened body; the Mhuwe was dead. Weston watched it smoulder and burn for a long time, just to make sure.

PART FIVE
CHAPTER SEVENTEEN

I

Sheriff Forster urged his horse toward the main road that entered his town. It had been a few long nights for the Sheriff and the town of Barclay, not knowing what had become of his deputy or the company of bounty hunters he sent out to find the escaped prisoner, the Indian they called Faraway Sue. In spite of all that, Forster's real concern was with whatever was lurking in the forest killing and eating his people. That was a deadly concern.

Derby Jarvis and Brent Kavanagh greeted him at the head of the path with tired eyes and rusty rifles. Forster had sent out shifts of men to guard entrances of the town the night after the small posse of fugitive hunters didn't return. Derb and Brent looked to the sheriff in hopes they could get some rest.

"Derb, how's it been?" Forester said with a nod to Brent.

Derb was lanky and a little too red around the nose and dry eyed for Forster's liking. "Not much happening, Boss. But we heard some strange noises about an hour ago and saw some smoke rose in the distance. Isn't that right, Brent?" Derby sat on a carriage wagon they'd set up as a makeshift barricade and checkpoint for anyone wishing to enter the town. Brent was a gruff man with a large, unkempt beard, and dirty hands and clothes. He nodded his affirmation.

"Smoke, eh? I would've liked to have been made aware of it as it happened," the sheriff said in his booming voice, eyeing the duo under his bushy eyebrows.

Derb shrunk away from him, pressing himself harder into the carriage seat. "We didn't think t'were nothin', Sheriff. Figured you'd be by before long anyway. When was the last time you slept?"

It was a true enough statement and a pertinent question. Forster hadn't slept much since the night the posse didn't return. He'd wanted to go out there himself and find them, take a few local lads, but he knew that'd be no good. As Bill Weston had pointed out, he had the rest of the town to think of. And while he wasn't going to send any more men out into the forest to die, he figured he could put some to work on a watch around the town. Still, no sight or sound of those men made for some terribly sleepless nights. And, with nothing better to do, the sheriff added support to the guard he had ordered in the town.

"Next time, someone let me know," Forster said with a grunt and started off towards the next guarded entrance. The town was quiet in the early morning light, and the roads were clear for the sheriff's gallop through its streets. There were four entrances into Barclay: two shared the same main road and went directly through the town while another was a small trail that the loggers used to go directly into the forest where they plied their trade. The final entrance into the town was an old trail that the miners had once used to get in and out of town when all it had was the General Store and a boarding house. That was the entrance that he headed for now.

He took a tight path between some houses, his horse snorting in objection as its haunches and Forester's legs rubbed too snugly on the stone and wooden walls. At the end of the path, two more men sat smoking and laughing, leaning on some barrels, and their rifles slung over their shoulders. Ambrose Cassidy and Ike Holt gave the sheriff a strange look as he pushed his horse through the narrow space, one that Forster took some delight in.

"Sheriff," Ike said around his cigarette. "Leading the cavalry today?" Ambrose broke out into another round of laughter.

"Anything new?" The sheriff looked down upon Ike, a small man in just about every sense of the word, but with an endless supply of mouth. No wonder he and Tom Baker had got on so well.

"Nohm," said Ambrose, trying to get his laughter under control. Ambrose was a brawny logger that spent too much time in the bar and far too little time working, in Forster's opinion. "Saw some smoke earlier out yonder, but nothing serious."

"Did you hear anything?"

Ambrose and Ike gave each other a sidelong glance over their cigarette smoke. Then they both shook their heads; they hadn't. Forster grunted and carried on past them, moving to the next guarded entrance and hope that some news had developed.

The past few days had not only been hard on the sheriff; the people of Barclay were suffering as well. As rowdy and robust a bunch as they were, the townsfolk were living in compounded fear. On one hand they had an escaped prisoner; on the other they had a killer on the loose. Many people started to put these two together, and that bred theories that there was some wild band of Indians who were tearing people apart and wanted to free one of their own to join in. It was foolishness, of course, and most of it came from the heavy drinking folk, but it was out there all the same. The sheriff would have had to been deaf to not hear the townsfolk's thoughts on his part in the whole mess. He let the Indian go, they said. He was in cahoots with the bounty hunters to get a quick pay off. He had hired some evil bastards to come murder some people so he could try and solve it.

"What a load of hogwash," he said aloud. Of course, the death of Greta Dubois didn't settle things down at all, and then the missing posse that went out in search of Sue. It was a fucking mess, is what it was. A fucking mess.

He took a roundabout way to the next entrance, riding around and through the town. The folks of Barclay were starting to push their way into the light of the morning slowly but surely. Loggers were walking out of the town in two straight lines, the burly, bearded men all walking with axes over their shoulders and smiles on their faces, but they wouldn't go far into those trees. No one went very far anymore. Farmers and store owners would come after the lumberjacks, ambling about the streets to reach their opposite destinations. The sheriff pushed past them all, trying to smile and wave to those her could, put up a reasonable facade that everything was okay.

"Sheriff," a voice called from behind him. He halted his horse and turned back, casting a wide glance to make sure he caught sight of whoever was hailing him. Derby Jarvis was running up the street, manoeuvring around anyone that got in his way. He looked harried and out of breath.

"Sheriff," Derby panted as he reached Forster and leaned against the sheriff's horse. "Sheriff, you oughta come see this." He pointed towards the entrance that he and Brent had been guarding. Forster turned his horse around and broke it into a mad gallop towards the main entrance of town.

It only took him a few moments to get there, parting the townsfolk that stood in his way like Moses did the Red Sea, and he swung down from his saddle even before his horse could come to a complete stop. He ran to the carriage that Derb and Brent had been using, but Brent was nowhere to be found. Forster looked around, his heart beating savagely in his chest, and caught glimpse of someone at the edge of the trees just out from town. Forester took to his feet and ran towards them.

Brent turned as he heard the sheriff approach. His broad back swung away from the scene he was taking in, and he gave the sheriff a tempered look. On the ground at Brent's feet was Bill Weston in dire shape. He had bumps, scratches, and bruises all over his head and face. One of his hands looked as though it had been broken, and there was a large gash opened on his left thigh, blood flowing from an attempt at staunching it. Weston was only semi-conscious: his eyes heavy lidded and rolling up in his eye sockets as he attempted to take in what was happening around him. His eyes swung to Forester as he knelt down by him, and with effort the pools of gold flecks focused for a moment. Weston tried to speak, but he fell into unconsciousness. There was a noxious smell of smoke on him, and as Forester looked him over, he noticed that he was burned in several places including his hands and chest.

Forester and Brent supported the body between them, Weston's arms across their shoulders. Derb had made it back in time to help them struggle with putting Weston's dead weight over the back of Forester's horse, without causing the man anymore damage or spooking the horse too much.

"Keep an eye on the road and let me know if anything else happens," Forester said once they had Weston situated. He took his horse by the reins and guided it back into town towards the doctor's residence. What did Weston know, continued to play on Forester's mind as he walked, and when would he be able to find out for himself? The man had been trying to say something when he saw him. What was it? Hopefully the doctor would be able to speed his recovery along, if Weston was able to recover at all.

II

He reeled and wavered, his vision plagued by random things he could not recognize. A wooden ceiling, an empty chair, white bed linens, and the sheriff. Always behind and in between them, was the image of the beast's jagged teeth clicking together a hair's space away from his face.

"It's no good, Bill, you can't kill evil," came the voice of Jim Phillips, his voice rasping and hollow. "Real evil, evil like that creature back there in those woods, that persists. It's eternal."

Weston turned his head on his soft pillow, looking toward his dead friend who now occupied the lone chair in his room. Phillips' skin hadn't stopped bubbling, and it ran slowly over his left eye, exposing his sugar white skull. The corpse smiled at him.

"It's okay, Bill. You just can't save everyone, but you already know that, eh?" Phillips' nose seemed to collapse in on itself as he looked up to the ceiling, his skin sloughing off him like candle wax. "Tell me about Mary again?" A chuckle, low and rasping.

"I never…" Weston started, but was greeted with an

empty chair. His room still filled with the smell of smoke and burning fat. He dug the heels of his hands into his eyes hard, and forced darkness to come over them. The pressure seemed to focus things for him. Where was he? How did he get here?

"Some damn fool dragged you here, I expect. Just like I used to." A hulking shadow stood in the corner of the room, its broad shoulders tucked resting on the walls that joined there.

"Dutch?" Weston managed, black spots disappearing from his vision. The big man nodded his head, a fresh gush of blood spilling down his chest from the large section of missing flesh on his neck.

"Howdy, Bill. How could you do it?" Dutch stood over him now, his wide mouth cocked to the side in a grimace. "How could you leave it like this?"

"Dutch... I." Weston's voice echoed in his own head; like a marionette, his mouth was moving, but he couldn't control the words.

"The creature. I sacrificed myself for you. I took your place, and you let it live. How could you do that?" Blood dripped from his neck and chest, striking Weston on his bare arms.

"I did it, Dutch, I killed it. It's dead."

"No, it's not. You let me die, you let us all die, and here you are alive and well, same as that beast. You're a coward, Bill."

"Dutch..." Weston's voice cracked. He tried to raise himself up, to meet the corpse of his friend face to face. He wanted to explain, wanted to tell him how sorry he was, how he could make it right, but no words would come.

"It's alive, just like those butchers that killed Mary."

Weston screamed then. Screamed and thrashed in

his bed. His voice strained and his muscles tensed. He screamed until he could feel hands on his arms and chest, hands on his head and neck pushing him down into the bed. He saw Dutch and Phillips, their gore covered faces smiling down on him as they pushed him back. Pushed him down so he couldn't move. But it wasn't Dutch or Phillips. He didn't recognize either man who was on top of him, and he fought against them, pulling himself up to their shoulders. And he saw it. The Mhuwe stared at him from the corner of the room, squat down on its too long legs, sucking blood and flesh off its clawed fingers. It looked into his eyes and gave him an evil smile of sharp teeth and malice. He succumbed to the strangers then, a fresh round of screaming that gave away to darkness.

III

Despite the constant assault of nightmares, Weston soon discovered he was out of the forest, and back in Barclay. He had been brought to the local doctor, Burrows, who wasn't much of a doctor really, but more like a medic for the logging company. The doctor hadn't had to deal with wounds such as Weston's often. Most of his cases were axe or saw wounds, and the occasional fall. Predominantly he didn't have to do much of anything. Most of those wounds lead to death before he could be of any help. Nevertheless, he took to Weston's ailments rather quickly once the sheriff gave him a bottle of rye. There wasn't as much to work out as they had expected; just the large wound on his thigh, his broken fingers, and some scratches and bruises.

"Easy," said Burrows once Weston was up and aware.

Sheriff Forester visited him regularly. They were short

visits, mostly talking about what the sheriff was up to, how his wife was doing in all of this. Though the sheriff tried to keep things light, the town of Barclay seemed to be going through some hard times. Weston would often press him for details, tidbits of information, and even offered to help. Forester would just laugh it off, clap him on the shoulder and leave the room without another word.

They hadn't talked about the forest, or about what happened there. The sheriff simply wouldn't bring it up, and Weston didn't feel strong enough to talk about it on his own. He didn't know if he could explain the deaths, if he could explain the monster that they all had stared in the face. Weston didn't even know if he could trust himself to believe his own memories. Maybe it was all a nightmare.

Weston wasn't sure how many days he sat in that bed in the doctor's house, for the days seemed to all meld together only interrupted by his nightmares and the visits from the sheriff. Otherwise Weston spent his time trying not to think about what had happened to him in the woods. He found the best way to avoid this was to try and stretch his sore limbs. It wasn't much at first, but he was able to walk around his room and that was good enough. When he tired of that or he just couldn't walk anymore, he tried to read. Most of the books he had access to were those owned by the doctor, so they either detailed anatomy or biology, or spoke of different types of trees. Like it or not, they kept him distracted.

His stay in the doctor's house ended when Sheriff Forester came into his room frustrated, red-faced, and breathing heavily through his teeth. He paced around the room for a moment without looking at anything in particular and then slammed the door. His thick, gnarled finger pointed at Weston.

"All right, boy, we need to talk." The sheriff threw his hat on a small bedside table, dragged the chair through the room, and sat across from Weston. "I've tried to keep quiet. I've tried to give you time. The doctor said you were having some pretty nasty dreams. Flashbacks or some such, but, god damn it, Weston, I need to know what I can do."

Weston stared at his hands. They were still bandaged and sore, and his right was completely bandaged, two fingers in makeshift splints. His left was full of cuts and bruises and sores. He made fists. "I can tell you what I know, but I'm not sure I trust my own recollection." Weston told his story then, of the foolhardy ride into the old mining camp, of the deaths of his companions, and reluctantly of the beast.

The sheriff, diffused of his anger, now sat back rubbing his thick growth of stubble with one rough hand. "Let's say I believe that you're not crazy, son." The sheriff's deep voice was slow and thoughtful. "You say you killed the monster that did all this? Burnt it to a crisp. Sat there and watched it burn before heading back to town."

"Yes, sir, that's what I'm saying," Weston said with some relief. He expected to hear all kinds of thoughts on how crazy he was, had expected the sheriff to want to throw him in a cell and hang him for the deaths of all those people. He never thought he would hear anything so close to understanding, so close to belief in his crazy memories.

The sheriff stood up and paced around the room again. He looked at Weston and held up one finger, one minute, and walked out the door. Apprehension snuck back in to Weston's gut then. This was it, he'd be dragged away. Perhaps he'd even killed on the spot. But, then again, what was the point of living if you were this crazy.

The sheriff came back a few moments later with some clothes under his arm. He picked up his hat, placed it firmly on his head, and put the clothes on the table next to Weston. "Here, put these on. I want you to see something," the sheriff said before leaving the room again.

IV

The clothes fit well. It surprised Weston how good he felt being in clean clothes. It felt even better being able to walk about outside. He inhaled the cool, fresh air and pulled his jacket tight around his waist. Barclay was covered in a fresh layer of snow; the bright white reflecting off the roofs of the buildings gave everything a refreshed and new looking feel. It was almost as if it wasn't the same town as before.

"Feel good being out of the bed?" the sheriff said as he motioned for him to follow.

"Yes, sir. Feels just fine. I do miss the feel of my guns on my hips though," Weston said, trying his best to keep up with the sheriff's long stride while limping on his still wounded leg.

The sheriff chuckled, "I bet you do." He looked at Weston over his shoulder, a smile on his face. Weston saw a hard look in the sheriff's eyes that made him uneasy.

They walked down the main street of Barclay, and though it was bright daylight, and couldn't be much past noon, they didn't run into any other folks on the way. It turned out to be a short trip that ended in an unwelcome sight. The sheriff stopped and gave an appraising glance of Greta's house, the corner of his eye trained on Weston's reactions. It didn't seem to have changed at all since Weston last saw it the day they went in search of Faraway

Sue, but the door stood open and two unruly men stood on either side of it, rifles in their hands.

"What's goin' on, Sheriff?"

The old man raised his eyebrows and gestured for Weston to move on ahead. "Come on, boy, I'll show you."

The snow crunched under their boot steps as they approached the small house. Weston didn't recognize the two men who stood on either side of the doorway; their drawn faces were that of men over worked and tired, their eyes sunken into darkened folds. They gave the sheriff a firm nod of recognition but scowled at Weston as he stepped through the gaping portal.

It was as he remembered, a small house, messy now as it had been the day Sue had escaped his custody. The bedroom door was closed to hide the blood of the deceased Greta and keep the cold air out from the broken window in the same room. Weston faced the sheriff, gave him a shrug, as he continued to study his surroundings. Nothing seemed out of place. The sheriff raised his thick grey eyebrows once more and led him to another door, opened it, and motioned for him to go through.

It was a small room, smaller than the bedroom Greta shared with the Darrio girl, but it had a small bed tucked away in the corner, a chest, and a four-drawer dresser. Weston stepped further into the room, scanning it for anything the sheriff had a notion to show him. Everything was kept in pristine order and nothing seemed out of place. He turned to the window, looking out upon the forest from which he felt he had just escaped. The snow was sparse in the field between the house and the forest, but the white took on a cotton like appearance in the still green grass. It reminded him of the cotton fields of California, near where he and Mary had settled down.

Weston turned away from the window and he saw it. It was hard to find in the glaring sunlight, but it was there as he turned his head: three bloody fingerprints. They were faint and it looked like blood may have been dried before the fingers ran down the window. The fingerprints were strange. Though they were obviously dragged across the surface of the glass, the prints didn't seem quite right, like they were longer than normal. And then he knew.

He turned to the sheriff, pointing at the bloody prints on the opposite side of the window. The sheriff nodded. "Yup, but that's not all." He motioned for Weston to come closer. He pointed to the floor where a splash of blood seemed to have fallen just under the bed. As Weston got closer, the sheriff moved the bed with a grunt, and there were more bloody cast-offs there, hidden and out of place.

"Familiar, wouldn't you say?" The sheriff moved the bed back, a grimace of disgust forming under his thick moustache.

"Yeah." Weston felt sick. He killed the Mhuwe, he knew he did. He watched it burn, watched its skin bubble and char, watched its hair turn to ash and horns blacken. He had killed it. *It's no good, Bill, you can't kill evil...* The words of his dead friend swam around in his muddy head.

"Near as we can figure, these are what's left of Susan Breslin. Do you remember her, Mr. Weston?"

Weston nodded. He didn't know the name, but he knew who it must be. Greta's companion, the young woman who aided her elder in taking care of the Darrio girl. The last time he had seen her she was crying outside of the very house he was standing in after finding her mentor butchered and her ward captured and eaten by the Mhuwe.

"Is this the only one?"

"Since you returned, yes. The first since Greta in fact." The sheriff crossed his arms.

"But how?" It was all Weston could say. Everything else was jumbled in his mind.

The sheriff gave him a ponderous look over the bridge of his nose. "Well, son, I was hoping you could help me with that. What did you really find in those woods?"

"I've told you, Sheriff. But if I was wrong, if I didn't kill that thing, then it will be back. It will kill again and again. It won't stop killing, not until every person in this town is dead. Eaten." Weston made to push past the sheriff who grabbed him by the arm, stopping him short.

"Where do you think you're going?"

"I'm getting out of town. If you were smart, you and your people would get out of here too. It's coming, Forester, this is just the beginning." Weston stormed out of the room and made for the door.

The two men guarding it turned when they heard him coming and blocked his way, their faces sour and determined. Weston paid no heed, ignoring their murderous stares. As they grabbed him about the neck and arms, he lashed out at them, trying to clobber them around the face and head. Sheriff Forester ran out of the room and separated them all, cursing down his men and giving Weston a cruel grimace.

"Let him go," Forester panted, smoothing out his jacket and adjusting his hat.

Weston nodded to the sheriff and left the small house. He hoped to never see it again.

V

Weston made his way through the town, barely aware of the strange stares he was receiving from the few people who seemed brave enough to leave their homes. Flurries of snow continued to fall around him, small snowflakes like those he had witnessed just a matter of days ago, upon his first look at the god forsaken town of Barclay. He wasn't sure where he was headed, but he needed to get away from the house and from the sheriff. With any luck, he'd be able to get away from the town before the beast returned.

What a fool he was to believe that he had killed a being such as the Mhuwe, a blood-soaked devil that hungered for pain and torment as much as it did flesh. Then again, perhaps there was no beast. Perhaps he had dreamt the whole thing. If that was the case, he thought, what happened to the others? Did he kill them, and his weary mind supplemented a savage beast so that he wouldn't go insane? Unfortunately, that was not a question he could answer himself, not now at least. But he had a notion of how. He looked around; he was close to the doctor's house, but that wasn't where he wanted to go. He picked up his pace, his legs still aching, and moved towards the sheriff's office.

The office was closed up and locked. The only windows in the building were the iron barred cages that stood at the back and a small glass window at the front. Neither of those would suit his purpose. Once again, he gave his surroundings a once over. The streets this far into the city were still deserted, with even the small porch that stood outside the general store empty of the old gossips who sat there most of the day chatting. He crossed over to the general store now and looked into the window. It didn't show any signs of life inside. The town had taken quite a toll as of late and they were closing in on themselves, trying to keep their families safe from whatever was out in the world trying to kill and maim. Another door locked.

Weston searched the porch where the old men sat; he just needed something with a point, a stabbing tool. He got to his knees and ran a hand under some of the chairs -- nothing. He went around the side of the building, into the alley that separated the store from the jail. At the end of the small space, there were two snow covered barrels. Inside the barrels were a number of loose parts and scraps from the store. A lot of garbage and junk. The Mr. Barclay that ran the store now must have been quite a pack rat. Weston had no doubt that the store had the same feeling inside. He dug around in the barrels for some time, emptying one of them onto the snow-covered ground of the alley. Among the wreckage, he found a six-inch shard of metal; it looked like a straightened fragment from the bilge hoop of another barrel.

He held it up to his eyes. "This should do."

The street was still deserted after his brief stay in the shadows of the alleyway. Weston didn't want to waste any more time and jumped up the steps leading to the door. He adjusted the metal shard in his hand and jabbed it viciously into the keyhole. The shard stuck, and Weston's hand recoiled, the sharp edge of the metal having dug into the palm of his good hand. Still, the shard's job was nearly at an end. He wrapped his hand around the metal one more time and forced it to twist to the right. The door swung open, drops of his blood painting a trail into the office.

Though it was dark, Weston remembered the layout of the office well and found what he was looking for without issue. His guns were laid out on the sheriff's desk, and his bowie knife as well. He unfolded his belt and holsters and strapped them around his waist. Their weight felt good at his hips; he felt whole once more. He strapped the knife around his chest, making sure it was in his usual spot before he checked the guns to see if they were loaded, but there he wasn't so lucky. Did he reload them after his final encounter with the creature? He couldn't remember. He did another quick search of the sheriff's desk, and he found some loose charges that would fit his guns, but there was only seven of them, not enough to load both guns. Weston shook his head as he fully loaded one of his Colts, and then put the final round in the other. It was a pitiful sight, but it couldn't be helped for now.

Weston stole out of the sheriff's office, closing the door behind him. He didn't want to arouse suspicion. Once someone got a closer look at the lock and the bloody metal shard that stood out from it, an alarm would be sent up. Weston aimed to be out of the city before that happened.

There was no one to hinder his path until he came to the town entrance next to Greta's house. There were two men set up on a stagecoach, the same two who had accosted him earlier, laughing and jabbering on about things Weston couldn't quite hear. He approached low to the ground, as quiet as he could, his guns at his side. He didn't want to use them but would if he had to.

"Ike, I'm telling you, brother, this fine little thing rode up to me and started blabbering on about some priest and her dead brother. Or, maybe, it was the priest's dead brother; I don't remember. But, let me tell you sumthin', that lass was stacked from head to toe. I just wanted to eat her up."

Weston skirted the edge of the carriage the two men

were sitting in. They were both facing forward, looking out into the forest. It was a good idea, though it didn't save that young woman, nor would it save anyone else. Weston knocked on the side of the carriage. Their conversation halted; listening.

"What the hell was that?" A whisper from the man who had been speaking was followed by a rough grunt from the other.

He was still leaning into the wagon when the head peered over the side to look down on him. It was a ruddy face, youthful under the sparse beard that covered it. Surprise crossed the man's eyes and his wide mouth dropped open in mid-shout as his arms scrambled for his rifle. Weston grabbed the man by the collar and pulled him over the side. He fell to the ground with a thud, cutting his shout off before it had truly rung out. Weston paid no mind to the fallen man after that, and instead he pulled and focused his revolver on the carriage edge above. Ike soon stuck his bearded face over the side just as his friend had done a moment before. Though the barrel of his shotgun crossed the threshold with his face, it was not pointed at Weston who stuck his revolver in Ike's bearded face. It wasn't long before Ike was on the ground with his unconscious friend, his mouth bound with his own dirty handkerchief, his arms and legs bound with the coats of he and his friend. His eyes delivered a cold hatred upon Weston as he moved away from the carriage and back into the forest.

CHAPTER EIGHTEEN

I

The forest welcomed him back, enveloping him in the growing shadows of dusk. The tree branches reached out for him, hoping to caress him once again in their tangled grip. A slow shiver ran up his spine and prickled the hairs on the back of his neck.

He hurried up the path out of Barclay. It was familiar to him now; the mud ridden road would have had his footprints still imbedded in it if snow hadn't fallen in his absence. He didn't bother to remain quiet, nor did he attempt to pick up any tracks of the beast. If it had somehow lived, it wouldn't have left any.

Weston soon realized that the forest was much more alive than when he had left it before. The flutter and call of birds rose around him, as did the nervous scampering of rabbits and squirrels, and he even thought he caught a glimpse of the yellow eyes of a lone wolf tracking prey. The animals had returned. It cheered Weston. A weight lifted from his chest and he stopped to enjoy the sounds, his eyes cast to the sky, the orange sunset breaking through the tangled branches of the forest's tight canopy.

It wasn't long before he came to the break in the tree line and found the clearing. It was as he had remembered, though snow had hidden the evidence during the previous nights. Cursing, Weston waded into the ankle high snow, hoping that what he sought was still there.

His memory had grown vague of the exact details of how he fought the creature, and he began to scan the ground for anything that seemed out of place. The snow, of course, was a blanket that made this more difficult than it might have been just hours earlier. Weston's fingers grew colder and colder as he dug through the snow, displacing rocks that looked unusual and loose branches or twigs. He focused his search in the center of the field, sensing that was where the creature met its end, but it proved to be little help. He sat there, knees in the snow, and searched his mind. *It had to be here,* he thought. And then a deeper, colder thought: *But what if it isn't; what if it never was?*

"Now that is a good question," Phillips' breathy, smoke filled voice echoed from behind him. Weston turned, not surprised to see four men silhouetted against the risen moon at the entrance to the clearing.

"Certainly is," said the thick, congealed mockery of Dutch's voice. "A question I believe you and I had once posed ourselves." There was a hollow chuckle then that rang through the four dead men.

The four men began to encircle him, but Weston remained where he was, powerless to stop them even if he had the nerve to do so.

"Well, Mr. Weston, don't you make a pitiful figure, sitting there by your lonesome in the snow."

"What are you doing here, Deputy?" Weston turned towards the stout corpse, its stomach a gory mess of blood and intestines.

"Why, I'm one of the men you had killed out here." Baker's face cracked into an oily smile that held no mirth.

"I have no guilt over your death, Baker. You were a fool and a coward, you--"

"I deserved the death I got?" The ghost of the Deputy erupted and flew in his face, large teeth and claw marks appearing on his face, sloughing off flesh and muscle as it did. "I deserved to be eaten alive by a fuckin' chug monster?"

Weston turned from the dead man, eyes looking down upon his open hands.

"Bill, you're in real trouble now, pal. If you can't find something here and now, they'll think you've gone crazy. You'll be in a noose before the end of week." Phillips crouched down next to him, his burnt and charred skin popping as he did.

"I'm sorry, Jim. I'm sorry." Weston stood and walked further into the flatland.

"You can't get away from this, Bill. You're going to pay for it one way or another," Phillips called after him, a cold chuckle on the air.

Weston looked over his shoulder and saw the ghosts were gone, replaced by the slanting rays of moonlight.

"I like this place much more now that the animals have returned," Faraway Sue's deep voice rolled over the wind. He was staring at Weston further into the field, a shadow amongst shadows. "Perhaps your search would be better accomplished over here."

Weston walked towards the shadows, his feet crunching in the snow. He could see Sue motioning to him, telling him to come closer and closer. Weston kept walking, his eyes on the ghost of his former captive, trying to get a good look at the Indian's kind face. He moved closer, his eyes squinting in the dark, the features of the Indian just coming into focus when his foot hit something and he tumbled to the ground.

"Kitanowit provides," Sue said, and his shadow faded from sight as a hearty laugh carried on the wind.

II

Forester pushed into his office, the warmth of the wood stove slapping him in the face. He cast an annoyed glance at the doorknob, a metal shard protruding from it, before he slammed it closed and entered the small building.

He did his best to ignore the two men who sat furtively before his large oak desk. It was a gift from his brother-in-law, the desk, something that was made as a wedding gift. As he sat down, Forester took in the smooth surface and the sheer craftsmanship of his wife's brother. The desk was a thing of beauty, there was no doubt there; immaculate in almost every sense except for the bloody drawer. Forester hated that drawer, and not only because it looked out of place, like it was an afterthought, but also because it stuck. Not that he had much use for a drawer. He used it as little as was possible, but when he did have to use it, when he had to dig around for a pencil or one of his record books, he would have to work on opening the cursed drawer like a drowning man struggling for breath. He would beat upon it and pull on it until it opened. Every time it did open, it made a treacherous screech that caused shivers to go up Forester's spine. It was a black mark on an otherwise magnificent gift, and the sheriff couldn't seem to make himself get past it.

It was Derb who started to talk, as Forester knew he would. He started to blubber something, but Forester cut him off with a look. Derby had seen better days: his face was scratched and bruised, a large bump forming on his forehead where he had landed from his fall. His lips were split, and between breaths he dabbed a dirty blue handkerchief to it with a horribly scraped hand. He also looked to be missing a tooth. If the sheriff wasn't so angry, he might have laughed.

"So, let me get this straight," the sheriff leaned forward, his elbows and hands on the desktop surface. "Bill Weston, a man who only a few days ago was lain up in an extended fit, snuck up on you two, knocked you out," he pointed to Derb, "and then tied you up," he pointed to Ike who was scowling into his beard. "Does that sound about right?"

Before they could answer, the sheriff spoke again, "Do you even understand what it means to guard something?"

Derb butted in, "Well of course, Sheriff, but you told us to guard against someone coming in, not someone going out." Finished, he dabbed his lips with his handkerchief, a look of pride on his face.

"Derby, the less you talk the better. Have you even considered that he might be part of the reason people are dying 'round here, and you just let him go?" The sheriff stood and began to pace around the room. His guests hung their heads, awaiting some more debasing or perhaps even a slap or two. The sheriff looked mad enough.

"Get out," Forester said finally, before opening the door and shooing them into the snow dusted wind.

He returned to his desk and jiggled at the sticking drawer for a moment before tearing it completely off the desk frame, red-faced and cursing. He drew a bottle of whiskey from the now detached drawer and poured himself a tall drink, swallowed it, and poured himself another.

Forester couldn't be sure if it was the drink or just the

days he'd gone without rest, but he fell asleep in his chair with his boots crossed on his desk. He woke with a start, the raging wind blowing hard outside. It was dark in the office, for his lamps had gone out while he slept. He stood and stretched; whether he meant to or not, he needed the sleep and he felt all the better for it.

He lit a match and used the flickering light to guide him through his office. The sheriff didn't need the light of course, he'd spent so much time in this old office he could have walked through it blindfolded. Things being as they were though, he felt better with some light. With the match held between finger and thumb, Forester guided himself around his desk with his other hand, gliding his fingertips over its surface.

He left the desk and had begun to cross to one of his lamps when the match went out. He cursed, stood for a moment deciding whether or not to light another match or wait until he reached the lamp, then reached in his pocket once more. With another lit match in hand, he crossed to the lamp and checked its oil reserve. Still plenty there for tonight, he thought and hoped it wasn't some nonsense with the wick that he'd have to fuck around with.

The lamp lit without issue, and he placed the glass cover over the wick carefully; already he could feel the heat coming from the small flame. The sheriff turned to walk toward his other lamp and Weston was there, a strange package under his arm. Forester jumped with fright and almost collapsed into the wall behind him.

"Jesus Christ!" Forester shouted, dropping his matches and reaching for his chest.

"Howdy, Sheriff," Weston said, tipping his hat. "I brought you something; didn't think you'd mind."

The sheriff had straightened and was tempted to grab

at the gun at his hip, but he refrained, a frown overcoming his face.

"Didn't think I'd ever see your face again," he said, picking up his matches and moving to the other lamp. "Not after that shit you pulled earlier."

"Had to do something, Sheriff, and I needed my guns to do anything. Sorry about the door." Weston stepped further into the office and laid the package on the desk.

"I guess we should feel lucky you didn't kill poor Ike and Derby while you were on your way out of town. You dropped Derb on his head, and that boy wasn't smart enough to begin with." He lit the lamp and took it from its perch on the wall.

"I had the feeling neither of those boys would've let me go on my own peaceful way. No harm meant to them, just the way things panned out." He pulled out a chair and sat down, making sure he was facing the sheriff who could now see a gun in Weston's hand.

"So, what'd you bring me, Mr. Weston?" The sheriff moved towards the desk, each step lighting up Weston and his package more. Weston was covered in sweat and dirt. Tree and branch cast-offs clung to him, and his pants were wet from the knees down.

"I think you best have a look." Weston gestured towards the desk and the package that lay there. The sheriff looked at the thing laid upon his desk, but his eyes couldn't make much sense of it. For a moment he thought it was a simple rack of antlers, a good size notwithstanding, but only antlers. As he moved closer though, he saw that they were still attached to something, but it was far from any elk or deer skull Forester had ever seen. The face was flatter and more human like, though it was larger than he'd have imagined. It was the teeth that threw him off. They were jagged, sharp teeth that looked as though they had been filed that way. One look at those and his eyes and mind were trying to reconcile what exactly he was looking at, and they both came up with nothing.

The sheriff sat down at his desk and laid the lamp next to the skull he now took it to be. There were still pieces of charred flesh stuck to the bone, and it had an overall blackened look as if it had just been dragged from a fire. He took a deep inhale of breath between his clenched teeth.

"Well now this is interesting," he said and bent to study it closer. Weston put away his weapon and smiled.

III

It could be a fake, Forester thought, walking around the desk for the fifth time trying to take in every little detail he could. When he was a boy he had gone to a travelling carnival with his mother and father. The sights and sounds were amazing to behold, but the most amazing by far had been the sideshow attraction of oddities. Forester's mother refused to enter the tent, claiming that the attractions were abhorrent to God and all his works. That didn't stop Forester and his father though. They delved into the tent without hesitation. It was dark, the objects and people were strange, and Forester huddled close to his father who only offered a gentle chuckle in response. The only thing that the young Forester didn't shy away from was the medical oddities. That attraction had strange jars of human and animal foetuses, a two-headed snake that rested behind a glass cage, and pictures of even wilder things. At the centre of it all was the entombed and deformed skull of a man that was claimed to have been possessed by a demon. You could tell, it was pointed out to them, because of the monstrous bumps and growth along one side of the skull, an obvious attempt by the demon to make the man look more demonic. Forester had shuddered then and he did again now, looking at the strange skull that sat in front of him.

Of course, Forester's father, being a very logical man, explained to his upset son that most of those attractions had been faked. He explained that many of the items there had been stitched and sewn and glued together to make two things seem more horrific as one thing. It was a relief for the young man that would become the aging sheriff of Barclay much later in his life.

He hefted the skull, picking it up by the antlers and looking at it from every angle. It was heavier than he'd have thought, and there were no obvious signs of glue or anything that might have been used to set bone together. The flesh that still clung to the skull was real enough, the sheriff wagered, and refused to touch it to make sure. He placed it back in his desk with relief. "And you killed this? By yourself?"

Weston grimaced at the question and shrugged. "Between all of us we had done some damage to it, but I think the fire is what did it in."

The sheriff sat down with a thud and poured up two glasses of whiskey. "Tell me the story again," he said and slid a glass towards Weston.

Weston went through the story once more making sure to leave out the interactions he had with his dead companions. There was a long silence after he had finished, both men staring at the grinning skull that rested on the desk between them. The sheriff sighed and twisted his still full glass in his hands, the amber liquid sloshing close to its edge.

"It's hard to believe," he said at last, eyebrows raising to look at Weston across the desk. "Even with this," pointing one gnarled finger at the skull, "it's hard to believe."

Weston nodded, playing with his own empty glass.

"What can I do with all of this, Bill?" the sheriff said, his eyes pleading. "How does this help anything; how does it stop the killing?" The sheriff's voice was strained and tired, his face drawn and grey.

"I'm not sure it means much of anything, but whatever killed that young girl last night wasn't this." Weston nodded toward the skull.

"Something new then?"

"Maybe, or a new version of the same."

"So, how do we kill it?"

Weston shrugged. "Fire seems to do the trick where bullets only seem to piss it off. Though getting close enough to light it ablaze will be a bitch, trust me on that. But that's not the hardest part. Finding it, now that's going to be a challenge. If it's anything like this one, it will only come out to hunt and feed."

"And we know what it eats."

Silence overtook the room again, the oil lamp casting shadows over each man's drained face as they pondered the problem at hand. During the war, Weston and his company of fellow soldiers had faced some tough situations. Often, when in the field, they were undermanned or under-armed for the battles they were supposed to wage. It took a lot of strategy on his commanding officer's part to stage the battle so that they came out victors. One of those victories came to his mind now.

"I think I know what we can do, Sheriff." Weston laid his glass to the side and stood before the desk.

The sheriff drained his glass. "Let me hear it, boy."

IV

It wasn't a plan they expected to work, but it was the only one they had. As Weston had explained to Forester, during the war they often found themselves outnumbered. To even things up, Weston's commander would order them to take position in a secluded area surrounded by forest and leave a skeleton crew to hold the position. While they did that, the remainder of the soldiers would hide in the forest waiting. If the enemy had scouts, they'd only see the small contingent of men, and it'd give them a sense of superiority. They'd march in confident in taking the smaller group and have an easy victory, but when they walked in, secured their positions, and dropped their guard, the rest of Weston's men would pounce. "Surprise and positioning," Weston's commander had said. "Baiting the trap," Weston had replied. For this creature, the only bait it wanted was flesh and blood. Weston took that honour.

"You've been through a lot, boy, you don't need to do this," the sheriff had said, his voice gentle enough, but his eyes told Weston another tale. The sheriff wanted to keep his people safe, and he wasn't about to sacrifice them for a harebrained scheme like Weston had devised, no matter what his words said. Weston couldn't blame him of course; too many people had died already.

"I got this, Sheriff." And both men nodded as they made their separate preparations.

The night had almost come to an end by the time they had finished planning and Weston hoped to get some sleep. He didn't think the creature would be back again so soon after feeding; it was ravenous, but a whole body was a lot to get through.

He walked into his room at the hotel, the first time he'd set foot in it since his first days in Barclay. Weston, Dutch, and Phillips didn't carry much with them on the road, but whatever they had was in here. It was a singular room, not overly large but somehow accommodating three beds in a manner that still left some room for moving to and fro. It was an end room and took up a corner of the hotel. Two windows cast a pale light onto the floor, illuminating little. Weston fell into one of the beds in the room, its springs groaning under his weight. The sheets and pillow smelled fresh enough, and that put him at ease. He didn't have the courage to look through his dead companion's bags and instead left them where he found them -- by the other beds they had claimed as their own.

Rest didn't come for Bill Weston in spite of his hopes, and as the light of the new day cracked through the windows of his room, he was sitting on the edge of his bed cleaning and reloading his wheel guns. It was an old habit he had, something that helped him think, though what he had to think about wasn't very appealing. He'd be out there alone, drawing the creature to him. He had gotten lucky once, he wasn't so sure his luck would keep a second time.

His guns back in their holsters, Weston studied his wounded legs, rubbing around the particularly sore knots and bruises. The stitches in the gash on his left leg had held up to the stress of the day before and it didn't look infected; he'd have to thank the Doc Burrows when it all was said and done. And what would the good doctor be doing tonight, he wondered. Would he be in retreat with the majority of the townsfolk, or would he be amongst the sheriff's volunteers? Weston didn't think there'd be many in the latter group, but it was all they could do now.

Once the sun broke the horizon, Weston ventured downstairs and ordered a hot breakfast of coffee and oatmeal. The old woman that served him offered him some eggs and bacon.

"No thanks, darling, I'm not much of a morning eater," Weston said with half a smile.

The old woman shrugged and went into the kitchen to make his order. She was a short and stout woman, who may have been handsome in her youth and still had a sly twinkle in her faded blue eyes. She returned a moment later with his coffee and then left him to finish his breakfast.

Breakfast wasn't something Weston had ever gotten used to; he was more accustomed to the sparse breakfast he had on the trail than a home cooked endeavour most folks preferred. The coffee and jerky diet provided by Dutch suited him fine. Mary wouldn't have that, of course. No sir, she'd cook him a large meal for breakfast, lunch, and supper. She used to say it wasn't healthy for a man to eat scraps like a hungry coyote, that she wanted her man strong and thick, not starved and sickly. Truth be told, Weston often got sick from too much breakfast, and it usually delayed his tasks by a half hour or so while he dealt with stomach cramps. He'd never tell her that of course. He always obliged Mary.

The oatmeal was fair enough. A little too hot for Weston's liking, but he gobbled it down as quick as he could all the same. Between mouthfuls, he wondered when it was he had last had solid food. Sometime on the trail, he supposed. Dutch and Phillips liked to have a good cook up every now and again, after a successful job or a particularly long trek. It cheered them some. Weston supposed it made them feel a bit more normal.

He left the hotel after a second cup of coffee. The street was deserted once again, but Weston was unsure if that was from the killings, the early hour, or the sheriff's doing. Snow gusted on the wind, and he drew his coat about him. It was going to be a long day.

V

The night came on quick, and Weston walked the streets of Barclay alone. He had spent the rest of the day going over the details of the plan with Forester and his volunteers. About ten or so arrived to help out to Weston's surprise, and even more of a surprise was that number included the two men Weston had accosted in the carriage the day before. Even the good doctor Barrows had come out. He recognized a few more men from about town, mostly burly lumberjacks armed with axes or old muskets. It would do. It was Weston's hope that none would need to take part in any fighting but were to be prepared just in case it came down to that.

Weston and the sheriff organized them into pairs and gave them positions around the town. The sheriff had arranged for Evans, the man Weston had beaten the night Phillips was clawed, to lead a group of townsfolk to the hotel and keep it guarded for the night. Some refused to leave their homes and boarded themselves in before the night fell. The sheriff made sure those people had enough supplies to get them through the night, weapons and bullets included.

It all ran smoother than Weston could have hoped for; it ran smooth for a plan Weston was having more and more doubts about as it got closer. As it turned out, it was becoming a solid plan, with every person attached to it doing their part. That didn't mean it was going to work,

Weston reminded himself when he allowed himself a moment to think amongst the activity of the day.

By supper, everything was sorted and Weston found himself eating alone in his hotel room. He'd opted for a light meal again, some chicken and buttered bread. It was good, but he didn't eat much. Instead, he sat on the edge of his bed and stared at his hands.

It was dark outside and lamps were being lit. It would soon be time for him to take his position and hope the plan would work. Trepidation dragged on him though, sought to keep him sitting on his bed and have him wait until the night was over; to break out at first light no matter what the consequences. He sighed.

"That's the Billy I know," Phillips' corroded voice crackled in his ear, and he felt the bed shift with the weight of someone new sitting at the end of the mattress. "Ready to run out on the people who really depend on him. It's good to know some things never change."

Weston turned to look at his dead friend. All that remained of Phillips' face was blackened skin that was flaking and peeling. His blue eyes were too big, the flesh around them having fallen away some, and he looked more like a skull than man. "I didn't run out on you," Weston said, returning his gaze to his clenched fists.

"That's a matter of opinion, friend." Dutch's large foot sunk into the bed on the other side of Weston as he leaned on his knee and looked down upon him. Dutch remained the same, a stream of blood gushing down his chest from his neck with his face sallow and eyes sunken, but otherwise he was the same old Dutch.

"I fought for you, Dutch," Weston said without looking at the apparition. "I was going to bring your body back to bury."

"But you didn't," Dutch hissed through clenched teeth. "There wasn't enough left of me to bury."

"Same ole Weston, all high and mighty. Get off your pedestal and take a look at the little people in your life." Baker stepped in front of him, blocking the light slanting in from the windows.

"I don't care to talk to you, Baker. You're not my problem."

"That's not quite true, is it, Bill?" Phillips was in his ear again, and harsh smell of smoke and burning hair assailed his senses. "You were our leader. You always led us into the fray. We're lucky we survived as long as we did."

Weston supposed it was true enough that he became an unwilling leader of the three men. After all, it was he who brought them all together. It was Weston who brought them their first bounty. It was Weston who led them out of the East and into the West.

"That's right, Bill. You did get this small little gang together. You brought us here. You led us into the forest. You got us killed." Dutch gargled when he spoke, and he pressed one massive hand to the side of his neck.

"No..."

"Yes, Weston, you piece of shit. You killed us."

Weston felt a thump in his back, the thud of a boot into his ribs, another thump and thud, and he covered himself up; took the beating.

The knocking on his door got louder and he sprang up in bed. He was alone again, the stench of old blood and burning hair still carried in the air.

"Mr. Weston, you ready?"

Forester, just in time. Weston stood, his body aching all over; he could feel welts rise in his skin. He shook it off, rubbing at his legs once more.

"I'm ready," he said, opening the door and walking out. The sheriff didn't look like he'd gotten much rest either, and the day of preparations did little to help. He leaned on the door frame of Weston's room, his face lined with concern.

"What were you doing in there, Weston, saying your prayers?"

"Forget it, let's get moving." Weston stormed down the hall and into the night.

VI

Weston stalked the empty streets of Barclay, an open torch in one hand, a revolver in the other. He'd been in the open for nearly an hour without a sound. Forester was holed up with Evans in the hotel protecting the town, but he couldn't quite be sure where the others were. He only hoped they were where he needed them to be when the time came.

The flame whooshed past the empty alleyway as he drove it in to catch a glimpse of anything, but he was greeted with nothing. He could feel anxiety and impatience well up in him in equal measure, and an angry sense of disappointment. The plan and all their preparations, it seemed, were for not. He let the hammer down easy on his Colt and holstered it, listening to the creak of the worn leather as it welcomed the cold piece of iron.

Only once did he see movement, near the church where Phillips had been attacked. It was close to one of the boarded-up houses, a flash of colour in the dark of the night. Weston pursued it down the alley, his gun at the ready. He saw a shadow turn a corner and he jumped to confront it, torch and gun in front of him. He frightened one of Forester's volunteers, a stocky young man he recognized from the town. He was one of the many lumberjacks of the town; he thought his name was Butch. Weston almost had his head split with an axe for his trouble.

Aside from young Butch, he had seen nothing. No movement, no sound, not even a breath of wind. The creature he had faced in the wood and walked away from had been swift and quiet. It left no tracks unless it wanted to and could imitate anything or anyone in order to get what it wanted – food, sustenance. It had wanted to eat human flesh, and this new beast would need to as well. Weston knew all that, but he still felt he missed something. He felt that what they were doing just wasn't enough.

VII

Weston found himself walking past Greta's house once again, taking time to study its open door and shattered windows, hoping that the creature may return there yet again. Again, he was met with nothing. He stared down the main road that crossed in front of Greta's house, looking into the darkness beyond the torch's reach, the outline of trees swaying in the moonlight. He squinted his eyes, not seeing anything in those shadows, but feeling a need to move closer, to check the shadows out.

He took out his gun again, making a whisper on the old leather, and moved the torch ahead of him. There was something in the shadows, a solid blackness that didn't retreat from the torchlight. He saw the flash of a pale limb in a shimmer of quick movement, and he raised his gun firing once into the air. The movement held still for a moment and Weston could hear the scurrying and shuffling of boots around him, a glugging sound, and then a short whistle.

"Got'cha," Weston said, and tossed the torch towards

the whistle. In a blast of air and a whoosh of pressure, a ring of flame appeared around Weston and his adversary. A wave of heat assaulted his chilled bones, and his eyes began to water. He wiped at them with his free hand and heard the volunteers around him exhale in a combined sigh. Clearing his eyes, Weston moved forward with his gun at the ready. The plan was in motion and now all he had to do was finish it.

Eyes cleared of tears, he stared forward at the creature, his jaw dropping along with his gun. The plan had fallen to pieces.

CHAPTER NINETEEN

I

A high-pitched tittering pierced the thick air, drawing Weston's eyes to the creature that stood before him, despite the effort he asserted to look away.

The girl wore nothing but a slip of a dress that may have been white at one point, but now was stained with dirt and blood. Her thin legs and bony knees were exposed underneath the slip and were dirty and scratched; her feet were bare. Bethany's golden hair was a mess of tangles, congealed together with mud, tree sap, and more blood. Her hair fell around her oval face, her bright red lips stretched into a horrible smile revealing a mouth full of fangs under her dark, sunken eyes. Sprouting from her forehead, piercing through rings golden hair, were fawn-like horns.

Weston levelled his revolver at the girl that stood before him, his hand weak and slow to cooperate. She continued to smile and titter, blood-stained saliva dripping from her mouth. He cocked the hammer.

The apprehension outweighed the heavy and hot air, nervous coughs broke forth from the growing number of men that had run when they heard the signal gunshot. Weston's gun was heavy in his weak hand, but he fought to keep it upright, not sure what the girl was capable of.

"Beth, darling, are you okay?" Weston said at last. The girl was still staring at him with her black eyes, swaying back and forth. "What has it done to you, girl?"

The girl tittered some more, and Weston began to wonder if she could talk at all anymore or if the creature had stolen that from her. She uncrossed her hands from behind her back and extended one deformed and elongated finger, a sharp brown talon replacing its fingernail, and brought it to her lips. "Shh."

With clawed hands outstretched and her jagged smile still pasted on her face, the creature that was Bethany began to move toward Weston, its tittering going faster and faster. Shouts from the men outside the firewall turned to instructions: "shoot the beast," and "kill her" chief among them.

Weston took aim with his revolver and fired twice, but he was so lethargic that he didn't think the weapon would hit its mark. A roar went up from the crowd as one of his shots found a home and spun the girl in place, sending her to the ground. A screech of pain echoed from her bony chest. Weston turned on the crowd to see those who cheered so loudly at the dispatch of a child, but the haze of the fire concealed them. Still, anger rose in his guts, and he let forth a frustrated scream, his boots digging into the ground under him. *What have I done,* he thought against reason, and holstered his gun again.

The small form cringed on the ground, and it made small cooing noises, like an animal in pain. It sniffled as it quivered on the cold ground. One long fingered hand scratched at the dirt underneath it as if trying to distract itself from pain.

Weston moved closer, hands empty and extended ahead of him. "Bethany, child, please. You'll be fine. We'll help you, just stop fighting me." Weston knew his words were hollow. The only man he knew that had any knowledge of the blasted creature and its condition was Faraway Sue and he lay dead in the very same field where he had vanquished the first beast.

The cooing noises continued, and Weston thought he heard within them the sound of an upset and sad young child. A baby looking for its mother. He kneeled next to the form of Bethany, meaning to pick her up and cradle her in his arms, much like Greta had been doing the night he visited them with Phillips and Dutch. He stretched one long arm over her back and made to use his other arm at her knees to turn her and cuddle her into his chest.

She attacked.

She twisted like a snake in his grip and slashed at his face and eyes. He dropped her and pushed her away from him, avoiding harm by a hair's width. Bethany was up on her feet in an instant and began slashing and biting as she charged toward him. Weston backtracked as best he could from his knees, but it wasn't fast enough, and she caught his chest with her razor-sharp claws. He fell backwards to the ground, his hands jumping to his chest to protect the wound and kicking both legs out to push her back once more. His boots impacted squarely on her chest and sent her reeling. He struggled to his feet, one hand still locked on his wounded chest. The wound felt cold; a coldness that seemed to spread like gripping tentacles across his chest and neck. He gritted his teeth against the pain and saw that the girl had gotten to her feet yet again. An icy smile cracking her small, round face, she began to move towards him with her claws flashing in the harsh orange light of the fire that surrounded them.

It was then that Weston heard the gunshots. It started

with a solitary shot from those surrounding the fire that struck the ground between Weston and the girl, dirt and grass spitting up from the impact. That gunshot, however, was followed by several more shots and those were accompanied by hoots and hollers from the gathered volunteers. Weston managed to gain his feet at last as the girl became distracted by the gunfire all around her. She lashed out at the bullets as if she was unaware what was happening to her, like a wild animal assailed by mosquitoes. Most shots missed their mark and sent skittering pieces of ground into the air, but one or two were fair and landed on the transformed girl. Her reaction had greatly changed from his initial shot, and she seemed to not feel the bite of the bullets in her skin (though dots of black blood rose where she'd been hit) nor the impact of it.

"Bethany…" Weston said, moving towards the girl. She roared, a roar like that of her mother the Mhuwe, and danced away from him. When she jumped over the waning fire, it was like nothing he had seen before. She launched herself into the air and completely cleared the high flames that Weston had hoped would contain such a beast. Bethany quickly disappeared into the shadows of the forest, her tittering carrying on the frosty wind.

II

Weston fell to the ground and let the volunteers work at putting out the surrounding fire. He heard their guns firing a few more shots as Bethany ran into the forest, but he had no worries that the bullets would affect her more than they had. He stared into the star polluted skies clutching his chest, feeling the trickle of fresh blood through his fingers. It was the girl.

The fire was out, and Weston had managed to sit himself down on the small patio of Greta's house when Forester arrived. Weston had sent for him when the fire was well within the control of those gathered. Forester rode up on his big grey horse, his face riddled with concern. "I heard ye were wounded. How are you, boy, still alive?" His booming voice echoed as he dismounted and made his way to Weston.

"Just a nasty scratch." Weston moved his hand from his shredded shirt to reveal the four jagged lines that stretched along his chest in a diagonal, a slow leaking of blood running down to his stomach. The icy feeling had returned, and he shivered when he removed his hand from his chest.

"Jesus Christ," the sheriff said in a low cadence mostly to himself. "Here, Charlie," he called to one of the men still beating down the remnants of the fire with a heavy old blanket. "Go fetch the Doctor. I think he might be around the church." Charlie ran off with a nod.

The sheriff took a seat next to Weston, removing his hat as he did and running one big hand through his grey hair. "I heard tell that it wasn't what we were expecting?" he said, looking on as the final flames were being doused.

"It was Bethany." Weston returned his hand to his chest and pressed there. It felt better when he did that; the pressure seemed to bring some heat back to it and he felt a desperate need to keep himself warm.

"Bethany Darrio?" The sheriff turned fully to face him now, his eyes wide and mouth agape. Weston just nodded and bowed his head, taking in the lines on the palm of his free hand. "Shit," the sheriff said, dropping his face into his hands and caressing his temples with his fingers. Weston felt the very same.

They sat that way for some time, a tepid silence crawling over them as they watched the remaining men gather belongings and return to their posts. None came to bother them though, none came to ask if the plan was done, or what they should do now. They just went back to their posts to wait. Weston wanted to tell them it was over, to gather their things and their families and leave the accursed place, to put Barclay in their dust and make out for another town, another state, another country if they could manage it. He wanted to say that, but he just sat there, hand over his chest, trying to ignore the cold feeling that now spread to his extremities.

"So, how are we going to approach this?" Forester said after some time. He'd raised his head from his hands and was staring at Weston, his lips pursed under his bushy moustache.

"I can only think of two options, Sheriff, and I don't like either." Weston rubbed his engaged arm with his free hand absently. "First, we can leave it all: abandon the town and everything in it. Everybody leaves, tonight. No waiting." He paused and locked eyes with Forester. "The second option, we hunt it down and kill it," Weston said it like he was spitting bile; he could feel the distaste grow across his features.

"Fuck," said the sheriff as he stood up to pace along Greta's patio, his boot heels clicking on the wooden boards. Weston agreed with him and resigned himself to studying the palm of his hand once more.

"How did this happen?" the sheriff said, slamming his hand into the outer wall of the house. "How did that thing manage to change that little girl anyway?"

"Near the end, Jimmy said he was turning into a creature too. He said he could feel it in his bones, could feel the hunger come over him. Maybe it was passed on through the damage." Weston paused as he noticed the sheriff scanning his wounded chest. "Or maybe it was through a bite. Hell, Sue even said that this creature, the Mhuwe, only existed because it gave in to temptation and ate human flesh. I didn't know much about Jim before we met, we didn't speak about it, so who knows what he had to go through, what he had to survive up 'til then. As for the girl, maybe she was left up in the little house with her dead parents for too long. Maybe she got a little hungry and..."

"Shut it," the sheriff said tersely and turned away from him. "I get the idea. We don't know how it was passed on, but it was. Fine, but I'm still having the doctor look at you if he ever gets here." He walked over to Weston and looked down on him. "Any idea where we might find the creature?"

"I just might. Are you sure you want to go down that route, Sheriff; I don't have a great feeling about all this." Weston rubbed his chest harder; he could feel the pain sting his skin.

Sheriff Forester nodded his head, but his eyes could not meet Weston's. Neither man spoke of it after and any more conversation about it was left there in the cold alongside with the dead bodies the creature had claimed since it laid siege to the small town.

III

It wasn't long before Dr. Barrows showed up huffing and puffing behind the younger Charlie. He had a slick coating of sweat on his brow and panted heavily while muttering something about not being as young as he used to be.

He checked Weston over, and bandaged up his

wounded chest as best he could. He was very apologetic about having to use strips of old cloth and bedding to wrap Weston up, but he'd forgotten his supplies with his bag back at the church.

Patched up, Weston thanked the doctor, shook his hand and hopped on a horse the sheriff had wrangled for him. It was a brown Quarter Horse colt, strong and compact and made to ride. Weston instantly fell in love with it. The sheriff chuckled to himself as Weston swung into the saddle and allowed himself a smile as he patted down the great animal.

"He's a beaut," said the sheriff, clucking his tongue and guiding his horse toward his office. Weston followed suit. The horse rode well, and it helped to distract him from his need to place his hand at his chest, but it only took a few moments to make it to the sheriff's office.

Once there, the sheriff turned to him. "I think I have everything we'll need in here. Are you sure this is the way we'll find her?"

"I can't be completely sure, Sheriff, but the first place she attacked in town was ole Greta's place. Leads me to believe she is a bit of a sentimentalist," Weston said with a shrug and motioned for the sheriff to lead on.

They followed the same path Dutch had sussed out for them just days before. More snow had fallen and what little tracks were there were long gone with the weather. The sheriff led them on at a slow pace, more out of necessity than comfort. The snow made the trail slick at best and they were not traversing a flat path as some were wont to be. It was a craggy hillside they crawled up, making their way to the small farmhouse with two dead inside and one alive.

It was a dark path, the stars and moon covered by the

growing tree canopy, but the sheriff had his lantern at the ready and it helped them see well enough in its hazy orange light. Weston still felt some familiarity with the path and began to pick out some of the landmarks as they passed them, and in some cases didn't need Forester to point out exposed tree roots or low hanging branches, he just knew.

The ride was quicker than he expected, but Weston supposed his long trek deeper in the wood would be a terrible comparison to any trip in the future. They dismounted just as they did when they first found the house, which still lay dark and quiet, the door hanging ajar just as Greta's was. They moved silently without the horses and made their way to the front of the house without much sound, though Weston had no doubt that any sound they made Bethany would have heard. Weston had elected to take the bag of supplies that the sheriff had put together before they left, while the good doctor was still bandaging Weston's chest.

They stopped at a gate made from sticks and bark, and Weston handed the bag over to Forester, his hand rubbing his chest. "Check around the house but keep your distance. If it's in there, it will probably know by now. Stick to the plan, but if there's trouble on my end, you're better off heading back to town and getting as many people as you can out of there."

"I'll stick around as long as I can," the sheriff whispered, one wide hand gripping Weston's should before he made for the far side of the house. Weston waited for him to get out of sight and then pulled his guns. He stood tall and walked toward the small farmhouse, its darkened windows like black eyes, dark and lidless and void of emotion as it watched him saunter towards the door. *This was the end,* he thought; one way or the other, this is the end.

Weston took a deep breath and threw himself into the house.

IV

Weston swung Mary around their small dining area, dancing with her like a fool, laughing and stomping. Mary wailed with her own laughter and she hit him playfully about the chest which felt oddly cold.

"You foolish man," she exclaimed. "Let me be," and with another smack, "let me be." A wry smile grew across her full pink lips and he grabbed her again swinging her around the room.

"Are you sure?" he said between laughs, but she would only laugh and call him a silly man or some such thing. Finally, both of them out of breath and sitting cuddled together at the dining room table, he took her small, pointed chin in his big hand and drew her eyes to his own.

"Please tell me you are sure, Mary, I don't think I could bear it any longer."

Mary sat up straight at this, hands pressed into his thighs to brace herself, and stared him directly in the eyes. Weston could not believe the beauty in that pale blue color that shimmered at him every time they were close. Mary stared him right in the eye and said, "We're going to have a baby, William." Her cheeks were red and flushed, her hair a tousled and a mess, and her smile intoxicating.

Weston grabbed her about the waist and pulled her to his lap, a giggle rising up from her supple breast. "I love you, Mary Sinclair," and he kissed her soft, pale lips. It was everything he remembered, everything he had dreamed, and he didn't want to stop kissing her. Not ever.

"But you had to didn't you, William?" The smoky voice of Phillips grated in his head, and Mary was gone, his arms empty and his vision filled with the charred and melted features of his dead companion.

"Did I interrupt you, Bill?" Phillips said, taking a seat opposite Weston at his old kitchen table, in his old house that he shared with Mary. "Why, I'm sorry about that, but there is much to do. So much to do." Phillips tapped his fingers on the table top, a rhythmic thumping over the table.

"Leave me alone, Jim, please." Weston's face drew into a scowl. Phillips had never been to this house, not his real house, and seeing his charred and undead visage taking up space at his dining room table soured his memory of it somehow. He rubbed at his chest.

"Well, Bill, I'm not sure about the other fellas, but I have some doubts on that matter. On the one hand, the little mite is pretty resourceful and powerful. She almost had you there, didn't she," Phillips said, pointing to the place on Weston's chest where his hand was now gently rubbing. "On the other hand, you don't want to kill the girl. She's only a little girl after all. A little angel brought down from heaven, with horns popping out of her head and a hell of a taste for people." Phillips laugh was coarse and dusty.

"I'll get the job done," said Weston, trying not to stare at Phillips. It began playing on his mind though. Would he be able to go through with killing the poor girl? It wasn't her fault she became such a thing, it wasn't her doing. Shouldn't she have a say?

"Better be careful there, Billy, you might pop a stitch." Weston started to ask Phillips what the hell he was talking about but looked down to see his hand furiously scratching at his chest, spots of blood growing across the make-shift bandages applied by Dr. Bowers.

"Oh, and that's another thing. She scratched ya', Bill. What will become of you after all this avenging, eh?" Phil-lips ruined face offered a lopsided smile. "You're going to turn into monster, Bill, if you don't stop this. Believe me, it takes one to know one." With this he moved his jacket and shirt to reveal to wide gaps in his shoulder where flesh and bone used to be carefully preserved even under his horribly charred skin. His laughing started again, louder and longer.

"I'll stop it, Jim. I'll stop it." Weston looked down at his chest, both of his hands were now tearing at his bandages; not finding them there, they began to tear at his wounds, his skin, his bones. He wanted to scream in pain, in anger, but whenever he tried it was drowned out by the hideous laughing of Jim Phillips.

Weston jumped up from the table and ran to his door, hands searching inside of him now, his teeth aching to be-gin to chew on something, his stomach growling, a hun-ger was growing inside him. He ran to his door and burst through it feeling the warmth of the sun as he fell.

V

Weston fell into the farmhouse. Dizzy and confused, he leaned into the wall next to the door to get his bear-ings. He consciously avoided touching his chest, though the fierce cold had returned.

The entryway was empty aside from the toppled fur-niture, but there was no evidence that anything had been disturbed since he had last entered the house. Still, Weston readied his guns and crouched low, keeping watch for any movement in the darkness of the farmhouse. Everything was still and quiet save for the creaking of the house with the wind.

Perhaps she didn't come here, Weston's mind ventured, but Weston didn't truly believe that. The creature had changed her, but she was still a child, a child that sought security and safety when afraid, or under attack, or hurt. Weston didn't have to push himself too far to believe that was the reason Bethany had stalked Greta's old house for her first meal. She had been comforted there, kept warm and safe, and well fed. Weston pushed forward into the small house, keeping as quiet as he could.

Besides, it wasn't her whereabouts that worried him so, but the beast's reason for creating her in its image. It had already marked Phillips with its bloody curse, why mark a small child as well?

The kitchen was empty and hadn't seen activity since the sheriff stood guard days before. There were still chairs toppled next to the tiny table, which Weston stepped over carefully while watching the entrance to the small hallway and the bedrooms.

Perhaps it didn't know it had infected Phillips, or maybe it wanted a younger plaything. Weston didn't want to presume to know the thoughts that flashed through the creature's mind, if it had thoughts at all as opposed to a sinister need; instincts driven by an urge to spread its horrible disease.

Weston remembered the thumping he heard the last time he traversed the small hallway, the girl banging her head against the wall in the farthest room, distraught and shocked out of her wits. There was no sound now aside from the soft scuffing of his feet travelling over the plain old boards of the homestead. Every so often a board would squeak under his feet, and he would hope the girl could not hear him.

It was a short walk to the girl's bedroom at the end of the hall. The door was ajar, but Weston couldn't remember if they had left it that way when they left or not. He pushed the door open with one of his guns but was met with more blackness. His eyes had adjusted to the darkness already, yet they strained as he tried to see into the room. He could make out the shapes of the furniture in the girl's room, could make out some toys from the little light that spilled into the hallway. Nothing moved. He stepped further inside, trying again to see everything inside, but there was nothing out of the ordinary. Weston moved back to the hall.

He stared at the creeping stain of blood that spread across the floor from the door of the last room in the small house. Weston moved towards it, slowing his steps and trying not to pay attention to the cold feeling crossing his chest. He holstered one of his guns and opened the door a crack trying to ascertain what awaited him.

The girl was there, standing sidelong to Weston before the open window. Moonlight spilled into the room, exposing the wounds and sores, scratches and blood that covered her. Yet, her face was serene, her big eyes staring fixedly at the wall before her. Weston couldn't be sure, but she looked as though she had grown since he saw her just hours before: her legs looked longer and skinnier, as did her arms. Her once round face now long and drawn, her cheeks sunken. Weston entered the room and drew his weapon once again, his two guns facing the girl.

"Bethany," he said in a hoarse whisper, wondering what was left of the child that had lived in this home with her parents.

She didn't turn to him, but her eyes flickered his way;

watching him. They were black eyes, devoid of expression. They stood out all the more because of her lucid, pale skin that seemed to glow with the moonlight that caressed it. She tapped her clawed fingers on her legs as she watched him.

"Bethany, sweetie, do you remember me?" Weston moved a step closer, watching the girl for any movements. It occurred to him then that if the girl had wanted, he would be in a world of pain at this moment, that his bullets would work just as well as his words were now.

"Bethany, girl, do you know where you are?"

She turned and stared at him then, and he could see all the changes that had overcome her. Her shoulders were broader, but thin and brittle looking as they seemed to shrug into her chest. Her torso had gotten longer as well, and the dirty white slip she had been wearing was little more than a small shirt to her now. She tipped her head to one side, large black eyes still focused on him, and he saw her antlers now on full display. They had changed the most of anything, had grown and bloomed and spread thick fingers of bone in sharp angles from her forehead. The girl's mouth, pink and sore looking, split open and a blackened tongue lolled forth.

Weston turned his eyes from the creature that had been Bethany, the girl. She was gone. Her mind completely taken over by whatever curse or disease the Mhuwe had passed to her. She didn't even look to be human, nor did she act it.

"I'm sorry," he said at last, arming his revolvers and levelling them at the creature before them.

He had expected quickness, but the blur of motion that he barely saw when he fired his revolvers was speed that he had never counted on. The creature was on him in a moment, her long gangly arms extended before her to push him through the air. Weston crashed through the door of the room and into the wall on the opposite side of the hallway. Pain flooded his back and chest, and he gasped for breath. He tried to curl his legs underneath him, but his body could only focus on breathing and refused to follow any commands until at least that function was in use once again. Eyes watering, he took a quick peek around him. His guns were on the floor nearby, but he couldn't reach them, not yet. He tried to crawl forward, clawing the floors with his hands, but it was slow work and the beast was emerging from the room, head now tipped to the other side, a sharp-toothed grin gracing its face.

There was no question that he was no physical match for the creature, not with speed and endurance levelled against him, but he just needed to take up some time; it couldn't be long now.

The thing that had been Bethany stepped out of the room. Before her she saw one of his guns and kicked it to the side, distaste or disgust crossing her strange facial features. Weston was on his knees and reached to brace himself against the wall as he stood. The creature watched him for a moment and stepped forward in a slow manner that had mocked his own. When he was on his feet, still using the wall for support, she moved closer still, her black eyes wide and watchful. Weston could see his other gun out of the corner of his eye; it had slid out of the hallway and was nearly in the kitchen. He'd need to make it there -- he needed his gun.

He gathered his strength and ran out of the hallway, bending to grab his gun as he moved. A tremendous scream rang out around him, amplified by the close quarters of the small hallway. Weston believed that at any moment he would feel the girl's sharp claws stab into his back or the jagged bite of her teeth as they entered his neck, but it didn't come. He slid across the floor of the kitchen and, grabbing up his gun, turned to face the creature now on one knee and braced to shoot. The creature's face was anguish and pain, her long fingers wrapped around one of her thin legs which seemed to have broken of its own accord. The knee of the creature now appeared to be bent backwards, her bare foot stretching out and cracking as well. A thunderous snap echoed in the house and another howl rang out, hurting Weston's ears. The creature's second leg had begun to follow the example of the first.

The girl seemed to be in complete agony: she was unable to move, and, for but a moment, Weston thought that she had stopped breathing because the pain was so deep. Weston knew she would recover, and so he took advantage of the situation and emptied his Colt revolver into the struggling creature. Six small holes seemed to emerge on the creature's chest and head; the bullets not able to pierce her skin fell heavily to the floor and more black blood oozed from the fresh wounds. The beast cringed at the shots but was still more preoccupied with the pain in her transforming legs.

"It's time, Forester, god damn it," Weston said as he struggled to load his weapon again. The creature was panting in harsh, wet breaths that made gurgling sounds in her throat; the pain was subsiding. He finished loading his gun and fired six more rounds into the creature as it lay there recovering from the sudden changes in its body and the pain that came with it. The creature moaned, but the bullets had the same effect as those he had fired just a few minutes before: more black wounds and a slow, oozing black blood.

Weston reloaded again, fumbling with bullets from his belt, and wishing he had brought a rifle or a shotgun. He slammed the gun's chamber shut and took aim, but the creature was gone. Weston cursed out loud and swept the farmhouse with his eyes but found nothing but shadows.

The acrid smell of smoke wafted into the farmhouse as he moved through it one more time. Finally, he thought, allowing himself a moment to smile; it was almost over. Weston moved back into the hall and towards his lost Colt. He was midway down the hallway, his gun in full sight next to the far wall, some light spilling in from the window above it, when the attack resumed.

He was slammed from behind, the creature's shoulders and arms flailing as they plowed into the back of his legs and knees, once more sending him sprawling. Weston held firm to his gun this time and was able to recover in time to fire a round into the creature that was dashing towards him. His aim was true, and the bullet hit the beast in the shoulder, causing it to rear up and pause its momentum. In the back of his mind, Weston realized that the creature was now running on all fours, its strangely transformed backward legs aiding it like an animal's legs would by pushing it forward. These new legs increased the creature's speed instead of hindering it.

Weston scrambled forward to reach his fallen revolver, the smell of smoke stronger now as its wispy tendrils began to leak in around the open seams of the house. The creature roared behind him, so much like its mother, and he felt its full weight land upon his back. Claws pierced his jacket and dug into his flesh followed by a rush of warmth that gurgled onto his skin. Then all he felt was cold. The creature's weight hadn't changed much from when it was a mere child despite the unchecked growth that was evident in its gangly frame. Weston had no trouble moving forward with the creature on his back, though the claws that it continued to push into the flesh and muscle of his back gave him pause coloured by fresh screams as he did continue on.

Without looking, he stuck his gun behind his head and fired the remaining bullets at the monster that clung to him. The sound of impact on the walls and ceiling let him know that his aim was far from true, thought the creature had stopped pushing forward with her claws for a moment. A moment was enough, and he was able to grab up his other gun, feeling the heat on the outer wall as he did.

The creature was still attached to him, its long claws refusing to give leeway. Weston, in a desperate attempt to shake it free, stood from the ground, feeling the minimal weight of the creature pulling at his body and flesh nonetheless. Once on his feet, he threw himself backwards against the nearest wall. The impact was hard and it stunned him for a moment; he heard a crunch from behind him and hoped he had loosened the creature's grip. He moved from the wall again, but the beast still clung to his back as a grotesque tittering rising from its throat. He launched himself into the wall again and again, each time feeling the heat more and more, but each time he came away with the monster still attached. He attempted it one last time and pushed it hard into the wall, hoping to hold it there and relieve some of the weight that was now dragging on him. A high-pitched scream came from the creature behind him and he could feel the claws release from his back. He pushed back into it more but felt a sudden flash of pain in the side of his neck as the monster's teeth sunk deep into his flesh.

Weston fell forward but made sure to land on his side so he could keep his eyes on the beast. It flailed around, flames sticking to the slip that the creature was now shredding in an effort to remove it. It was the wall; it had become a moving lake of flame that climbed towards the ceiling, fluid and terrible. It was about damn time, he thought to himself as he fought back a cough.

He dropped his empty Colt and pressed his hand to his neck. Blood flowed freely from it, but all Weston could feel was the cold tentacles wrapping themselves across his chest, neck, and back. The former girl had succeeded in finally removing the slip from her emaciated torso, and now stood with her pale skin glowing in the dim light, a growl rising in her throat. Her slug-like tongue lashed out between her lips and sopped up what was left of his blood on her face. She moved towards him.

She was awkward walking upright on her new legs, but she didn't need to be fast. Weston's energy was draining from him, his eyes felt heavy, and he was having a hard time standing. He levelled his weapon at the creature and emptied it into her at a range where he would not miss. The creature flinched with every shot but continued to move forward. Weston dropped the gun and used his hand to help him to his feet. The walls of the farmhouse were now all engulfed in flame; the heat and smoke were staggering, and Weston was having an even harder time seeing and breathing than he had before. And yet, the glowing, pale form of the creature continued to move forward.

"This is the end of it," Weston said aloud and used all his strength to run forward and tackle the beast. He wrapped his arms around the monster's deformed legs and drove his shoulder into its stomach so he could lift it up. He did this without slowing and he carried the creature for a few feet before stopping suddenly, using the momentum and whatever strength he had left in his arms to throw the creature back into the wall. Immediately the beast reacted to the fire and began to screech in a high-pitched noise that was too close to human for Weston to stand. Flames licked the Mhuwe's limbs and body, its bob of hair disappearing in violent bursts of smoke. The creature seethed and dropped to the floor, still covered in flame, its glowing pale skin turning a black charcoal that bubbled and cracked. Weston sat on the floor hard, both hands clutched at his still bleeding neck, and he watched the thing that had been Bethany die.

VI

The fire blazed around him. He could feel its pressure on his skin, could smell the smoke in his lungs, but the heat was absent. Weston shivered from the cold that crawled under his skin and he could feel his sweat run over his gooseflesh. He pushed away from the flaming walls and the dead Mhuwe with his heels, feeling the rough boards under him run across his wounded back.

"You did it, Billy." Phillips stood over him now, his ruined face held up in a mockery of a smile. "You really did it. The monster, well, she's dead. And you, well, you're going to die too. Everything works out. Everyone's happy." Phillips shuffled through some of his cards, burn marks spotting them in brown in black.

"Boss, if you die, it'll all be over. No more suffering, no more pain. No one to die for you, no one for you to kill." Dutch appeared behind Phillips, placing one of his massive hands on Phillips' shoulder.

Weston could not respond. He gulped in breath as

best he could, but it was followed by a great coughing fit that pained him more than he could have imagined. Each cough caused the ice in his veins to crack and rally against him, and it felt like glass had exploded and coursed through his body.

"Yeah, Bill, that is a horrible feeling. Felt it myself for a while there. But have you felt the hunger yet?" Phillips started to do some tricks with his cards, eyes content to watch them as they turned in the air.

No hunger, not yet. Just cold. He turned to his stomach and got to his knees, but one large foot pushed to his side again, a hoarse laugh erupting from the spirits of his former friends. Somewhere in the background he thought he could hear a knocking

"Weston, I ain't got no pity for you and your Injun loving, high falluting ways. You deserve death as much as any man before you," Baker said, fixing the collar of his jacket. "Perhaps more." He joined in with the others and gave Weston a small kick to the stomach, a malicious smile gripping by his face.

Weston scowled at the former deputy and spit a stream of blood where the deputy's boots had once been, though they seemed to be much more transparent than before. Weston got to his knees one last time, but, even though the spirits left him be, he could not stand. He crawled towards the door, the spirits laughing at him and his pain.

"Think about it, Bill. It's better this way." Phillips was crouched before him now, his face returned, rejuvenated. Weston stared at the man he had once known, all the familiar creases and wrinkles, the familiar bushy beard. He stared into those perfect circle spectacles that reflected only the flame that crawled up the wall behind Weston.

"What do you think that cold feeling is anyway? You're

becoming one of them, Billy. If you leave here, more people are going to die. One more monster let loose on the world. There's enough of them out there, isn't there, Bill?" Phillips' voice was sad and haunted, and though Weston knew this Phillips was trying to manipulate him, he also knew he was right. He'd been feeling different since he was slashed open, and it only made sense that what happened to Phillips and Bethany would happen to him.

He took another look towards the door; the ghost of Phillips had disappeared once again and he caught a glimpse of the closed door, smoke billowing around it. Weston rolled to his back and closed his eyes. The ghosts were gone, and he was left with the sounds of the fire burning and the wood cracking. He tried to picture Mary then, her eyes, her mouth. The world didn't need more monsters.

Weston felt the blood draining from him; it was slower now though, a trickling from his neck and back and nothing from his chest. He faded in and out of consciousness, welcoming the black, hoping that sleep would counteract the pain and he would burn to death in the cradle of a gentle dream. But he heard a knocking. A distant knocking that wasn't clear but was consistent and annoying and it wouldn't let him sleep. The knocking became a hollow drumming, skilled and precise, and a melodious humming followed along with it. Weston couldn't contain himself anymore and he opened his eyes to search for its source.

He wasn't surprised to see Faraway Sue before the door, sitting on a chair he had pulled over from the dining room table. His soft chestnut eyes were on Weston, and his humming continued, his foot tapping to the beat. Sue was dressed differently than he had been in life. He was wearing a white shirt and black trousers with black suspenders holding his pants up over his boots. At his hip he wore a hatchet where his pistol had lain, and he had a long wooden necklace that fell over his chest. He wore a full Indian headdress of long eagle feathers dyed red that danced over his jet-black hair. Sue nodded to Weston as he hummed and relished a smoke from his pipe.

Sue stopped humming and removed his pipe from his mouth, the thick white smoke flowing from his lips and mixing with the grey smoke of the fire. "You've given in then?" Sue said simply.

Weston couldn't answer him, he still gasped for breath and his voice had left him with the bite marks on his neck. But yes, he had given in.

"It's an easy thing to do." Sue placed his pipe in his mouth and looked up at the ceiling studying the fire and smoke that had climbed there. "You know, I found it easy to leave my tribe when I was very young. They were trying to teach me things, teach me traditions, stories, history. But I was young and what does all that mean to a young buck who wants to hunt and fish and fight and kill?" Sue winked an eye at him and smiled. "It means nothing. And it was easy for me to leave, so easy. I just said I was leaving, and I did. Nothing easier than that." He nodded his head and rocked in his chair some. "And life was grand. I did hunt and fish and fight, oh yes. Did I kill? Well, if I had to, but that wasn't easy, not by a long shot. Then everything else got hard." He took another long drag on his pipe and exhaled it. He began to hum again, it was a pleasant sound and Sue smiled a little as he did it.

Weston fixed his eyes on Sue and his long pipe. *I don't want to become one of them,* he thought.

Sue nodded. "The Mhuwe curse is only carried by

those who committed a great sin. The worst sin, but if you feel that you truly have contracted its curse, stay here and die. If not," Sue stood and extended his hand, "let us leave this place. It's getting far too warm."

Confusion and fear ran over Weston's mind. He'd lived in a world without Mary for long enough, perhaps it was time to end it. On the other hand, what would she think of him making the decision to end his life? Weston reached out a hand to Sue who smiled broadly around his large pipe. The knocking had returned; it was loud and seemed closer now. Weston tried to push it out of his mind and focused on Faraway Sue, clawed with his hands over the wooden floors to reach the outstretched hand.

The knocking proceeded to get louder and louder until a deafening crack was heard and the door to the house split open with Forester falling atop of the pieces. Coughing, the sheriff looked around the room and raised himself to his feet. Fire had eaten away at the inside of the house and an inferno had grown in the back where he had initially set the fire; the heat slapped him hard and took his breath away. He saw Weston in a pool of blood reaching out to the wall just beyond the doorway. He ran to Weston and, with effort, lifted him over his shoulder and got out of the house as quick as he could.

Weston looked back into the house as the sheriff struggled to lift him to safety. He saw the four spectres in there, each standing by themselves, but as he had remembered them in life. And then they were gone as the house collapsed around them.

CHAPTER TWENTY

I

The sun rose into a blue horizon dispelling the purple and blue leftovers of the night before. Weston made a stiff turn to watch it from his firm bed in Doc Barrows' humble office. It was longer this time they'd said, longer lost in unconsciousness. So long that they didn't know if he'd ever wake up. Yet here he was watching the sun rise one more time.

He didn't have many visitors, though the sheriff dropped in on him once or twice. The first visit was the longest, with the sheriff filling him in on the comings and goings since he last went under.

"What do you remember last?" the sheriff had said, gently prodding his memory.

"Sue. I remember Faraway Sue." Weston knew that was preposterous, but it was what he remembered. "Sue humming one of his songs."

The sheriff gave him a patient look and patted him on the forearm. He sat back in his chair, removed his hat and told Weston what had happened. The sheriff had busted down the door to the farmhouse, though why it should have stuck so, he would not have been able to tell him. Half killing himself in that respect, the sheriff was able to recover and drag himself and the badly wounded, nearly unconscious body of Weston out into the snowy farmland before the entire house collapsed around their heads. Weston nodded along to this, not because he remembered, but because he could understand this being the case.

It was the fire that saved them, in more ways than one. After the sheriff had helped Weston escaped, he was nearly knocked out from the smoke and heat, and he wasn't going to be able to heft the injured Weston all the way to town, even with the help of the horses they'd left just a little ways down the path. The fire though, the glow and smoke of the fire, had brought more people from town. Those volunteers who had agreed to set and put out the fire in town seemed to have been only warmed up by their previous endeavours and were itching to do more of it. When they arrived, they sent Weston and the sheriff back into town to see the doctor.

"Is it done?" Weston said after a brief silence.

"It's done." The sheriff nodded. "I went back there myself as soon as the doc had a good look at me. The boys were still putting out some of the flames, but there was very little left to the house aside from ash and ruin." Forester picked his teeth with the fingernail of his pinky finger and said, "I spent the next two days going back there. Some of it I just spent waiting, watching the ruins, checking for any signs of life. The rest of the time I spent poking through wreckage trying to find any sign of the body. Even a skull like the last one."

"Did you find it?"

"Nohm. Found nothing in there. If it died in there, it burned away to ash with the rest of the house." The sheriff's face seemed troubled for a moment, but he changed that with a sigh and a shrug. "There have been no more deaths anyway, so that must mean something."

Weston nodded again, that was a good sign. The creature needed to feed. It was more than just a compulsion; it was more than a need. It was everything; a survival instinct ingrained into its very bones -- its very soul. If there hadn't been any more killings, then that was a very good sign indeed.

"And how are you?" the sheriff asked, eyes not looking directly at Weston, but facing him all the same.

"Do you mean, am I having sudden irresistible urges?"

"Well?" The Sheriff turned his eyes to him then. They were cobalt blue eyes that had turned cold. He had crossed his arms and Weston noticed that one hand had slipped inside his jacket.

"No sir, no strange desires or feelings. Even the bloody cold feeling has gone away. Perhaps the good doctor is better than he ever thought he was." Weston smiled.

"Oh ayuh. Being an ill-used sawbones for the logging company will do that to a man." The sheriff chuckled a moment and then the room fell to silence.

They made some small talk about the town and how it was recovering. Certainly, those that lost loved ones were having a hard time, but some had the satisfaction and relief of burying their own, having the whereabouts of the hunters Weston had found several days ago. Otherwise, most were still on edge. Many did not believe in the silly tales of those that saw a child monster entrapped in a ring of fire doing battle with a single man. They both chuckled at that, though neither could be sure why. The sheriff left shortly after that, excusing himself to take care of town business. That was fine with Weston, in his mind their business had already concluded.

II

Weston left the care of Doc Barrows just two days later. It was against the doctor's wishes of course, but Weston would hear nothing of it and threatened to leave through the window if the doctor didn't stand clear of his way.

He was surprised to find that his room was still in his name at the hotel. He supposed that had something to do with the sheriff, and he aimed to thank him special for it. He took his time looking through his room, dumping out the belongings of his companions and their last prisoner as a team of bounty hunters. Weston didn't know much of his brothers-in-arms before he had met them. He supposed that was what drew them together as much as anything else. They all had a past that they were trying to run away from. Weston had a dead wife and child that he couldn't face up to, but what had Phillips run from in Mexico, or Dutch in Holland?

While he picked through their things, he found precious little in the way of clues that might lead him to an answer for those questions. Though he did find some photographs in Phillips' bag: a beautiful woman sat up prim and proper, a book in one hand, and a ruler in the other. On the back of that particular photograph the name Sarah was written. Who was Sarah, Jimmy? The other photograph of interest was one of Jim Phillips himself. He was missing his beard in the picture and Weston was surprised at the thin and angular features Phillips displayed. Phillips was standing beside a large gallows with three men hanging from it, taking their final dance. More questions than answers broke from Phillips' belongings it seemed.

Dutch's belongings were less complex but just as telling. There were some books written in his native tongue, some letters in that language as well, as written in the cursive of a woman if Weston had ever seen one. Mary had written like that, he thought as he put everything away.

Sue's belongings were scant to begin with and were only made up of things that they had took from him after they captured him. He had a hatchet (not unlike the one Weston thought he saw him wielding the night of the fire), a pipe, some pipe tobacco, and a small locket with the picture of an older man and a younger woman in it. Weston held the locket for the longest time, not looking at the pictures inside, just holding it within his fist, feeling the ridges and bumps that made the ornamental filigree that covered its surface. Finally, he put it all away.

The only surprise he found with his belongings was a pair of Colt revolvers. They weren't his, but they were fair replacements for those that must have been irrevocably damaged in the fire and farmhouse collapse. He studied the guns: old and well-used but kept clean and in good shape by whomever owned them before. Sheriff Forester seemed to be at work yet again. That was another one that he owed the old sheriff.

Weston sat upon his bed; the mattress was more comfortable than the firm one he had to endure while living in the care of Doc Barrows, and he was tempted to try and sleep, but he had slept enough these past few days and he wanted to see some things for himself. He found some of his own clothes and changed into them, strapped on his new guns, pulled on his jacket, and left the room taking a lantern with him.

The night had come on while he did a search of his room, and though it was crisp and cold, it was a clear night with plenty of light provided by the moon and stars. His walk through town was uneventful, and though there were many people walking the streets, most did little to acknowledge him and left him alone. Weston found his way easily enough through the path next to the sheriff's office. There were still signs of foot traffic from the past few days, most, more than likely, from the night of the fire and the rest the slow footsteps of the sheriff as he made his way up and back doing his daily checks as he had told Weston.

Weston lit his lantern as he got under the tree cover, but truly the clear night provided as much or more light than his oil lamp did; still it felt good to hold the flickering orange light in his hands. He moved through the path, much more beaten down than when it had been when Dutch first steered them up this path, and less snow cover. As before, however, he could pick out the subtle signs of where he was and where he was going. As strange as it was, Weston felt comforted by all of this, by knowing the area. Like home, perhaps.

The trek didn't take all that long, despite not having a horse to carry him. He was somewhat winded by the time he stood before the ruins of the old Darrio farmhouse, and he blamed that on being too long in Doc Barrow's bed.

The sheriff had been right: all that was left of the farmhouse was ash and dust. Weston wandered through the wreckage casting his lantern here and there at things that appeared to be solid, but most were just remnants of the old house and its furniture. There were certainly no bones in there, no bodies, and no blood. He breathed a sigh of relief and returned to the front of the house, staring at it as if he was staring in the front door. It was all gone.

He turned to leave and tossed the oil lantern into the middle of the ruins; a small fire started burning there that spread out with the splatter of the oil. He hoped it all went ablaze once more, that it all burned again so that nothing was left of that accursed house or anyone who lived there. Re-birth by fire.

On his walk back through the path, an eagle feather rolled past him on the ground. In the light of the moon, he thought it looked stained red.

III

He didn't hear anything from the sheriff or the townsfolk about another fire up at the Darrio farm, and there was a doubt that sprang into his mind about the fire actually catching. But he didn't make an effort to go back and start again. He had no need or desire to do so.

The night he returned from the setting his own fire was the best sleep that he had in many years. His dreams were not plagued by horrible memories, nor was he bothered by the ghosts of his dead friends. He hadn't been contacted by them since he was almost killed in the fire. He wondered then, and would often wonder for the rest of his life, if they were just figments of his imagination or the vengeful spirits of those who felt he had wronged them. Whatever they were, and whatever their intentions, he found that he felt empty without them. He missed having them so close, missed being able to talk to them, or even hear their voices. When he awoke after that night, he stared for a long time at their bags and belongings, trying to figure out what to do with them.

After talking to Forester, he made arrangements to buy the Quarter horse he had ridden the night of the fire. With the strong beast in his possession, he loaded it up with the belongings of his lost companions and rode into the forest once more. Again, he found his way without issue, recognizing the paths he had taken several times now. The small clearing where he had killed the Mhuwe was still there, the snow having displaced a little and the high grass easily found once more. He urged his horse into the centre of the field and dismounted, taking a short shovel that he had bought at the general store with him. Weston wasn't able to follow the path he had left those few nights previous, but he felt his way around until he thought he was in the right spot and began to dig. The ground was hard and frozen, and the dirt moved slowly, but he got the work done despite his aching wounds and muscles. He dug three holes, not six feet deep, but a good three to four if Weston was to judge. With that done, he deposited the bags into the holes one at a time, covering each in their own turn. He didn't leave any markers for the shallow graves and didn't think he would ever come back to try and find them, nor would anyone else. It was just the right thing to do.

Weston gave his new horse a pat on the nose before he mounted him again and gave him some of an apple he had bought. He debated returning to town to give the sheriff a proper farewell, thank him for all of his help and perhaps share another drink, but he didn't think it would matter much. Weston and the sheriff had made an unspoken agreement and that agreement was at its end now. The sheriff would understand, he was sure of it. Weston leaned down and patted the horse on its strong neck. It was a good horse and he wanted to see what it could do on the open trail.

AFTERWORD

To my family, Ashlee, Emily, Brianna, and Conan. Without whom I'd have no inspiration to write.

To my parents, without whom I'd never know the fun of telling a story.

To my friends and peers, Steve, Jon, and Kevin (for reading this at the early stages); Write Club (for providing inspiration and great conversation); Jenn (for putting up with me at work, and pimping out my writing wherever you could); and Jud Haynes for designing a beautiful cover.

To the publisher, Engen books, without whom this wouldn't have been published at all. Matthew LeDrew and the Engen crew (Ellen Curtis and Erin Vance) have been very supportive throughout this process (even letting me send this in way too late).

CHILLERS
FROM THE
ROCK
EDITED BY
ELLEN CURTIS
& ERIN VANCE

EDITED BY ELLEN CURTIS & ERIN VANCE
DYSTOPIA
FROM THE ROCK
A COLLECTION OF SHORT FICTION

THE XANDER DREW SERIES

Prologue: The Long Road (May 2014)

Book One: Cinders (April 2015)
Book Two: Sinister Intent (November 2015)
Book Thee: Faith (December 2017)
Book Four: Family Values (December 2018)
Book Five: Fate's Shadow (forthcoming)

The early years of **Xander Drew** as he struggles with the evils of his small rural hometown of Coral Beach, Maine. Cursed with the heart of the Womb and the gift of seeing the world around him for what it really is, Xander must learn the hard lessons about the nature of humanity to traverse the minefield of criminals, gangs, and abusers that stand between him and ultimate happiness -- but most of all that **sometimes it takes a monster, to catch a monster.**

"THE WRITING OF ITS GENERATION- - VISUAL, TO-THE-POINT AND IN-THE-MOMENT."

- *The Northeast Avalon Times*

The Coral Beach Casefiles series by Matthew LeDrew:

ABOUT THE AUTHOR

Jon Dobbin is an award winning author living in the St. John's, Newfoundland metro region.

He is a father of three, the husband to an amazing wife, an educator, and a tattoo and beard enthusiast.

Dobbin's work has appeared in the *Chillers from the Rock, Dystopia from the Rock,* and, *Kit Sora: The Artobiography* collections.

The Starving is his first novel.

CPSIA information can be obtained
at www.ICGtesting.com
Printed in the USA
LVHW091659220120
644442LV00005B/880